# THUNDER ROAD

# THUNDER ROAD

# Ted Dawe

Copyright © 2003 by Ted Dawe
Cover and jacket design by 2Faced Design
Interior designed and formatted by E.M. Tippetts Book Designs

ISBN 978-1-943818-44-0
eISBN: 1-978-1-943818-84-6
Library of Congress Control Number: 2017940281

First published by Longacre in 2003
First hardcover edition June 2017 by Polis Books, LLC
1201 Hudson Street, #211S
Hoboken, NJ 07030
www.PolisBooks.com

POLIS BOOKS

## Also by
# Ted Dawe

*Into the River*
*K Street*
*And Did Those Feet*
*Into the World*

This book is dedicated to the memory of four people. To my cousin, Jak D'Ath, who rides beside me always.
To my grandmother, Rewa D'Ath, who taught me what love is.
To my friend, Dora Ridall, who never doubted me.
To my Rangatira, Niko Tangaroa.

*Ki a koe toku Rangatira kua wheturangatia Nau te Kākano nei I Whakaawe*
*No reira Haere Haere Haere atu ra.*

To you, my chief, among the Stars and Heavens You have inspired me, I am now the seed.
Farewell Farewell Farewell.

*The highway's jammed with broken heroes On a last chance power drive*
*Everybody's on the run tonight*
*But there's no place left to hide*

From 'Born to Run' Bruce Springsteen

# FOREWORD

*I'm no writer. I'll tell you that for nothing.*

*I just thought, it's me who should set the record straight, so here I am doing it now.*

*Doing it for Devon.*


*Where to start?*

*I was born. No, what the hell does that matter? My parents?*

*Ahh, forget it. No need to go that far back.*

*When I was little my father used to say, 'Trace, there is a right and a wrong way of doing anything'.*

*I could live with that.*

*When I was about 13 or 14 it had changed to 'Trace, there's my way, and the wrong way'.*

*I couldn't live with that.*

*So when I was 15 I shot through.*

*I've done a lot of dumb things between then and now, but leaving home wasn't one of them.*

*I reckon you've got to know when to stay and fight and when to walk away.*


*As a kid I would lie in bed and listen to the cars gunning it down Dyson Road. I knew each car, its make and who owned it from the exhaust note. Such sweet sounds! My mates were all into heavy metal music, dope or rugby. For me it was an engine begging for mercy (there is no mercy), the steep rising pitch of the turbo, the screaming tyres and the curtain of white smoke hanging behind me: all the stuff that spells street racing. Nothing compared to that. Anything else was second best.*

*We were partners, Devon and me. All this stuff I'm going to tell you took place when I first came to Auckland. So much has happened. It's like it was a lifetime ago and just yesterday at the same time. It takes me a while so you're going to have to be patient. There's so much to tell.*

# CHAPTER
# ONE

**A**FTER A COUPLE of years working as a plumber's mate on a building site, I knew that it was time to look for something else. The guys I worked with, Jesus, they looked beaten. As though life had already ripped them off. Each day, Wally, my boss, would fill his lunch box with flattened out copper pipe, smuggling it home to sell on.

'I've got nearly a hundred kilos in the garage.'

One afternoon the crane broke down and couldn't be fixed for four days. A load of heater pipes arrived that were needed on the fourth floor. Me and Patrick, being the only labourers on the site, were told to carry them up. The plumbers and the fitters wouldn't touch them. Patrick stood next to the pipes, pondering his next move. He was over 50 years old and there were limits to what he would and wouldn't do. After a spell in the site office he disappeared out the back. I waited by the pipes, wondering what would happen next.

After a while, Eric, the site foreman, came out. He paused in the doorway for a moment to light his pipe. He looked awkward. I knew what he was going to say before he opened his mouth.

'Patrick has some holes to drill so I guess it's going to be you laddie. Best to carry them up the stairwell.'

I was so pissed. The unfairness of it. The youngest gets the shit job.

'Can't be done, Eric, it's a two-man job.'

'No, it's just a slow job, that's all laddie.'

'That'll take days.'

'That's what you're paid for, lad.'

'To do the work of a crane?'

He closed in on me. 'To do whatever fucking jobs need to be done. So get started, eh?'

As I HAULED a pipe up to the third floor, I could hear the voices of the men mimicking Eric's Geordie accent.

'So get started, laddie.' 'upwards and onwards.'

'Don't make a fuss, lad, we need those pipes.'

I smouldered away angrily to myself. The injustice. There were limits. Just because I was the labourer didn't mean that I had to do anything they said. That was slavery.

I WALKED TO the window and looked out across the scaffolding. There was Patrick, de-nailing some timber on the far side of the yard. The work given out only when there was nothing else to do. I climbed out and sat down on the planks, feet dangling. I didn't know what to do next, or what was going to happen, so I pulled out my smokes and waited.

Sure enough, before long Eric emerged from the site office and looked up at me. He waved his arm angrily. I waved back.

'Get on with it, laddie.'

His voice sounded weak from this distance. I didn't respond. He strode purposefully across the yard towards the bottom of the building.

'Get on with it, Trace,' one of the plumbers called out, only half joking this time.

I could sense a back-down of sorts. I stood up and looked at the three men in the gloom of the building. There was something a bit hesitant about them this time, like schoolboys crumbling under a challenge.

'Fuck you too,' I said. They weren't my mates. Eric arrived.

'Too good for this sort of work, lad?'

'I'm not doing it.'

'Two choices, lad. Think carefully.'

'Do it yourself, Eric.'

'Pack up. You're out of here.'

'So that's it?'

'Seems so,' he said as he walked off.

There's always a moment when decisions have to be made.

This was one of them.

We were just coming out of winter; the last three months were the coldest I could remember. Every morning, at seven, chipping away in the gloom with a cold chisel, the afternoons spent waiting for the five o'clock whistle ... I guess all they wanted was my obedience, so when I wouldn't carry those pipes, something else was made clear to me.

'You're off? Fine, we'll replace you tomorrow.' Which is another way of saying, 'You're shit. See ya.'

I'D HAD ENOUGH of small town life, so I set off for the smoke. I'm one of those guys who sees everything that happens as an opportunity. This was an opportunity to get the hell out of the whole hometown/family scene at the same time.

I got this real buzz of freedom as I stuck my thumb out on Highway one and an even better one when I heard the gasp of airbrakes. A big furniture truck. He was going all the way to Auckland so it was like I was there already.

THE TRUCKIE PUT me onto a room in this big old house run by a woman called Mrs Jacques. As it happened she had a spot, a room share, cheap as, in the front overlooking a busy road. Cars hooning up and down all day. Ideal.

Mrs Jacques was in her late fifties and had the battered look of an over-ripe peach. The sort that are marked down in special trays out the front of the fruiterer's. She had known tragedy and wasn't afraid to talk about it. In half an hour I had her life story. An hour after that I had forgotten most of it. She took pains to spell out that she ran a tight ship, her husband, 'bless his soul', had been in the navy. That she would 'brook no jiggery pokery'.

There were two other guys living there. I shared a room with Devon; he was out of town at the time, so I had it to myself for a couple of days. I could tell from the things scattered around he was into the same sort of stuff as me. Car stuff, brand badges, posters, books and mags. A few porn type mags, too, in among everything else.

There was a framed picture on the chest of drawers: this really pretty girl sitting on the bonnet of an Escort. It had been taken at some beach. A pair of sunglasses and a bottle of beer that I guess he had put down to take the photo, waited on the roof. There weren't many clothes in the room, but there were cartons of junk under the bed and an oily smell which made me think of engine parts.

The other guy, Sergei, was a music teacher. He gave piano lessons in the front room. Although he must have been over 30, his face was smooth and unlined like he had never been out in the sun. Maybe it was because he was a foreigner (he came from Poland) that everything about him seemed extreme: bushy beard, wild hair, staring eyes and this really dramatic way of talking. Full of spit and hand movements.

Whenever he spoke it was like he was making an announcement, broadcasting to the nation.

Mrs Jacques adored him. He was like a visiting celebrity, not a boarder – first class all the way for him. He was a big man with small hands and feet, narrow shoulders and wide hips. Too long sitting at a piano, I guess. He didn't walk around the house, he surged from place to place. Like he was on wheels.

The large room across the hall from us was his: it was there that a procession of small kids, arriving by bike or being dropped off by waiting parents, received their weekly instruction on the 'pianoforte', as he called it.

I reckon Sergei had seen heaps of films about 'The Great Composer', the misunderstood genius. When we watched TV that first night he kept claiming to have written the theme music for this show or that ad: 'Did you hear that, Mrs Jacques, that introduction … it was a steal from my theme music for… there is not an original composer in this entire country… a nation of stealers… plagiarists… .'

It took a few days to get used to him. The bang of the piano lid was usually followed by Sergei bursting from his room, hand glued to his forehead, throwing himself into an armchair. Mrs Jacques would get really wound up.

'What's wrong Sergei? Is it not going well today?' Trying to make him feel better. Terrified he might leave.

'Don't ask, Mrs Jacques. I don't know how much more of this I can take. Every note I play seems flat and toneless. Music for a coffin.'

'Creative work is the hardest work there is,' she said.

'All my energy is stolen by tuition, no wonder nothing I write these days is any good.'

Mrs Jacques hovered sympathetically; I tried to read the paper.

It was sort of embarrassing.

'Mediocrity! I'm surrounded by it. When I think of what I might be able to write, if I wasn't driving talentless, unmotivated schoolboys towards some Grade Three pianoforte qualification.' He paused, gathering steam. 'Just so their shallow mums and dads can tell themselves that they are doing *the right thing* by their children. I would rather teach a dog how to knit.'

He leaned back in the armchair, eyes tightly closed for a while, then sprang up and surged back into his room where he attacked the piano so savagely I thought it might explode. I could see his face reflected in the hall mirror. Completely rapt. Eyes locked shut. Head rocking backwards and forwards, sometimes swooping low over the keys, other times facing up towards the ceiling as if trying to suck down the creative energy. It was better than TV.

WE WERE AN odd crew, but somehow we got by. Maybe because this was where I started out in the big city, I put up with all the crap that came along. I didn't know any better in those days. I do now.

# CHAPTER TWO

FOR THE FIRST few days I went hard-out looking for jobs. Anything would do. Cash was always short and my savings wouldn't last long. I figured no more building sites. Tried that. I checked out a couple of office jobs: office junior and dispatch clerk – but sitting behind a desk writing wasn't for me. Too much like school. Near the bus stop there was this big hardware shop, with a card in the window.

POSITION VACANT
Paint Sales & Tinting. Apply Manager.

So I did. Started work straight away. It would do for a while until I got myself sorted. The hardware shop was one of those that expanded to become an everything shop. The hardware sections were stalked by guys who were like professional knowalls. I used to hear them approach someone digging through a box full of shackles, and before you knew it, they had solved their problem. They were like this about everything else too. At smoko, reading the paper, they would do the same with national issues.

The main guy was Ernie, this 60-year-old English guy who saw himself as a thinker. He would kick everyone else into action.

'If they want their land back, well then, they should give the cars back too. And the TVs. And the telephones. Can't just have the good bits and not the bad bits.'

'And the rugby,' someone else would chip in.

'Can't use whiteman's magic in one place but then want the good old days somewhere else.'

'And the TAB.'

'I'd respect 'em if they said "fuck 'em" to the schools and the hospitals, but they don't. They want those, thank you very much.'

'And the Lion Red.'

'Yeah. They wouldn't get far then.'

It always surprised me that Joe, the old Māori fork-lift driver, didn't say anything. He just sat there.

Sometimes young people were the new topic of discussion. 'If they raised the drinking age back to twenty-one again….' 'And the driver's licence… .'

'And the school leaving age….'

'Yeah – well, they can't handle it. Read the paper. It says the same thing every day: "they can't handle it". I had my first pint when I was sixteen. My father bought it for me at the local. I was taught to drink. The kids here….'

'They should teach them to drink in schools,' I offered. They all looked at me to see whether I was taking the piss, then decided I wasn't.

'Not such a silly idea. They do all the other jobs that the parents should do. Sex education … sorting out their emotional problems.'

'We never had emotional problems.'

'Hadn't been invented.'

It was hard to sit there and ignore it. Not get drawn in. It was like listening to my father's opinions. The world was falling apart, and he was the only one who knew why.

The job itself was OK. It took about a day to learn how to do 90 per cent of it. The hardest part was colour matching for people who came off the street carrying some old can that had been under the house for ten years. Most of them seemed to think that there was one colour called cream.

A COUPLE OF days after I got the job, Devon turned up. I was beginning to think I knew all about him by this time, from his stuff in the room and what the others said about him. I hadn't noticed his car outside, I was still lost in my 'end of the day' thoughts as I walked into my room and found this guy lying on my bed smoking. He was 19 too, had longish hair, olive skin and these weird green eyes. What is it about brown skin with green eyes? You can spot them from 50 yards away.

I stood there staring down at him; he reached up, offering the flat of his palm for a slap.

'Hey man. It's Trace, right?' He sat up. 'Mrs Jacques has been threatening to stick someone in this bed for three months. I thought it would be Sergei, Version Two.'

He seemed so at home lying there on my bed, like he owned the place … that blew me away. The confidence, where did it come from? He was about as tall as me, but as skinny as a rake. Lived on cigarettes and coffee.

Mrs Jacques walked past and called over her shoulder. 'Smoking outside, Devon.'

He looked at me with a grin. 'She'll be Jakes. No jiggery pokery.' Nothing seemed to get to him.

We wandered out onto the verandah. He offered me a smoke. 'A stick?'

'Thanks.'

'So where you from?'

'Down near Hamilton.'

'Just came back from there. Cow country. If you can't milk it, forget it.'

'What were you doing down there?'

'I had to cover the big farm equipment show at Mystery Creek. It was a long week.'

'You're a reporter?'

'I'm meant to be, but I'm more like the Boy Friday. The gopher. Go for this ... go for that. How about you?'

'Paint shop. I was a builder's labourer but I had a *situation* so here I am.'

'What was it?' I told him.

'Ah, the glass dome.'

'What's that?'

'I've got a theory about it, I'll tell you later. Got wheels?'

'Not yet.'

'I place them right up there, next to sex. Better in some ways.'

'Where's your car?'

'Around the back. Come and look at it.'

On the back lawn was the little Ford Escort from the photo: bright orange, rear wing, Recaro seats, fat tyres on spoked mags, tinted out windows.

'What drives it?'

He popped the bonnet. The motor crammed the bay. There had been heaps of modifications. Double Webber carbs, extractors, fancy cam cover.

'Wow! What a beast!'

'Two-litre motor, with all the right shit to make this baby dance.'

'Did you do all this?'

'No. My man Martin. I've only had it a while. My ambition is to flick it on before I kill it. What do you reckon my chances are?'

'I haven't seen you drive.'

'Come on then,' he said, throwing open the door, 'time for a tour.'


I GUESS I had ridden with wild drivers before. Hell, I had driven some fast beats after midnight, but never like this. Devon made the little car suffer. It wasn't the speed as much as the aggression. There is a code with us drivers: you don't criticise and you don't show fear. I felt plenty of both as we howled around the busy streets, passing cars so closely some drivers pulled over and jumped out. I didn't know the area so I never knew what was around the next corner. The way Devon cornered, you'd think the roads had been cleared by track marshals. Eventually we reached a long straight road lined on both sides with two-storey warehouses. Devon looked at his watch. 'Six minutes. I've done it in five.'

'It was pretty quick,' I offered.

'There's pretty quick and then there's five minutes … which is low flying.'

He slowed right down until we came to a stop in the middle of the road. He sprang out of the car and threw the bonnet up.

'What's up? Overheating?'

'Nah! Just an excuse to park in the middle of the road.'

Such cheek. It was liberating. Road rules were for other people.

'What do you notice about this street?'

I looked down it. It was nearly six p.m. so there was not much traffic. Dead straight. Factories on both sides of the road.

'I dunno.'

'This is Whaitiri Street, but we call it Thunder Road. It's where we race mostly. You come back here at midnight on Saturday night, there can be a thousand cars along here. Lining the street with their headlights blazing. Full of people drinking, smoking, dropping tabs and, in the middle of the road every thirty seconds or so, two cars head to head, winding their tachs up to nine thou … sorting out the order.'

I looked at the street again. This time I noticed the burn-out marks for the first hundred metres of the straight.

'What's that?' I said, pointing to a big stained area.

'They drop the diesel there and set it on fire. For the flameouts.'

A red Falcon ute chugged up alongside. It had flames on the bonnet and real low-profile tyres. The two vehicles were now blocking the whole street. In the ute there were three guys about our age. Two of them were twins. The other one by the passenger window yelled out to Devon, 'Hey man, how's it hangin'?'

'Ay! The Taylor Twins and Rebel.' He gestured to me. 'Come and meet.'

The twins had been to the same hairdresser I'd say; their red hair was short on top, long at the sides. Rebel was a solid little guy, muscles and a spider tattoo coming out the collar of his T-shirt. He looked like a heavy bastard. The sort you don't want to mess with. There was a green trail bike roped on the tray. The sound from the bass driver was shaking the neighbourhood and the cab was a fug of cigs. The three of them were all smoking, hard-out.

'Who's this?' asked Rebel with a flick of his head.

'It's Trace, he's living at my house. Showing him the strip.'

The three of them all fixed their eyes on me, sort of weighing me up, then Rebel offered me a palm for the bro handshake. The other two followed.

'Where are you from, Tracey?' said the Taylor with thenchipped tooth. 'up from the sticks?'

'It's Trace,' I said.

The other one turned to Rebel with a grin. 'Sure man, that's what I meant.'

'The Waikato.' I didn't want to be too exact.

'Hicksville!' Rebel grinned with contempt, and then added, 'Got a car?'

'Not yet.'

'Planning to?'

'Yep.'

'When you're ready … see me. Midnight Autos. I do the deals.'

We all laughed. It had that corny, TV, used-car salesman sound to it.

There was the bleep of a siren, then a voice saying, 'Move on!' over a loudspeaker. A cop car had pulled up behind us without us noticing. Me and Devon jumped back in and the ute shot off in the other direction. We pulled over to the side to let the cop through and he came alongside.

'What are you up to, Devon?'

Devon flashed a charming grin. 'Sorry orificer Carmody, those young men were asking for directions.'

'I'll give you directions if I see you hangin' around here.'

'Yeah I know it. Do not pass go … do not collect two hundred… .'

Then Devon flashed the hang loose sign at him. 'It's cool,' and gave a little blip on the accelerator. Drag talk.

'Don't even think about it. This could eat your *old lady* car over any distance.' The cop grinned smugly and then, to prove it, he planted his foot. The police car disappeared down the strip like a sped-up film.

'I know that guy. Story goes he used to race this strip and now they've got him on the other side. That's a special patrol car just for chasing down the dudes. It can really move. He's taken some of my mates off the road.'

We drove back slowly. 'Who were the other guys?'

'They're your genuine Westies. Petrol's in their blood. Born to race. The stocky dude, Rebel, real name's Billy Revell. He's a hard bastard. Been inside. "Rock College" he calls it. He runs this car and parts outfit … Midnight Autos,' Devon said with a laugh.

'What's funny about that?'

'You want a set of mags, he says, "I'll get you a set from Midnight Autos." Because that's exactly what he does. He goes out at midnight and rips them off parked cars. The Taylors hang with him a lot now. I reckon they're in on it too. He hardly ever drives himself – well, not during the day time, anyway.'

'Lost his licence?'

'Yeah, for about sixty years. He reckons by the time he gets it back, we'll all be cruising around in space craft.'

I had to laugh. Devon had such an easy way with him, he seemed to be able to talk to anyone. Crims and cops, back to back. Made them all seem like cool guys.

BACK AT THE boarding house Mrs Jacques was in watching TV, really loud. Sergei was in his room making freaky sounds on the piano.

'Listen Trace,' Devon stopped me in the hallway outside his room, hand cupped behind his ear, 'sounds like Beethoven … decomposing.'

After a few hours with Devon it was like I had always known him. Dev came from the East Coast. His great grandfather, Diego Santos, jumped ship a hundred years ago and began the Santos dynasty. Devon was really proud of the Spanish thing and claimed he would go back there some day… back to the old hacienda. Drink Bull's Blood and eat paella. He made it sound like it was just around the corner, and I was invited.

We clicked. Held nothing back, there was no point. I've always been a bit of a fatalist. If it's meant to happen, it'll happen. Devon showed up in my life at just the right time. He was what I needed, and as it turned out, I was what he needed too.

# CHAPTER THREE

GUESS THE next big thing that happened was Karen. Bob Bryant asked me to work weekends until five. He had this trainee/manager angle that he dangled in front of me. Seven days straight was tough going but I needed all the money I could get. The good thing was that most of the usual staff didn't come in. A different bunch did the weekends. They were a cool change from the weekday stiffs. The old, burnt out guys. The nightmare mums.

Three of them were about my age: at last, I thought, people I can relate to. Two guys and a girl. The guys were university students: Jason, who was tall and thin with a crew cut and glasses, and Richard, who had long brown hair, and an annoying way of not looking at you when he spoke to you. They'd gone to some private school together, and they were always talking about their teachers, what marks they had got in the school exams, and most of all, which of their mates were dicks. There were big dicks, dumb dicks, fat dicks, sad dicks and total dicks. I had never heard the word dick used so often. Where I came from, anyone called Richard was always called Dick but this Richard didn't seem so keen.

The girl, Karen, was quiet, shy I guess, and still at school. Pretty though. Even with her hair tied back and wearing the company smock. One of those girls who played down her looks. I couldn't take my eyes off her.

They all came to work in a mint old Jaguar: Jason's father's. 'Dad uses the work car.' The three of them had all known each other, like, forever.

I was looking for a chance to break through with Karen, but casually, so it didn't look like I was hitting on her. You've got to let girls think that they're the ones in control. Their guard always goes up when they think that you're coming onto them.

The two guys just stuck together and made smart comments about people and ideas I had never heard of. They had their own way of talking: accent, lingo, it all left me on the outer, like a loser. Seemed deliberate. Karen worked on the cash register so she was pretty much on her own. The two guys were stocktaking at the back of the store, my end. Whenever I had to talk to one of them, they exchanged looks after I had finished: some sort of code. It didn't take a genius to work out that I was in the dick category … if I was lucky. I probably didn't even rate.

Most of the time I was stuck in my paint-mixing bay. I needed a reason to leave it. Richard and Jason were doing a slow stock take on the shelves, so they were free agents. There was something about their oh-so-casual manner that said, 'This work is meaningless' … or maybe even, 'I don't really need this'.

In part I agreed … it was crap work. But I needed it. Their talk went along these lines.

Richard (reading from a sheath of notes): 'Latch locks, galvanised, assorted, do we have a tally yet?'

Jason: 'Wait varlet, tally approaching. I make it seventeen that's a one followed by a seven.'

Richard: 'Are we talking assorted?'

Jason: 'We are. I'm not paid to particularise.'

Richard: 'Remember Mr Bartram in history last year? "Selwood, the significant cognitive shift I am waiting for is when you learn to move from the particular to the general." '

Jason: 'I can't see Mr Bartram working in a hardware shop sorting *galvanised* latches obviously.'

Richard (mimicking): 'obviousleh.' Jason: 'obviousleh. Yeh! Ho ho ho!'

Richard: 'Bismark *galvanised* Europe with a complex system of alliances.'

Jason: 'Napoleon marched to Moscow for a *galvanised* clasp.' At this point they would both laugh loudly. Even that sounded as if it had been learned at school. The braying, in-group laugh.

It really got up my nose.

We had lunch in shifts. Richard and Jason went first, Karen and I second. On my first weekend shift I looked forward to it because I hadn't had a chance to talk to her. When I came back from the Vietnamese bakery, she was sitting at the lunch table eating a packed lunch. Her nose was buried in some big, fat book. I wanted to break through, but she was sort of selfcontained and aloof.

There may have been a chance, but I had left it too late. Awkwardness had arrived and the moment was gone, so I sat at my end of the table, eating my lunch in tense silence. The time began to drag and soon I couldn't bear it. I went downstairs and lurked out the back, feeling a failure, having to eat my lunch among the rolls of wire netting and pallets of cobble-stones. Thought I might as well just go back to work.

The afternoon dragged after that. Gone was the possibility of making new friends. They were just three more rich kids doing a bit of work for fun money, so far up themselves it was unreal. Sometimes Jason or Richard would come over and ask where something was, and

I would just point and go on with what I was doing. I thought, 'Fuck you! Why should I bother?'

By five o'clock I could tell that even my quiet hostility was the basis of 'oh so amusing' jokes. At the end of the day we all left out the back way together without exchanging so much as a glance.

BACK AT MRS Jacques' I wanted to have a shower but Sergei was in having a bath. I could hear him singing 'Deep River' through the wall. You could tell he was listening to the fake low tones of his own voice. No sign of Devon. He hadn't come home the night before, so I figured he had forgotten his promise to take me to Thunder Road.

The phone rang, for Sergei, so while he stood in the hall, nattering away wrapped in a towel, I got my shower. At last, a chance to wash off all the filth and tiredness of the day. I emerged feeling fired up so I put on clean clothes, scrabbled together a few bucks and set out. I had gone about 50 metres when Devon's exhaust note sounded at the end of the street. He swung over to the wrong side of the road and threw open the passenger's door.

'Planning to shoot through without me, eh?'

'I thought you'd forgotten.'

'As if ... get in man!'

I was surprised to see that the back of his car was full of clothes: he usually kept it spotless.

'What've you been doing, man?'

Tapping the side of his nose with his finger, he flicked a glance at me. 'I've got involved with this lady. It's complicated.'

'What's the story? Is she married?'

'Not when I'm with her.'

It was a bit like that with Devon. The only things that mattered were the things we were doing right then. The past and the future took care of themselves.

He pumped up the sounds and we buried ourselves in its regular pulse as we weaved through the 'burbs. That night changed much of the way I thought about things. I often wonder why. Some of it's to do with what Devon later explained as the 'glass dome' theory. But maybe more importantly it was this other world. The one we dived into. The world of cars, of dope, of speed, of no rules, no old people and nothing beyond the scenery flashing past. The world just a blur in our peripheral vision.

Devon had this idea. It goes like this. Young guys like me and him, we're held back. First by our parents, then by schools, and finally, when we leave home, the rest of the world makes it clear early on that we are crap. Most of the time you just accept it, you think it's the way things are. But every now and then you get this little flash, where you see that it's all a game … none of it matters. My run-in with the foreman on the building site was one of those, Devon says. The really important thing is what happens next. If you roll over and take it, then you're dead already. The brainwashing has worked. The rules are made up by the winners, just to keep them on top. You have to bend the rules, otherwise it's just a lifetime of kissing arse. If you can bust through the glass dome, then you're a free guy. When I walked off the building site, Devon says … that's what I did. My first step towards becoming free. Cool!

On the way to Thunder Road we dropped in to see this guy, Martin. He and his girlfriend, Gail, lived in a tiny house in the poncey suburb of Parnell. All BMWs and cappuccino bars. Their place was nestled between two big apartment complexes. It stank of piss from one end to the other. They had a kid who was called Martin too. Big Martin and little Martin. Little Martin looked like a wild boy: long stringy hair, a bit dirty and not enough clothes on. I guess he just pissed wherever he wanted to. Freedom.

Martin was the mechanic who had done the work on Devon's Escort. He had a garage rigged up for it and the driveway was jammed with dead cars. All the long grass in front of the house was a sea of rusty old parts.

Gail was an artist. The walls of all the rooms were covered with her visions. They looked like pictures of bad acid trips or heavy metal album covers. I liked the way she and Martin didn't seem to give a shit about what people thought. Or about how they raised little Martin. Or the car parts filling the section in this posh part of town. Or painting every wall with images of hell.

Martin was an American. He wrote poetry because 'it pours from my soul like a river ... like I have no choice man, it's just there'. He read us some. It sounded like Bob Dylan to me, but I liked it. 'Fixing cars ... just puts food in our mouths ... we gotta eat man ... there's no love in it for me.' He and Gail were serious tokers so Devon paid for everything with dope. That night he was after a bottle of Jack Daniels to fuel us while we cruised.

'Dope,' Devon explained, 'is our currency. The trap's thinking it's a doorway. It isn't. It's just a window. The freedom it gives is just an illusion. Real freedom takes more effort, more guts. When the dope wears off you're still in the same room.'

THAT NIGHT WE drank and talked, cruising the streets, eyeing up other cars and other drivers. The later it got, the more street racers appeared. At 11 p.m. we headed for Queen Street. The mum and dad traffic had thinned and the beastie cars were gathering. RX7s, Skylines, worked Holdens, Evos, Integras and grunty old Falcons with bucking hydraulics. There were small cars too, like Devon's: 323s, CRXs, Civics and Lasers, everything you could think of. There were even a few cars that were worth big money, like Porsches and BMWs.

A blue Mercedes with four kids in it pulled up next to us at the lights. Devon had his choke out slightly to produce the rough chug-chug idle that suggests a racing cam. The Merc slid in beside us, silently biding its time, the guys in front, girlfriends in the back. The driver kept blipping the gas pedal and peering our way, anything to get our attention: but unworked, the motor just went swish, swish, swish. Devon carried on talking to me as if they didn't exist. When the lights went green he floored the gas pedal and then shut off almost immediately. The Merc took off down Queen Street like a raped ape. A solo drag. What a shrink! A block later at the lights we chugged up next to him. The kid driving looked shamed. He'd blown it. He'd tried to race someone who wouldn't engage. A bit like reaching out to shake someone's hand just to have them whip it away. This time it was them looking away and Devon with the big 'Mr Friendly' smile.

'Just school kids in a D.C.,' he said.

'What's that?'

'A D.C.? It's a daddy's car. There's no respect in that. No one will race him except other kids like him.'

It was all like that. unwritten rules. Where I came from the races and burn-offs were casual, spur of the moment things. Here, no way. They were carefully thought out and cunningly planned. First it was staring and mini drags, just like we were doing: trying to guess what you were up against, and what chance you had of creaming the opposition. A game of show a little, hide a lot. By the time we all headed to Thunder Road, the pairings were mostly decided. Of course this was the way it worked for those lower down in the order. The top guys, those guys whose cars were really tuned, they all knew each other. They had a running tally of grudge and payback drags that went on until someone gave up or their car got totalled. It was hard core.

About midnight the whole main street of Auckland was packed with snarling drag racers, blipping up and down, and juiced-up wannabes making claims their cars couldn't possibly back up. There were cop cars too, checking out anyone who got too frisky and did anything stupid. Devon pulled the Escort over and ran back to a Holden ute parked on a bus stop. I could see him yacking to the driver. Suddenly I noticed the traffic had started to thin out and within five minutes all the racers, the cruisers and the parked, had gone.

Devon appeared, breathless, caught out. He stamped the clutch and jammed it into gear. We screamed around the corner, completely ignoring the red light. I waited for the siren to start up but nothing happened.

'They're just pleased to get rid of us. We'll hammer it over to Thunder Road.'

Devon hadn't been exaggerating. It was a carnival of headlights, smoke, and people thronging about. There must have been a thousand cars lining the canyon of warehouses and factories. The place was teeming.

'They've come in from all over. There are guys who drive up from Taupo for this, just for a chance to put their car on the line and have it out. This is something you're never going to see on the *Wide World of Sport*.' He used this fake announcer's voice.

We joined the procession of cars buzzing up and down. It was time to do a couple of runs backwards and forwards to show ourselves and check out the talent. There were knots of young guys sitting on the bonnets of their cars knocking back beer, cars with the boot open letting their sounds out to make their mark, there were even a few girls' cars, which surprised me.

On our way back through, this guy tried to take us. He was driving a lowered 323 with all the windows blacked out. Devon built up speed at the same rate as he did until we were doing about 120 kilometres through the narrow corridor of cars and foot traffic. It was wild! Cars crossing our path at the last moment, drunk dudes staggering around the edge: anything could happen. I realised that it was all on about the time the other guy decided to drop back. Devon backed off too, as soon as the other guy had flagged it.

'Smoked him,' he said with a smile. 'It's about power ... not just car power but guts and nuts too. That guy had the first but lacked it in the second.'

We cruised back towards the starting line, Devon with his window open, acknowledging other guys with his eyebrows or a toss of the head. I could see a slight sheen on his forehead that must have been sweat. He covered his nervousness well.

We found a slot near the start and went off hobnobbing. Devon seemed to know everybody and collected a few calls of 'Good blast, man,' and 'Way to go, Dev,' as we walked from car to car. Some time later a black Mercedes glided slowly down the course. There was a space by the start line that seemed to have been left for it. The windows were tinted so you couldn't see who was inside.

'Who's that?' I asked.

'That's Sloane. The Sloane Ranger. He runs the outfit.'

'What do you mean runs it?'

'He decides what goes down here.'

'Who races who?'

'Mostly who gets what.'

'Dealing drugs?'

'Everything, the whole caboodle. Whenever stuff changes hands Sloane's hand is in there too. Like the tax man, taking his cut.'

'How do you know all this stuff?'

'From Rebel. All the deals he does have to get Sloane's nod at some stage. The Midnight Autos ones too, I reckon.'

'I wouldn't have thought a guy like Rebel would follow the rule book.'

Devon smiled and patted me on the head. 'Look, Trace, people like

Rebel, this *is* their rule book. He understands this one. This was the one he learned all about in Rock College.'

A big Māori dude got out of the driver's side of the black Merc and walked around to sit on the bonnet. He was huge; must have been about two metres tall and 140 kilos. A monster. You could see the front of the car go down when he sat on it. He wore a black leather coat and had face tatts.

'Jesus, I wouldn't mess with him,' I said to Devon. 'That's Tonto. You know, trusty Indian sidekick.'

'Is that what you call him?'

'Shit no, I call him Sir. Actually, his name's Mark. I've never spoken to him or Sloane, they're a bit out of my league. There's a lot of money changing hands here, Trace. Money and dope and cars and favours. Sloane's got a network of stooges who do the deals. He stays pretty aloof.'

'Does he ever get out of the car?'

'I haven't seen him. My mate Bri says he's a stocky little shaven-headed dude with a goatee beard. A thug in a suit.'

We were interrupted by a yellow Skyline winding out some choice doughnuts right in front of our car. The smoke and noise were terrific. Devon didn't look. He seemed to be interested in something down the strip a way.

'Don't look too keen, Trace, he's just a try-hard grease monkey from Huapai. I smoked him a couple of weeks ago and he's been out for revenge ever since.'

He was right. The car stopped in front of us and this string-haired guy with a pock-marked face stuck his head out the driver's window.

'Hey Devon, show us what you've got.'

Devon laughed under his breath. 'Check out the mullet Trace, he's the real article.' Then he yelled, 'Hey Cal, I'm saving mine for the main event. You and me, we got this sorted.'

'I done a bit more to the mill … I reckon you'll be sucking in my smoke.'

'I don't think so.'

'I've taken out Steve Fenton's Torana. I'm ready to eat you for afters.'

'When was this?' Devon suddenly sounded interested. 'on Wednesday night.'

'That's nothing … if it doesn't happen on Thunder Road, it doesn't happen. Forget the little boys' drag games. Can you cook it here, on the strip?'

'I tell ya.'

We were drowned out by two Hondas winding up through the rev range. Virtually identical. Lime green CRXs, full body kits, both cars with Asians in them.

After a slight stuttering start they spun off down the line, distracting Devon and the guy in the Skyline.

Devon turned to me. 'Rice burners! They're taking over.'

There was a sort of wistful tone to his voice like he was describing the end of an era. 'Hop out Trace. I'm gonna cook this turkey, but it will be close. The car's gotta be as light as I can get it.'

I climbed out and stretched my legs in the cold air. I was surprised to see that Devon had fastened his seat belt. I hadn't seen him use one so far. Down by the start line things were hotting up. The swarming back and forth had stopped and cars were pairing off. There was an urgency as wheels were checked and engines were given their final test revs. Devon and the yellow car chugged in at the back of the line.

At the front, two identical eighties Falcons were preparing to start their run: muscle cars, the chrome super-chargers sticking up out of their bonnets like four-eyed aliens. I spotted Mark; he was leaning on the window of the black Merc talking to someone inside. This would be a good chance to get a squiz at the mysterious Sloane. I ran across the strip to walk up behind. It was busy out there, no time to loiter. As I got alongside, Mark straightened up and sauntered back to his position at the front. He signalled to someone with a careless nod of the head. The blacked-out electric window slid back into place.

At that same moment, the two Falcons burst on down the road. This was the big grudge match. The lights of the long line of parked cars on each side of the strip came on and followed the passing racers like a long luminescent Mexican wave. It was a close race, impossible to call from where I was positioned. All I caught was the tail ends of two cars screaming for traction before the headlong blast into the distance, matching gear changes all the way. Soon after that, two fully worked Mazda Rotarys lined up. They were followed by three motor bikes.

Then it got really busy. A pair of matched 323s, a couple of funky Starlets, a Godzilla against an Evo, an RX3 against a Celica in full racing kit. Cars filled up behind Devon and his rival so there was no pulling out. Now, just beyond the start line, I could see two guys about my age on each side of the road; they were the starters. One had a walkie-talkie and the other used a raised torch as the start signal. After all cars in front of Devon had done their runs, there was a break as the competitors threaded their way back up the strip. It was easy to tell the winners this time.

When the road was cleared again it was Devon's turn. It was all very sudden, no messing about. The lamp dropped and two cars wound up to the top of their rev range. Smoke poured up from the road, at first burying the wheel arches and then the whole back end of the cars. The first movement was slow, almost leisurely, as the tyres failed to make a good bond with the black top. Then they both found traction and danced off the mark, the distinctive round tail-lights weaving in the white smoke as they fishtailed down the track. The Skyline seemed to find power of a higher order. Even at a hundred metres it was clear that Devon was well and truly whipped. I felt a pang for him. Beaten so easily.

It was a long, tense wait before he reappeared. I shared his shame and humiliation. After about ten minutes he pulled up next to me: staring angrily ahead, hands gripping the wheel, cigarette locked in mouth. As I got in, the Skyline rolled past on the other side of the road, Cal's triumphant fist punching the air above the car's roof. There was nothing to say so we headed back to our space, each lurking in his own sullen, awkward, little world. We watched the racing for about another hour ... cars pouring down Thunder Road in pairs, the winners and losers threading their way back, triumph or dejection visible from a hundred metres. There was no 'hard luck' or that sort of bullshit. It was harsh but fair.

When all the pairings had worked themselves out the road was given over to stunts, burn-outs and wannabes doing hand-brake slides. Some time during this circus, Sloane's long battle-cruiser slid off into the night. Its regal, unhurried departure made a bigger mark than most of the other stunts by drivers who were doing everything but setting themselves on fire.

Later, the cops showed up. They'd evidently had enough. The talk on the strip was of another street in Penrose, but Devon had lost interest now, so we slunk home.

BACK AT MRS Jacques' we both sat out on the front verandah smoking and staring into the night. After a while, Devon perked up. 'It was always coming, it just came a bit earlier than I thought. I'm relieved, actually. It's time I got something with a bit more grunt. Something not so old.'

'I thought the Escort had lots of grunt.'

Devon leaned back and put his feet on the railing. 'I drove this car of Rebel's a while back, it was a Subaru rally car. A WRX. Completely stripped for racing. All hollow. It was like being tied to the back of a Jumbo jet. Your head pressing into the seat, eyeballs flattening out.

Since then the old Escort has been a bit of … what did the good officer call it? … *an old lady car*. He's right. It is.'

I tried to cheer him up. 'I reckon it's a cool little car, just a bit old maybe. Your carburettor is up against turbos and fuel injectors.'

Devon seemed to have made up his mind. 'I've been messing about in the little league. I want something that can mix it with the big players.'

'I guess you're going to need big money for that.'

He looked at me and raised his finger. 'Wrong thinking man. It's just going to mean bigger risks.'

I couldn't see where he was going with that and I waited for him to start into one of those big lectures, but it never came. He just stared out at the stars like he had made some sort of deal with them. Like it had been all wrapped up.

RISK DIDN'T SEEM such a big word back then. Back then I didn't know the difference between a walk on the wild side, and living on the edge.

# CHAPTER FOUR

**T**HE FOLLOWING MORNING I was up early because I was working. Devon was still out of it ... sheet pulled over his head, a skinny brown leg sticking out across the room. I dressed quietly and slipped off to work without a shower. It felt sort of sleazy but I was too apathetic to do anything about it. I was so tired and my brain was stained with Jack Daniels and dope residue. At work, the customers seemed to be talking to me long distance: there was a delay before any message got through to me.

My tension over Richard and Jason had gone. Half the time I forgot they were even there. All my brain power went into a close reading of the names and quantities of the tints. It was easy to stuff up and once you had mis-tinted a tin you were looking at 60 bucks worth of paint that no one wanted.

Just before lunch time this street kid came in and wanted to buy some glue. He banged coins down on the counter and told Karen to get it for him. I saw it all from where I had just levered the lid off a can of paint. Karen was at the counter all by herself. She looked scared. The other two, Jason and Richard, shut up and made themselves scarce.

She pointed to a sign that said 'No glue to minors'. At first the kid tried to be funny. 'I just want to glue my shoe man.' He pointed at his bare foot.

'I'm sorry, I'm not allowed.'

He was young but he was big. He picked up a two dollar coin and began to rap it on the steel counter.

He chanted softly, 'Get it. Get it. Get it.'

Karen was looking around for support but Bob Bryant was out to lunch and the others pretended not to notice.

The kid walked around the counter and began to look for the glue, treating Karen as if she wasn't there. I saw her face; she was terrified. There was nothing else to do. I sprinted down the aisle to where the kid was rooting through the boxes behind the counter. Getting a good grip on his hoodie, I dragged him clear of the serving bay. He didn't know what was happening at first and I had him most of the way to the front door before he turned on me. Wrenching clear he then danced towards me, one fist up and the other hand low, signalling, 'Bring it on'. One look at his dead eyes told me all I wanted to know. He was so far whacked it didn't matter. There was nothing I could say or do; I was for it. He fixed me in his sights and came towards me, head weaving slightly. He looked like he'd been in plenty of fights before. Surely a brain with that much glue on board must give me some advantage?

We circled each other, waiting for the other's move. When it came, it came at me out of nowhere. The king-hit that means 'It's all over baby … out of the ball park'. I dropped my head out of the arc and he missed my face, hitting me a glancing blow just above the ear. The unspent force left him off balance and he staggered forward into a pyramid of paint buckets. One of the tops came off and a balloon of white paint glugged out onto the polished wooden floor. As he struggled to his feet I snatched the half-filled pot and flung it in his face. He sat there blinking and coughing, trying to work out what had happened. He looked like a melting snowman. The fight was all over. He sloped off, the mess of coins still on the counter. All that remained was a painty trail out the door and down the footpath.

I stood there gasping, my heart beating like an over-revving engine. Karen slumped down on a paint can, her face drained of colour. She looked small and vulnerable. Our eyes met. I walked over and squatted next to her, my hand on her shoulder. I could feel her shivering through the thin nylon uniform.

Slowly things returned to normal and I became aware of a small circle of people standing around us: Richard and Jason, Janice, an older woman from accounts, a few customers. They were all replaying the incident.

'There were two of them … Māoris I reckon….'

'It was a hold-up….'

'He swung a knife….'

Bob Bryant showed up and took over. Janice led Karen, who was weeping quietly, out the back. The police were called. I had to give my version of the events again and again. Jason and Richard got to clean up the spilt paint – and ten litres is a lot of paint.

I didn't have to do much that afternoon. I had this hero status. I tried to play it down – it was a bit embarrassing really – but no one would have a bit of it. I was now part of shop folklore and that was that.

At five o'clock we closed up and made to go. I had been tied up with the police and Bob Bryant most of the afternoon so I thought I must have missed the others. As I walked out the gates I heard Karen's voice. She was in the back of Richard's Jag. They had been waiting. I walked over. There was something in Karen's eyes that I hadn't noticed before. Perhaps it hadn't been there before.

'Would you like a ride home, Trace?'

I noticed the two in the front looking straight ahead, a bit shamed maybe. I didn't reckon that the invitation was coming from them. Also there was something about me and Devon … I couldn't see the two scenes coming together. 'I've got … you know … a prior….'

'You've got a date?'

'No, a mate's taking me to the street races.'

The two in the front grinned and exchanged glances; Karen seemed a bit disappointed.

'It's just that I'm new to the city and this guy Devon's showing me around.'

She smiled. It was pretty. 'Maybe another time.' 'Yeah that would be cool.'

I went to walk off. 'Trace, one other thing.' 'What?'

'Thanks.'

Something about that last little word – my feet hardly touched the ground all the way home.

WHEN I GOT back Devon had gone. Mrs Jacques said he had gone up North for a week or so. He had mentioned that he was writing a piece called 'The Rural Beat'. It was a companion to his Waikato articles. I had forgotten. I was really pissed off. I had blown my chance to make something happen with Karen, and now I was stuck here with nothing to do except hang about.

It was hell without Devon around. Everything got up my nose. Mostly the piano music banging away … the same pieces again and again. The scales were really bad. It was like someone tapping on your head with a stick. After an hour or so I wanted to smash the piano with a sledge-hammer.

Our evening meals were put back later because of Sergei's routines. It must have been about this time that he discovered August, the child prodigy. Small, freckly, red-headed, but a 'huge talent'. He could sure do things to that piano – and he did them loudly and way past the seven o'clock deadline. The pair of them would emerge from Sergei's room, blabbing excitedly – like they were the same age. Sergei even deigned to walk out to August's parents' car, where he would spend ten minutes replaying the lesson.

Sergei changed too. Before he was always on about 'klutzes with fingers like soft bananas'; now he was floating on August's cloud of promise. He and Mrs Jacques would rabbit away at the dinner table.

'August just played a Polonaise by Chopin. Claudio Arrau couldn't have done it better.'

Other times August was the cue for a long story about Sergei's childhood.

'I can see myself as clearly as if it were yesterday … nine years of age … the Warsaw Conservatorium of Music … a cluster of grey-haired professors … they couldn't believe how such small hands could span the chords … .'

I sat silently eating my mashed potato and carrots and watched the two of them: Mrs Jacques, rapt, hanging on Sergei's every word, and Sergei, head slightly tilted back, listening to the sound of his own voice. It was like I wasn't even there.

It didn't take long for this to begin to get to me too. If only Devon had been back to make a few of his sarcastic remarks, everything would have been OK. But he wasn't. It was a nightmare. I looked forward to going to work, just to get out of the house.

SINCE THE INCIDENT with the street kid, Bob Bryant had regarded me with a new respect. He was doing little things that told me he had plans for me in the shop. What as, I wondered? Senior paint tinter? I hadn't minded the job up to that point but the thought that I might be doomed to work on there for the rest of my life was seriously scary. The guy I worked with, Dave, was good-natured but weird. I reckon he came from a country where soap hadn't been discovered ... or maybe where it had been replaced by aftershave. Man, he was strong and he was sweet. Even amongst the fumes of paint thinners he stood out. No one else seemed to notice, but I sure did. Especially when I was standing next to him as he reached for a high tin. Whoa! The other thing he did was bring out weird little phrases that cracked him up. His two favourites were 'Mouldy old dough' and 'ode to Billy-Joe'. I could never get used to that.

Most nights I stayed in my room and read. I hate TV and was trying to save money. I found myself looking forward to the weekend coming around and the weekenders coming in again. When Saturday arrived I was ready to go off to work early, way before the store was open. I had to wait for Bob to open up and then hung around inside with nothing to do. Nine o'clock came, and there was still no sign of them. Few customers too. It was nearly 45 minutes later that they arrived. Karen smiled and gave me a cheery wave. I thought Bob would sack them but he hardly said a word. It was that other principle in operation. The glass dome, different sets of rules. Even here.

When lunch time came around Karen was in the lunch room with her book closed when I arrived back from the bakery. She was waiting.

'How was your night, Trace?' she asked when I walked in. 'Eh? What night?'

'The night on the town with your mate.'

'Oh, it was cool.'

She listened attentively while I invented an exciting evening. It sounded hollow and I felt stink about it, but what can you do? I didn't want to seem like a loser, with no life. Away from the other two she came across sincere and interested. A different person.

'So where are you going tonight?'

'Well, nowhere,' I said and explained how Devon was away and I was trying to save money.

'What for? Varsity?'

I laughed at the thought. 'No I want to go overseas. Aussie probably, for starters anyway. How about you?'

'I want to get into Med School next year with Richard and Jason.'

'What is it, a family tradition?'

She blushed. 'Yeah I guess so. My dad's a doctor and he's been friends with their dads since we were all babies.'

'And that's what you want to do?'

'I guess. I have to be accepted yet, which means that I have to get huge marks in Bursary.'

'Will you get them?'

She didn't say anything, and then changed the subject. 'I told my dad about what you did last week. He said he'd like to meet you.'

It was one of those statements you don't know how to react to. 'What for?'

'For dinner.'

'What?'

'You know, food, drink, conversation… .'

'Whooo….' Images flashed through my head.

'It's no big deal.'

'Really?' I saw myself sandwiched between two old people, getting the third degree. 'When?'

'Well, tonight.' Then she added. 'If you're not doing anything.'

'Sure,' I said. 'That would be great.'

It seemed rude to refuse but I didn't fancy the sound of the dinner-with-the-doctor routine: I had more visions of interrogation. What does your father do? What school did you go to? What are you going to do with your life?

I spent the rest of the day regretting that I'd accepted: torn between dying to see more of Karen and hating anything that sounded like a polite social gathering with its tense talk muttered over the broccoli… .

All afternoon I was really trying not to think of the evening. Not to mentally rehearse imaginary questions and answers. Not to stress over which fork to use for dessert. When four o'clock rolled by I was still wondering what the arrangements would be. Would we all go straight back home in the Jag? Would I be 'one of the boys'?

It turned out to be a bit different from that. A few minutes before it was time to go, Karen slipped me this piece of paper with an address and time on it. It was clear that she didn't want the other two to know what was happening. I realised then that maybe it was tough for her too. I felt a bit selfish. She had pressures too. Just different ones.


BACK AT HOME I found Sergei in a state of high excitement. He and Mrs Jacques were sitting around the dining table while he described every tiny detail of a practice period. He'd had a 'huge session' with August and he was convinced that he had discovered the 'musical equivalent of uranium in this nine year old' ... it was going to 'put him on the map', he reckoned. The people who wrote him off years ago ... they'd have to sit up and take notice ... they'd be sorry that they underestimated him... that they never recognised his outrageous genius ... they'd seem such fools.

I listened to this ... well, half listened to it, while I read the paper. Sergei must have been suddenly aware of my lack of interest, as he turned his focus on me.

'Trace! How is the colourful world of paint?' Then he laughed loudly. Like he had cracked this really witty joke. He prattled on for a short time, pretending to be interested in something other than himself. But then it was back into yet another story that showed his brilliance.

After a while I couldn't stand it any more, I was, as Devon used to say, 'all Sergei-ed out'.

I took a shower and rummaged around looking for clothes to impress a doctor. I settled on clean jeans and T-shirt but I had to recycle some old socks because Devon seemed to have taken my other two pairs up North with him. All this so that Karen might like me ... it felt wrong, but what could I do?

# CHAPTER FIVE

HAVING NO CAR and a poor sense of direction I had to take a taxi to Karen's place. The price was a real body blow to someone desperately saving money. I resolved to walk home. Her parents' house was set back from the road, up a long curving driveway. It had big pillars holding up a massive porch by the front door. I remembered thinking 'appointment with royalty' when I rang the doorbell. Through the stained glass I could see a feminine outline approaching. It was Karen's mother ... she looked more like an older sister.

'Yes? Ahh of course ... it's Trace, isn't it? How lovely! Won't you come in? Karen's in the bath. I'm Helena. Come and meet Raymond.'

They reckon that you should look closely at your girlfriend's mother because that is usually what she is going to look like 20 years down the track. Well, the look wasn't too bad, I thought. Yeah, I could live with that.

There was this man sitting at one of those huge old desks, those ones with all the little shelves and drawers. It looked as if it weighed half a ton and was hundreds of years old.

He seemed older than Helena: balding, stooped, with those funny little half-glasses on the end of his nose. We both stood there for a while, awkwardly – he was adding up a row of figures – then he turned, looking me over carefully, like I was a specimen.

'So you're Trace?' I nodded.

'Where are you from, Trace?'

I told him and he nodded his head like this was really important information.

'And what do your parents do there?'

'My dad's a butcher and my mum helps in the shop sometimes.'

A faint smile briefly flickered at the corners of his mouth. 'And you, Trace, what are your plans?'

'I haven't got any really, I guess buying a motorbike is pretty high on my list.'

We stared at each other for a few minutes – he seemed to have run out of questions – then he barked 'Great!' and went back to his sums. The interview was over.

I felt Helena's hand on my arm as she led me back through to the sitting room. It was a big square room with dark panelling, a wall of books and these paintings, each with dinky little lights positioned over them.

She saw me staring. 'Which do you like, Trace?'

There was this one that looked as if it had been painted by some dude who was whacked out of his skull. It was of a room, but the walls and furniture were all over the place at crazy angles.

'That one.'

'Good choice. It's a Clairmont.'

'*So what?*' I thought.

'Are you interested in the fine arts, Trace?'

'I don't know. I've never thought about it.'

She cleared her throat. 'So what *are* your interests?'

I thought about it for a moment and then I said, 'I guess the art I like is done by mechanics, or bodywork guys. I like the look of a car or bike that's been worked, that means the business, that looks like it's breaking the sound barrier when it's standing still.'

She didn't seem to know how to answer that. I guess it wasn't the answer that she was looking for.

'So, tell me about your home.'

'You mean the place I'm living at?'

'No, I mean the place you come from.'

I was disappointed. She wanted to slot me too. Even though she and Raymond were quite different – she lively and frothy, he reserved and stiff – they couldn't help themselves.

At last Karen showed up. What a relief. She was dressed in tight jeans and a white blouse. Her hair was loose, tumbling down past her shoulders. I knew immediately why, against all my instincts, I had walked into this ordeal. I couldn't take my eyes off her. I thought she was pretty at work but here, it was like she had turned into something else.

Helena poured out white wine into these long glasses for everyone. I couldn't believe the look of the stems … they didn't seem strong enough to support the size of the bowl. My fingers and thumb kept locking on each side of mine, testing it, like you would a twig.

The wine was cold and dry and refreshing. I was thirsty. I skulled mine in two hits then got a refill. A couple of glasses later everyone seemed to be loosening up.

'You certainly seem to like the wine, Trace!' Helena said.

'Well I've never been much into it. I had it figured for old people's drink … but this is nice.' I held my glass out for another refill.

Raymond appeared.

'Ah! The king's come out of the counting house,' I said. I thought this was quite a witty remark, but the other two seemed to wince. It must have been about this time that I snapped the thin stem of my glass, sending the contents into my lap. Helena jumped up like it was some sort of disaster. Like I was on fire. She insisted that I come out to the kitchen and sponge down.

By the time we had dinner I wasn't hungry any more. Raymond claimed that the wine had run out but I figured it had just run out for me. Karen asked me to retell the story of the street kid. It seemed a boring story to me now so I spiced it up a bit, anything to get them to chill, to climb down, to see me as me. At one point I tucked my foot over my thigh. I noticed that I must have slipped my shoes off at some stage. When had that happened? Those socks sure smelled cheesy.

Everything was a blur from that point. I was properly smashed and maybe a bit loud. I can vaguely remember being put to bed in the sun room. Mind you by this stage I couldn't have found the front gate, let alone my way home. Some time during the night I awoke long enough to find that I had vomited on my pillow. I stared through the gloom at a mirror opposite the bed. My face seemed to be bathed in a green glow. It must have been at about five a.m. that I finally woke. The room stank of vomit. Apart from the pillow and sheets it seemed to be mostly on the clothes I had gone to sleep in. My head felt as though it had been in a hot vice all night. It pulsed. I had a red sore spot, a bit like a rash, on my back. Then, as I struggled to view it in the mirror, I saw the cause lying on the bed. I had slept on a hair brush … the rash was bristle marks. I knew I had made a complete arse of myself; all I could do was to try to limit the damage. I stripped the bed and went looking for a washing machine. I planned to throw the pillowcases, sheets and my clothes into the machine and wait around until it had finished. But then what?

A cheerful chat? I knew I couldn't face that so I stuffed all the sharp-smelling sheets into the pillowcase and set off on foot.

THE WALK HOME took nearly two hours. When I had thrown every scrap of clothing and bedding into Mrs Jacques' washing machine, it was time to go to work. I hoped the second walk would burn off my hangover. It didn't. I stalked into my mixing bay and pretended to be busy. Richard and Jason turned up at the usual time but this time without Karen. I knew then, if any further proof was needed, that every aspect of the evening had been a disaster. I had made the giant leap from hero to zero in one tiny step. Depressed, as well as feeling ill, I felt the day stretch before me like an uncrossable expanse. The torture of hearing Jason and Richard wittering on only made things worse.

Jason: 'If a galvanised clasp falls in the desert, does it make a sound?'

Richard: 'Sounds are only weak evolutionary excuses to justify the existence of ears. ugly things, ears. You notice birds and aliens don't have them.'

Jason: 'Birds have them. They just don't stick out like yours.'

Richard: 'That must be why you never see a bird wearing glasses.'

Jason: 'Ear ear!'

Richard: 'Take Van Gogh's ear for instance.'

Jason: 'Which one are you offering? Attached or detached?'

Richard: 'The one he sent to Gauguin maybe. Hey what did Gauguin say when he got a package from Van Gogh?'

Jason: "Ello! What 'ave we 'ere?'

At about this stage I gave up and told Bob Bryant that I was feeling ill. The flu I thought. I must have looked pretty bad because he sent me off without a second thought. I was home by midday and fell asleep almost straight away.

THE FOLLOWING DAY I was feeling better but decided I couldn't go back to work yet. I was too shamed. I hung around the house reading and sleeping. Mrs Jacques didn't like this one little bit and made no bones about telling me. If I was going to 'lie around like some member of the great unemployed' then I had better start looking for alternative accommodation because that was not the kind of place she ran here. 'No sir.' This was a 'respectable house'.

I was in a foul mood anyway and this did nothing to improve it. I longed to make a few remarks about her and Sergei and what they could do with their house, but something stopped me. I guess it must have been Devon. I knew that underneath it all things would be OK when he returned.

But where was he? He had been gone for a week now. He had stepped out of my life as suddenly and as unexpectedly as he had stepped into it. I had put myself in that position of relying on another person and now this was the price.

The only way around it was to go back to work and bury myself in paint tinting and lunch room discussion. My boss, Bob, didn't seem to mind the fact that I'd had a few days off but Dave went on and on. How he had to carry me … I was letting the team down … it was all right for me … when he was starting out it would have meant the sack … all this with scatterings of 'Mouldy old dough' and 'Ode to Billy-Joe'.

At smoko the topic was the declining standard of youth today and what it was like in their day.

In summary:

Today's youth don't know how lucky they are.

In the old days a good kick up the arse fixed most things.

The world's going to hell in a handcart.

# CHAPTER SIX

**T**HERE WAS A tap at the window.

Shit! It was Devon.

'Open up man!'

I opened the casement window and extended my hand. The top of a black plastic rubbish bag was placed in it.

'Take this!'

I hauled it up. It was quite heavy ... about 15 kilos or so. Then I pulled Devon up onto the window ledge.

He sat there getting his breath back for a moment and then lit up a smoke.

'What's happening, man?' I asked. 'Where've you come from?'

Devon grinned and sat there for a while enjoying my confusion.

His white, if kind of crooked, teeth showed up against his olive skin.

'What do you think's in the bag?'

I looked at it, then picked it up again, jiggling it, trying to pick the weight. 'Well, let me guess ... your clothes?'

'Nope. Try again.'

'Money?'

'Good as.'

'Can I look?'

'Be my guest.'

I unwound the thick gaffer tape around the neck of the bag and opened the top.

There was the overpowering, composty smell of drying vegetation. Because of the huge quantity, it took me a few moments to realise what it was. It was dak. Masses of it. I couldn't believe how much there was. The most I'd ever seen was an ounce bag.

'Shit a brick. Marijawacky. Are you into horticulture?'

'I've always had a soft spot for whores and their culture.'

There were going to be no straight answers tonight. 'True?'

'Do you want the truth?'

'Yeah.'

'Why?'

'Call me old-fashioned … I like to just touch base with the truth every now and then so I have some idea of reality.'

He shook his head and gave me a pitying look. Like I had no imagination.

'Weeell it's like this.'

'oh yeah.'

'Would you believe … that I carry this stash around for my own personal use, Your Honour?'

'Young man, that must be a shitload of big doobies.'

'Shall we adjourn for a cup of tea?'

'Adjournment granted, but we'll have to be quiet. Mrs Jacques has been a bit intense recently.'

I tiptoed out to the kitchen and went about making a pot of tea. Mrs Jacques' light was still on so I assumed that she wouldn't wake up too terrified if she heard me in the kitchen. As I waited for the jug to boil I found I was trying to suppress my giggling. I was so excited that anything would set me off. Mrs Jacques' apron, my grinning face caught in the reflection of the kitchen window … it was like I was stoned already just from looking in the bag. When I came back in Devon had rolled a thick joint that looked like a 20 dollar cigar. He stretched out on my bed with this obscene spliff sticking out the middle of his mouth, legs crossed, hands behind his head. The picture of relaxation. I quickly closed the door. It was understood that we were about to imbibe. The story was going to be slow coming. Devon loved the long twisting yarn.

'OK. Did you know that I had an assignment as a stringer based at the Whangarei Polytech?'

'What's a stringer?'

'A sort of local agent to feed back news to the big paper. Anyway I get this story … a chance to go with the cops up in the hills behind Whangarei.'

He changed his tone of voice and went into newsreader mode. 'I was given the assignment to cover the operation which has become…' he raised an eyebrow in mock seriousness, 'as I am sure you are aware … *a major PR exercise.* The police and the government collaborate in this to convince *a disbelieving world* that not only are they doing something about dope, but … an unbelievable but … but, they are making real progress *clipping back* N.Z.'s biggest horticultural money earner.'

'You sound as though you could have gone to *60 Minutes* with this one.'

'Oh I could have, but there was much to be done, you know, putting names and faces in the story, first person colour. And something even more important.'

He paused, waiting for a response. 'Such as?'

'A ride in a helicopter.'

'OK. OK. That, I can relate to.'

'We had this big grid map and we were out to spot the patches in the early summer period when the foliage of the dope plant is clearly paler than the native bush. I was on the left hand side and they had another spotter on the right. The pilot had a cop in the front whose main job was to spot and record our findings.'

I was amazed that he would stoop that low – even if there was a helicopter ride involved. 'So you're now an official spotter for the feds?'

'Yeah, a bit ironic considering how much of the stuff I've inhaled over the years. Which reminds me….' He pulled the joint out from behind his ear, lit up, then took a monster whack on the end. The tip must have glowed for a full 30 seconds.

'Careful Devon, it will come out the soles of your feet.'

He gave an involuntary snort. The smoke shot out from every orifice.

'Toke?' He asked in a high-pitched voice as he tried to hold his breath.

'Thanks,' I squeaked back, mimicking.

Devon breathed out and continued. 'Well, in part of the limitless jungle I spotted this thick dope patch. I held off calling out *dak attack*, our code word for the day, to see how long it took the others.'

Devon stared vacantly into space for a period. I guessed he was replaying the incident in his dope-addled brain. I nudged him back into action.

'To cut a long story short … thanks …' (taking back the joint) '… we flew … or chopped our way South … no one recorded anything. Now what made this more interesting was that we were quite close to the main road. And the patch ...' he took another puff '... and the patch was close to … the turn-off to Dargaville.' 'So you made a mental note. And then sneaked back and hacked it all down,' I said.

'Right and wrong. I snuck back and hacked out one plant, bush, tree, call it what you will.'

'Why only one? Shit, this is quite strong.'

'In another month it will turn your brain to jelly.'

'True? Why only one plant?'

'Good question. I was hoping you might ask me that.'

Devon lay back on the bed and looked at the ceiling for a while. And then almost immediately closed his eyes and went to sleep. I studied him. We were the same age but Devon was painfully skinny. He ate like a horse but never put on weight. Mind you, he did smoke incessantly. Why had my life been so dull since he had been away? He was trouble. He was unpredictable. He was out of control. But more than all of this, he was essential.

THE NEXT THING I knew there was this Bang! Bang! Bang! at the door. It was Mrs Jacques and she was highly pissed. The last thing I had done before I dropped off into Wonderland was to pull the chest of drawers in front of the door. I didn't want any embarrassing discoveries. Devon was still so out of it, he hadn't heard anything. The big black plastic bag was in the middle of the floor and the room stank of chopped vegetation.

'Trace, what's the matter? Why won't this door open? Who's in there with you? Why aren't you going to work?'

The questions came at me like machine-gun fire. I leapt up, my mind in a mad panic as I rushed around, trying to hide incriminating evidence. I threw the bag out the window. When I staggered over, hauled the drawers back and opened the door, her eyes were shiny and she was jumping from foot to foot as if the floor was red hot. 'What's going on, Trace? Who's there? What's that smell?'

When someone else has really lost it there is a bit of time to play with. I let her work it out of her system for a while. I felt like patting her on the head but restrained myself. No point in pushing my luck. With a smile I pulled the door open, showing the sleeping Devon and the room in its usual mess.

'What's the panic? Nothing unusual!' 'When did Devon get here?'

'In the middle of the night. I'm taking the day off. He's been tramping and has stunk the room out with his bush smell.'

I had this slightly outraged tone of voice. I was amazed at my own inventiveness. She was starting to back off. I didn't want her nosing around. Devon was bound to have left that jumbo joint to smoulder out on the carpet.

'Smells fishy to me,' she said, but went back to the kitchen. I could hear sniggering behind me and saw Devon's form jerking away in fits of laughter under the covers. He had just been faking, letting me handle it by myself. I was a bit pissed off.

Thinking on my feet is not what I do best. That was his area. 'Where's the dope bag?' he asked, sounding a bit edgy for once.

'Sergei put it out for the rubbish truck,' I answered in an off-hand sort of way.

That made him sit up fast. I pointed out the window. 'It's out there. You're going to have find some secure place to hide it. Somewhere that won't stink the house out.'

'I know that,' he replied, grabbing his keys and levering himself out the window. He scooped up the bag and put it in the boot of his car. When he turned around he found himself face to face with August. They had some sort of conversation, August in his grey shorts, red blazer and cap. The image of a little private school boy. They both walked up onto the verandah together. When August had gone into Sergei's practice room, Devon told me that he wanted to know what was in the bag.

'What'd you tell him?'

'Grass clippings.' He raised his finger as though teaching a lesson.

'Never lie unnecessarily, remember. "The truth shall set you free". He had this Sunday school teacher's voice on.

I shook my head at him. 'If you're not careful the truth will lock you up.'

# CHAPTER SEVEN

THE DAY STRETCHED before us like an untold story – full of possibilities and excitement. It was like I'd been bailed out of jail: I relished my new-found freedom.

Devon wooed Mrs Jacques with stories of the terrible living conditions he had suffered up North and how he was so pleased to be back 'in the bosom of the family that's more of a family than my real family'. I shrank a bit; it seemed mean to lead on people who believed you.

After breakfast Devon suggested that we go visiting, so we fired up the Escort and headed west. He wanted to know what I'd been up to while he had been away. I told him about the shop fight, the dinner party, the drunken escape. He hung on every detail. We drove on in silence for a while, then he turned to me and said, 'You're not tough enough to hang with the richies ... specially try-hard doctor richies. You see, Trace, they've got where they are because they've played the game. Every fucken twist and turn. They were raised carefully, tried hard at school, worked hard for their quals, grafted hard for their money... '

'You reckon being a doctor is hard work?'

'*They* do, that's the main thing. Then they slowly and carefully claw their way up so that their kids will have a shorter distance to claw. It's a bit like evolution.'

'So you reckon they're tough?'

'Shit yeah. They love the game. Anyone who doesn't play it or doesn't play it their way ... they're shit. You're shit man. I'm shit too. You had this curiosity value, because of the fight in the shop, but that was it. Don't think for a minute that you were ever in there. In with a grin. You never blew it, Trace: there was nothing to blow. You were just the floor show for the night and you played it to perfection, right down to guiltily skiving off with the sheets.'

I said nothing. I was feeling scungy and small about what had happened anyway but hearing Devon talk made everything so much worse. I was stupid, a real country hick, just when I thought I knew a few things. I sat staring miserably straight ahead as we wound through the nameless, bleak suburbs.


REBEL WAS OUR first stop. Mr Midnight Autos lived out at a sort of half-country, half-town place on the western outskirts of Auckland. It was a house that had been lifted up on concrete blocks with the whole downstairs made into a garage and workshop. There were two more big sheds out the back. The section was huge and overgrown, with a corrugated iron wall all around. Something like a gang headquarters crossed with a wrecker's yard. A lively Rottweiler was tied up by the gate. It seemed to know Devon but gave a couple of obligatory barks. He walked over and patted it as it stood up on its hind legs.

'Hey Boris ... good dog. This is the Bunker,' he said, turning to me.

'Why does he call it that?'

'Well, Rebel, he's a bit of a Hitler fan. He's read *Mein Kampf* for

Christ's sake. The Bunker was where Adolf and Eva finally bought it when the Russians closed in on them. You should get him talking about it one day.'

We tracked Rebel down in one of the big sheds and I saw what Devon had been on about. It was full of Nazi bits and pieces, most of it crappy replicas, but there was a big red flag with a black swastika hanging from the roof and Rebel had a real bayonet stuck into the surface of the desk.

Two identical MR2s side by side were getting the attention. It looked as if some serious mixing and matching had been going on. At the other end were a hoist, gas bottles, grinders, racing seats, sets of spotlights and piles of engines and mags. You could have built several cars with the bits. Rebel sat at a dirty old desk talking on a cellphone.

'What are we after?' I asked Devon.

'Man, we've got to get you a car. People aren't meant to walk.'

'I've got to get some bread together first. I haven't saved anything yet.'

He turned to me. 'Let me tell you something.'

'What?'

'You never will.'

'Yeah? So when do I get my car? I'd fancy a motorbike instead, I reckon. A big, old, oily Triumph. Something that really rattles and roars.'

'Oi! It's Jig and Trace,' Rebel said, finally tossing down the phone onto a torn, detached car seat.

'Hey Rebel, I need wheels for my man Trace here. He was on a date and had to catch a taxi.'

Rebel winced in mock pain. 'It shouldn't happen to a dog.' He looked at me. He had mean, hungry little eyes. 'What are you after, Trace?'

'Well I've got fuck-all money, so I guess that would limit it a bit.'

'A bit. It's not about money, Trace.' He fired a glance at Devon. 'You're just trying to save what you earn at the paint shop?'

'Trying.'

He and Devon exchanged smiles and head-shakes like I was some kid who had gone off the rails.

'So what would you like? Jig reckons a muscle car, an old Charger, four-barrel Holley carb, mags.'

'No. I reckon a motorbike. British. Triumph Bonneville maybe.'

He seemed to consider it for a moment and then said, 'Good call. Come with me.'

We walked over to the house and in the gloom underneath I could see a couple of bikes. One was the gaudy Kawasaki 250 Motocross that we'd seen on the back of the ute that first day, and the other was an old grey Norton Atlas.

'Take the Norton. It needs someone to run it about, no one's ridden it for a while. You'll have to get reg and warrant for it, but Jig can help you with that, eh Jig? You still got that tame mechanic?'

'Martin? Yeah he's got a book of stickers.'

'I just take it? What do you want for it?'

'I'm not selling it man, I'm *loaning* it to you. I don't have any plans for it at the moment. Fire it up.'

I turned on the ignition and tried to kick it over. The stiffness and the compression made it really difficult. It just chuffed, lifelessly.

'Try turning on the petrol,' Rebel said, pointing to the little tap under the tank. I felt a dork.

'Let me have a go, there's a knack.'

He pushed me aside and sprang down on the kick-starter. There was the slight chuff that signalled the willingness to fire. Second time around it roared. A big plume of blue smoke hung around us as the motor blew out the residue of old oil and dust. It was a beautiful, honest noise, a big, low-revving British twin: 750cc of the sweetest boof boof

boof boof I had ever heard. Deep and straight, no turbo tricks, just metal muscle. It sang in my heart. I couldn't believe it. What a buzz!

Rebel looked around for a helmet and found one of those bad-ass matt black jobs that gang members wear.

'Here! Wear this. This is the deal man.'

I looked inside it, at the soiled foam liner. I wondered what heads had been in it before me.

'Where did it come from?' asked Devon.

'Let's just say the guy who owned it won't need a helmet where he is. He lost it on the Te Rapa straights. Passing a car in the rain. Hit a milk tanker. This helmet was the only thing that wasn't scrunched. It came off.'

'Oh, great!' I said.

'Don't worry about it. Helmets are just another fucken government con job.'

Devon nodded in agreement. 'You shoot through, Trace. I'll see ya in about an hour.'

I could see that I was being got rid of, that there was some other deal going down, but I didn't care. I ambled out of the yard and back in towards town.

They both watched as I rolled the idling bike out the gates. The big Rotty gave my leg an interested sniff but backed off when I gave the Norton a rev.

'It's a beast!' I thought.

The clutch was incredibly stiff, as though frozen. I found first gear and let it out with a jerk. The bike reared, but didn't stall. We were off.

As I flicked up and down the gears I could feel things begin to loosen up. It was like the arthritic old joints of a sleeping giant. The dead weight of the bike disappeared as I found the rhythm of throwing it over low on the corners. It was like learning to ride all over again.

The traffic thickened up and I spotted the motorway more by

chance than anything. Time to open it up. I wrung my right hand back on the grip and felt the bite of the power train bonding with the smooth black road... .

*At about six and a half the torque flattens out and I click it on to third. The acceleration is still intense, fingers straining at the grips and helmet desperate to part company with my head. At 130 ks I chop into top. A cop car buzzes past on the opposite side of the motorway at 150. I'm gone at 170. I'm invincible, whipping past cars as though they were bolted to the highway. My eyes are streaming and I'm straining to see through slits. I see the green exit sign up ahead and begin the rapid clunk down through the gears. When my feet touch the ground at the lights they are numb with the tension and vibration, but my whole body is awash with adrenaline. I feel like a god wandering through mere mortals... .*

Riding that big old British cruiser had blown away the shame and the failure that had been sticking to me like a bad smell ever since Karen's place. All that really mattered was keeping in the power band and choosing the right line for the corner. A lesson for me, I thought.

BACK AT Mrs Jacques', I sat on the verandah staring at the Norton where it stood majestically on the front lawn. It was a beautiful object; no car combined such delicacy with such power. Some peasant had painted it all with matt grey paint. The first thing I'd have to do would be to get it resprayed in its original colours. It needed a wash so I attacked it with a bucket of water and dishwashing detergent. As I was scrubbing away at the layers of hardened crud on the tank I found the grey paint came off too. Underneath it was shiny iridescent red: the original colour. They had sprayed over a perfectly good paint job! An hour of hard scrubbing and careful scratching with my fingernail revealed the Atlas in its original glory. Crimson tank and chrome mudguards: a 200 kilo thunder machine, from the days when Brit bikes ruled.

When Devon returned he was amused that the bike had changed colour.

'A lot of Rebel's vehicles are matt grey,' he said. 'He must like the colour. Maybe it reminds him of the SS.'

'You don't think it could be stolen?'

'Stolen? Rebel? No! No, Trace! How could you? You ingrate!' Then he burst into laughter.

'Well, it's all right for you, Devon. I don't want to be riding around on a stolen bike.'

Devon held his hands out in the *calm down, calm down* mode. 'It's cool! My car's a Rebel car. I've been stopped heaps. He knows what he's doing, Trace. You've got to have a bit of faith, man.' He sang a few lines. 'I'll get you a warrant and reg next time I see Martin.'

'Why does he call you Jig, Devon?'

'Nickname. Short for Jiggaboo.'

'Jiggaboo?'

'Yeah, you know, nigger.'

'No.'

'Rebel and the guys he hangs about with hate blacks, eh. It's like one of their articles of faith. See a black by himself and they'll smash him. No questions asked.'

'You mean Māori?'

'Yeah. What do you think I meant? Nee grow?' he said with big emphasis.

'So he thinks you're Māori?'

'Maybe, he's not sure … so it's just Jig … to remind me … like I have a question mark hanging over me.'

'Are you?'

'My people are from Spain. Santos. That's a Spanish name, eh?'

'Oh. I assumed you were Māori, I guess.'

Devon's tone changed. 'Yeah, well I'm not. OK?'

It was one of those disappointing moments when you try to look past some major flaw in someone you admire. Try to pretend they didn't have it.

'Jesus, Devon. I've Māori on my mother's side. What's the big deal man?'

'Yeah, well with skin your colour people don't assume stuff, you know. It gives me the shits. I put up with Jig from Rebel, he's a mad bastard … and he's useful, but I get it a lot, and I'm sick of it.'

I put my hands up to say, 'Chill Bro!' I'd stumbled on some sort of big issue and I didn't want to pursue it. I didn't want anything to prick my little bubble of happiness. Somehow in the course of half an hour he had got me this glistening dream machine. I learned that day that there were two things you didn't question with Devon; the other one was money. It was always trade or payback. Cash in the hand was always avoided. What would the payback be for me? And when?

# CHAPTER EIGHT

**A** COUPLE OF days after I got the Norton I found the nerve
to drop around to Karen's place. I had blown it but I wasn't
prepared to flag things so easily. I hoped that beyond her
parents and the differences between our backgrounds we might
still have the chance of getting something going. Thought we
could rise above the fishhooks of family.

I had this idea that arriving with the clean washing might help
smooth things over. I folded it neatly, bagged it and tied it to the back
seat of the bike. By the time I arrived at the front gates I'd had second
thoughts. My nerves were wavering. Maybe another peace offering was
in order.

I knew this big rose garden that looked out over the sea. A good
chance to 'say it with flowers'. I went back and in a few minutes I had
hacked off a big bunch of stems with my pocket knife. On the other
side of the plots there was a bus load of old people wandering around
yakking, so I tried to keep a low profile. But maybe a knife-wielding,
rose-stealing motorcyclist isn't that inconspicuous, because a posse of
them bore down on me and drove me out of the gardens. One big old

guy made a staggering rush to catch me so I had to shove the roses down the front of my shirt to avoid 'an unpleasant incident'.

When I got to Karen's the second time I drove up the drive and parked my bike right outside the front door. Karen's mother answered the bell.

'Oh, it's Trace.' She looked back over her shoulder. 'And what can I do for you?' Her voice cold.

'Yeah, I guess I umm … blew things the other night. That wine sort of snuck up on me … I've brought back your sheets.'

She seemed to soften. 'And, umm, these roses.'

'How nice,' she said and then, 'Trace, you're bleeding.'

And so I was. The roses-down-the-shirt trick had scratched the front of my chest.

'Just a flesh wound.' And then, 'Blood and Roses. Good name for a band.'

She seemed pleased with my wit.

'That's really sweet, Trace. Look, Karen's not here at the moment. I'll give them to her when she gets back.'

I was going to say how sorry I was: for getting drunk, for breaking the wine glass, for vomiting over the bed clothes, for coming across like a hoon. But it looked like I wasn't going to get the chance.

I stood there on the step, wondering what the hell to do next, then Helena said something that was meant to resolve it once and for all.

'Trace, this year is a really busy one for Karen. She has Bursary coming up and a lot is riding on how well she does. We like to treat her like an adult as much as we can but in this instance …' she faltered, '… in this instance, Raymond has decided that it would be best for all concerned if she gives study her *undivided attention*.'

She said this crisply, like those politicians you see reading a prepared statement.

'Isn't she coming back to work?' She shook her head.

We stood there for a moment or two. I didn't know what else to say. She seemed to have a few things she wanted to say too, but nothing came. It was tense and embarrassing. I was only one step from her, but the gap seemed as wide as the Grand Canyon. I had this feeling that someone else had stepped into my life when I wasn't looking and had messed about with stuff. That I was crap, and a fool. I said goodbye and left.

EVERYTHING FELT HOLLOW on the way home. The bike's hoarse exhaust note and massive weight were the only things that had any solidity. The rest of the world was as thin as tissue paper and in danger of floating away.

As I arrived back at Mrs Jacques', Sergei was seeing off August at the front gate. He made some smart-arse comment as I climbed off but I couldn't hear it because I had my helmet on. August's mum, an upmarket blonde woman, was chatting to them both while her husband waited in the car. They both stopped talking and stared at me as I parked the bike. I stood there for a moment weighing up whether I should ask him to repeat it. A good excuse to give someone a smack in the mouth. I slunk inside, annoyed that Devon hadn't come home, and threw myself on the bed. I began to replay the scenes from my brief relationship with Karen, wondering if I could have done things differently. It was as if the family had dumped me for being me.

When Devon did finally return I could tell without getting up that he had a new car but I felt so shitty I wouldn't even look out the window. He walked in the door and shot a glance at me, seeming to take everything in.

'What's up?'

'I went around to Karen's place to take back the laundry, make amends maybe. It didn't work. I've become an instant leper.'

Devon grinned and shook his head. 'I've never been one to say "I told you so" but … I told you so. Wake up, Trace, it's the real world, not fairy-dairy-land. It's ugly out there. You had a brush with the rich and boring. Don't give a flying one, man. It makes you look so pathetic. You're better than that.'

'Devon, I reckon there are some things that you don't understand. You weren't there, eh?'

'I've been there. I didn't like it. I've done dumb stuff too. But not twice in a row. Rule number one: don't play by their rules … you always lose.'

'Yeah. What's rule number two?'

He thought for a while, and then, in a quieter voice said, 'Don't want it too much. You don't even know what it is you're after. Look, Trace, I *know* real rich people. They're not all like that. Just these "play by the rules" stiffs. They're killers.'

I must have looked a bit down, because Devon got up, gave me a thump on the arm and said, 'Come out with me, I'll take you to meet my old mate, Wes. He's the guy who first had the idea of importing used Japanese cars. Began shipping out four or five, now it's a shipload at a time. Lives on Parasite Drive. Swimming pool, Bentleys and Jags, dodgy houseboys. He does it the way it should be done. He's got style.'

I didn't feel like socialising but it seemed a better idea than lying around feeling sorry for myself. Devon was dying to take me somewhere. Outside was the reason: a Subaru WRX. A rally car for God's sake. You could see the faint outlines of advertising stickers beneath the matt grey primer paint.

'Do I see the hand of Rebel here?'

'Yeah, he's borrowed mine for a while. He probably wants something legit.'

It was a difficult beast to get into because of the roll bars and the tight racing seats. The inside had been completely stripped: the dashboard was a nest of gauges dominated by a huge tach. Devon fired it up. The motor snarled back with an ugly cackle. It was a bitch to drive: the clutch bit sharply and the motor's power was so raw it had to be tamed. Devon struggled to keep it within the legal limit; it jerked forward like an unbroken horse, champing at the bit. One thing was for sure, it would cover quarter of a mile in half the time the Escort took.

BY THE TIME we made the waterfront Devon seemed to have the knack of it. When he laid rubber now it was on purpose, not bad driving. We reached the cliff-top road, which was lined with huge white houses crammed together like a jaw full of jagged teeth.

'Paritai Drive, Trace. For people who have made heaps and heaps of money … and aren't afraid to show it off.'

Wes lived in a sprawling white stucco place, the kind they built in the thirties, but it had been added to by each new wave of money that had rolled in. The driveway was as stuffed with big British metal as Devon had said it would be. This young Asian guy answered the door. He looked like Bruce Lee and seemed to share some private joke with Devon.

'Hey Joey, where's the padre?'

'On a phone. Come through, Devon. He just asking about you las' week.'

In the front room were all the reasons why people paid a million bucks to perch on a big cliff overlooking Auckland harbour. The dark water scrawled with their reflection, the city lights sparkled all around us. A man in his sixties wearing a white bathrobe ambled in, muttering away into a portable phone. He mimed a greeting to both of us and signalled Joey to get us something to drink. Me and Devon sprawled on the big L-shaped bank of white couches and waited for the conversation to finish. Joey came back with beers in tall glasses, a tiny black coffee for Wes, then he disappeared.

'Wes' idea of a Jap import,' Devon whispered, grinning.

I was trying to get a fix on what Wes was talking about. It was mostly numbers. Money I guess. Eventually he held the phone away from his head and pressed the off button while fixing us with a conspiratorial grin. Although pushing 70, there was something mischievous, almost boyish, about him. His watery blue eyes were the only touch of colour. His smooth, unblemished complexion was unnatural on a man of his age. As though he had never been exposed to the harshness of the atmosphere. Like a baby maybe or a maggot.

He had this fussy way of talking, as if he was dictating to someone in the next room; everything was said slowly, and with great care.

'To what do I owe this late night visitation, dear boy, and who, may I ask, is this?' He waved a spotted handkerchief in my direction.

'This is my mate Trace, Wes. He's from the Waikato ... a simple country lad ... here in the big smoke to seek his fortune. Just like I was, long ago.' He made it sound sad, in that ironic way of his.

'Ah, the fecund land of mist and rain. I always knew someone lived there. So it was you Trace, all the time.'

I smiled, pretending to get the joke.

'And Devon is your guide to the fleshpots and hot spots.'

I nodded. He turned to Devon who had stretched out along the white sofa.

'Now tell me, Devon, what have you been doing?'

He leaned back and listened to Devon recount his recent adventures, though Devon didn't mention the dope stealing up North. I was surprised at how frank he was, and how much detail he went into, especially about girls. The old man leaned back on the couch, chuckling and squawking at every risqué incident. It was all told in the puffed-up style of Wes, as though Devon was playing a role, or taking the piss, more likely.

Devon finished and Wes sighed. 'Ah, what it is to be young.' After a few questions and clarifications he said to Devon, 'Now, young man, I assume this is not a social call. It never is these days. You want something, don't you? What is it?'

'Wes, it's like this. You know I've been living in cramped quarters with the lovely Mrs Jacques and the profoundly gifted Sergei? A humble domicile to say the least, but now I have teamed up with young Trace here,' indicating me with a condescending wave, 'I feel we need something more befitting our lifestyle and aspirations.'

'You require a bolt-hole, as it were, here in the city?'

'Well, OK, that is to say, in a word, yes.' Devon, mimicking. Wes stared at the big windows in front of us for a long time as though he was reviewing his options. He was quite a short man with a big stomach, and a completely naked head. I noticed for the first time that he had no eyebrows or eyelashes. There was no indication that he had ever owned any hair at all.

'As it happens, you may be in luck. You will have to do a little job for it though, just to show good faith.'

'No problem.'

'I have a little cottage in Parnell: part of my burgeoning property portfolio. A tumbledown dog-box, in the best part of town. The thing is going to be torn down as soon as I get planning permission. There is a family in it. I want them out. I bought them with the house, and I have the suspicion that the planning process has been held up because someone in the local council feels sorry for them because they are poor.' The last word he pronounced pooh-ah.

'Extraordinary! Pooh-ah! How dare they!' Devon exclaimed in mock outrage.

'A challenge for you, Devon. If you get them out, the house is yours until I get the go-ahead from the council.'

He paused, then fired off a challenge. 'Show me what you're made of.'

'Consider it done, m'lord.'

We all walked out onto the deck, as if the view wasn't powerful enough from the lounge.

'So you've teamed up with this rapscallion have you, Trace? I assume he is passing on his vision of how it all bolts together?'

I sensed that he was being a bit sarcastic so I looked to Devon for guidance. He was rolling a joint and grinning to himself.

'Has Devon told you much about me?'

'Only that you're the role model for what a rich person should be like.'

Wes laughed through clenched teeth, a scary, hissing noise.

Like an old reptile.

'Yes, I've made and lost fortunes. Money has long since ceased to be a source of enjoyment. I haven't physically touched money for years. I don't know whether I ever will again … *dirty* stuff, money … and yet everything I do revolves around it. It is everything.' He paused, trying to locate the next pithy phrase. 'Yet then again, it is nothing. Like this house, this land we stand on. So much money just for the right to sleep here. There is no *meaning* in any of this.'

Silence. We all stared at the distant lights. He turned to me, his face a smooth mask.

'What is it that you fear, Trace?'

I thought for a while. 'Lots of things. Big dogs, broken glass in long grass, losing my eyesight… .'

'Do you know what I fear?'

I shook my head. He continued to stare at me, his blank eyes drinking everything in.

'I fear nothing. I used to fear death, but I had a stroke a few years back and while I was on the operating table, I got a glimpse of the other side.'

He accepted a joint from Devon and took a leisurely toke. 'I was travelling down a tunnel towards some cool, green place. All I can remember is that I didn't want to come back. I wanted to be swallowed up in it.' He paused, remembering. 'But I was dragged back, by the surgeons at Green Lane Hospital. They were so pleased with themselves. They couldn't understand why I wasn't pleased too.'

'So after this you had no fear of death?' I asked. He nodded and passed me the joint.

'Everything has its price. Fear of death is a primal fear. When I lost that, I also lost the meaning with which death imbues life. It's just a card game to me now.'

out by the gloom of Rangitoto, I could see the red and blue lights of small boats moving slowly in the channel.

Wes turned to Devon. 'Are you happy now, my boy?' 'Yeah. I'm ecstatic,' Devon snapped back.

'Ecstasy,' Wes said wistfully. 'The height of happiness. The Mount olympus of personal pleasure.'

He smiled and looked at Devon and me. 'Ecstasy to you, Devon, may be just a little pill which lets you go on and on, but real ecstasy, that's something different. I have an image of ecstasy and it goes back to the time when I was about your age. Confident like you, certain I had the world by the balls. It's never gone away, not in fifty years.'

Devon fired me a 'here we go again' look. Wes closed in on me. 'In my memory there is this simpleton. This idiot. He could be nine, he could be twenty-nine. They have a sort of immortality, simple people: a fake one. This idiot is standing on a gate at the top of a hill, and he's waving a flag. Waving a flag in the sun.... When I looked at this boy's face, in it I saw a happiness I could never reach. I saw rapture. This kid was just a lightning rod for pleasure. Sucking it down from the ether. It made me sad. What a price for ecstasy.'

'Wes, dope can do that man. OK, you see it as a crutch,' Devon chipped in. 'I see it as a ladder...'

'It's just a weak substitute. This fellow was on another planet.'

'It's a vehicle,' said Devon. 'Dope takes you to that planet....'

'Yes,' said Wes, 'but there's a price. You kids don't realise that until too late.'

Wes reached out and put his hand on Devon's neck. It was a delicate movement and he slowly drew a little medallion out of Devon's shirt.

'What's this, Trace?'

I had a look. It meant nothing to me. 'I dunno. A black tadpole and a white tadpole.'

He laughed. 'Good guess. It is the Korean symbol of Yin and Yang. It was the first present I ever gave to you, wasn't it, Devon?'

'The only one, I think.'

'Ungrateful young pup! This symbol represents the relationship ... the duality of good and evil. There is never one without the other. Notice in the middle of the white tadpole there is a little black spot, and in the middle of the black a white....'

'I thought those were the eyes,' said Devon.

Wes looked at him suspiciously. 'I can never tell when you are being facetious or merely ignorant. No, they remind us that in the centre of any evil endeavour there is always some good, and vice versa. In the middle of any *so-called* good action there is a little bad. Something to muse on, eh boys?'

Devon tucked it back in his shirt. 'They're deep, those chinks.' I winced, but I sort of admired him too. He was rude, but he wouldn't put up with being lectured to. I had something to learn there.


As WE DROVE back, Devon asked, 'What did you make of that?'

'He's freaky. Is he always like that?'

Devon nodded. 'Never changes.'

'He seems a bit sort of you know … inhuman.'

'A bit! He's a fucken psycho. He's the scariest dude on the planet.'

'How'd you meet him?'

Devon paused for a moment, as if rehearsing an answer. 'I met him in the bus depot when I first came to Aucks. I was hanging with the streeties. You know … glue, stiffing drunks, breaking into parked cars.'

'Jesus!'

'Yeah, I've done some shit, OK. It's a tough city when you're fifteen, no money, no home.'

He was pissed at my response.

'So where did Wes fit in?'

'He found me, out of it one night, sprawled out on a bench. Took me home. Hooked me up with this job.'

'How did he do that?'

'Well, Wes is like … connected you know, someone in the newspaper owed him. It just took a phone call. I've been Jimmy Olsen, cub reporter for the *Daily Planet*, ever since. Superman in the weekends.'

'Shit, that was a lucky break.'

Devon laughed coldly. 'I paid for it, don't you worry. There's always payback.' He paused, as if remembering. 'If there's one thing he's taught me, it's that. Nothing's for nothing.'

# CHAPTER NINE

I T MUST HAVE been a month or so later that Devon's question came. I had tried to put it at the back of my mind. I came home from work to see this cute little truck outside the house. It was a red Ford F100 pick-up. The sort you see in movies about wholesome farmers in the midwest. It wasn't new but had a real spruced-up look. Devon was waiting for me on the front steps.

'Where did that come from?'

'The auction.'

'But where did the money come from?'

'Smoke money. It's cool. It cost nineteen hundred. I nearly got it for fifteen but these surfies began to bid against me at twelve and wouldn't let go. The bastards. They knew I wanted it. It's like poker you know, the auction. I was at the point where you say "I'll see ya". It would have been good to see whether they had the money but I couldn't risk it, I had my heart set on it.'

'What sort of mill?'

He lifted the bonnet and propped it open. There was this gleaming motor inside.

'A 350-inch V8. A modern one, overhead cam, four barrel, Holley carb. You should hear it at speed, it sings.'

'So what's happening?' I asked, thinking about all those dope plants sitting there in the patch that Devon had stumbled on. He knew what I meant. 'Harvest's got to be in the next week, ten days. Any later and it'll be gone. Right now it'll be in full bud.'

'Where are you going to dry it all out?'

'That's all covered.' His voice changed. 'What I want to hear from you is,' there was a long pause, '*are you in*?'

So there it was, out in the open, like we had already discussed it. We never had. Too big to talk about. So much rested on those three little words. 'Are you in?' More than the money or the risk, it was a pathway. A new direction.

Dare I leap?

Devon swung up into the cab and lit a smoke. He waited. I leaned over the shiny red mudguard, catching my vague, distorted reflection. I looked up and down the quiet street, at Mrs Jacques' old white bungalow and at our bedroom window. Then I turned to Devon and thought about the new life he had given me.

I nodded.


FOR THE NEXT few days the paint shop became a vaguely remembered film: my past life. Nothing mattered there. All my old interests and routines disappeared. They could sack me if they wanted, I had been chosen for something bigger than that. This person, Devon, had chosen me, Trace, to help him pull off this amazing scam. Mixing paint and staring into space didn't cut it. I longed to be there, sawing down ganja trees, swapping bags of dope for bags of money. Being a player. That was the world I wanted entry into. The last remnants of the old world were uprooted and now, in its place, was this vision, impossibly rich and colourful.


First thing was to organise the details of 'operation Herb' as we called it. We drove up to spy out the land and to get an idea of what to expect. Devon drove fast. We had all the juiced-up exuberance of party goers. I kept running through scenarios of what we would do when.... .

'I guess the big problem will be getting it all to the road?' 'Yeah, even with both of us going flat tack it'll still take a couple of hours.'

As we tore up the big hill just out of Waiwera, I caught the reflection of the moon in the Puhoi River.

'A full moon may not be the best time to do this op.'

'It'll help us walk in without torches,' Devon countered. 'If there are people in the bush ... well, that's important.'

*People in the bush,* I thought. Hell, neither of us had discussed that scenario.

'Will we be able to get a couple of hours undisturbed?'

'It'll be touch and go at this time of year. I bet they check it every night.'

'Maybe they'll have a guard there.'

'I doubt it.'

'Why?'

'Being caught on location by the feds in a plantation that size would have real serious consequences. I'm talking years inside. The courts really make an example of the big growers. It's a P.R. thing, you know, "the rule of law." '

'If there *are* guards we'll just have to take them out.' My fake heroic voice.

Devon would have none of it. 'oh yeah! Like how?' 'Tranquilliser dart guns will do the trick. Not much noise and twenty minutes or so to go hard.'

'You've been watching too many animal programmes on the box. Besides, you know those darts often kill the animals. They don't show you that.'

'Bullshit, they know how big a dose to go for. It's based on the animal's weight.'

'A lot of people think that, Trace.' Devon glanced at me with a condescending, take-the-piss smile. 'That's just to make the viewers feel good. They're wild things ... they die of shock.'

There was a silence for a while until Devon broached something else.

'I think, when we've got this dope safely stashed,' he said, 'I'll set up a team of motivated salesmen. We should place ourselves one step removed from the dealers ... that's where these things always come unstuck. It's the point of sale every time.'

'You have to swap dak for money at some time. That's when you're vulnerable,' I replied, like I knew it all.

'Trace. I've given a lot of thought to this. I've balanced out the trust and the self-protection angles. The dak is given at one time and place and the payment is picked up at another. A completely separate one.'

'What's to stop the buyer from just ripping you off?' 'Greed.'

'How? I don't follow.'

'You know. Killing the goose that laid the golden egg? Well, the idea is this. Sure, he gets a kilo for nix at an agreed price. If he never shows up again, we're down a few bags. But he's lost his place at the money trough. The only person who would give that up would be a really dumb bastard, and we don't want any of them, otherwise we're in all sorts of trouble.'

We drove for another ten minutes until we came to a turn-off, Mangatutae Road.

'It's not far from here, Trace.' 'Good name.'

'What?' 'Mangatutae Road.'

'What does it mean?'

'I don't know what it means all together but separately the words say *shit creek*.'

'So we're headed up shit creek, eh?'

'Whoa… .'

He pulled the truck over. up ahead we could see a ute parked on the side of the road.

'I don't like the look of that.'

'Growers?'

'Could be. There's no houses close to here. Growers or hunters?'

'Both maybe?'

'Well, either way, they'll be armed all right.'

'Shall we risk it?' I asked.

'Shit no. We'll park up and wait for them to go. It'll give us a chance to see who we're dealing with.'

'Back up man, there was a gateway at that cow paddock. We can get the truck off the road.'

'I guess the chance of a farmer being out at this time is fairly slim.'

We backed up. I opened the gate and walked in front of the truck, guiding it carefully to where the paddock was obscured from the road. The grass was damp and slippery underfoot and the cows regarded us warily as we crawled by. Sitting in the low manuka scrub on top of the bank, we could see the ute clearly in the moonlight.

'I wonder if there's anyone in it? If there was they'll have seen that whole manoeuvre.'

'Ifs and buts, man. What's the time, Trace?'

'Eleven-thirty.'

'If they're not back by three I reckon we should piss off. The farmer'll be getting these ladies in at about four thirty and it'll take us at least an hour … in and out.'

'I wonder if I should sneak down and check that ute out?'

'Too risky. There are three hours to go. I reckon we just wait it out.'

We lay in the manuka at the top of the cutting, smoking and talking softly. I kept watch. Devon made a bit of a bed for himself. He was philosophical.

'If it goes wrong at least we tried. I just know now that tonight's the night. Tomorrow it'll be all over.'

'Jesus, what've I got myself into?'

'Better than sitting at Mrs Jacques' watching Sergei clip his toenails.'

'Yeah? Waiting around for a bunch of homicidal dope growers to stagger out of the bush?'

Devon laughed.

It was a warm night and the air was full of that grassy smell of cows' breath. Sweet and nauseating. Devon was asleep. How could anyone go to sleep at a time like this? Every filament of my brain was buzzing with possibilities. I had this feeling that you have just before the race or the big game starts. Your body full of expectation.

Slipping away, I managed to work my way along the top of the bank towards the red ute. It didn't seem the right thing to let it go without at least taking its rego number. I took my time, making sure I made no noise. Every now and then my hands would rest on some tiny gorse plant and I had to suppress a squawk. I bunched the sleeves of my coat down to protect them.

At a hundred metres I could make out the number plate. I wished I had brought a pen to write it down. I would just have to memorise it now. As I turned back to where Devon lay snoozing

I heard a noise and froze. A black dog charged out of the bush. It headed straight for me. I braced myself for the onslaught.

'Heel, Nigger!' a clear call bellowed out. The dog stopped in its tracks then loped back to the ute, surrendering to the voice.

I raised my head. I could make out three men loading stuff on to the back of the truck. Whatever it was, it looked quite heavy. Their party was made up of two big guys and a smaller one. I couldn't see their faces but saw what might be a tattoo on one man's neck as he lit a smoke.

In less than a minute the three men had loaded up and then squeezed into the cab. The dog leapt on the back without a command.

I dropped down flat as they crawled past with only their park lights on. As soon as they were clear I jumped down onto the road and ran back to where I guessed Devon was sleeping.

'Devon! Come on man, let's go!'

'What are you doing?'

'Let's go … they're gone and they have taken a bunch of bags with them too.'

'What stuff?'

'Dope, I guess. I couldn't tell.'

Devon crashed his way down the slope. He was a person who prided himself on his agility but it was difficult to maintain that here. The two of us walked briskly back to where the ute had been parked.

'It's not going to be easy to find on such a dark night, but here goes.'

We clambered up the bank and over a derelict fence. Devon squeezed into the dense forest canopy, pushing aside the creepers and clambering over fallen trees that blocked our path.

'Are you sure this is the way?'

'I'm making for the ridge … then I'll follow it to the fork and head off to the south. I found it before, I can do it again.'

It was bewildering, pushing along in the darkness as Devon crashed his way through bush that seemed to have been undisturbed for decades. I followed blindly on his heels. How easy it would be to get lost in the bush at night. Devon *seemed* to know where he was going, but that didn't mean anything. A spiky vine whacked against my cheek and blood came immediately. Devon pushed on, not noticing that I had stopped. I had to run to catch up. Then, without warning, we were there.

A silver forest in the moonlight. A feathery grove of marijuana plants. Huge ones, like little trees, their sticky heads drooping slightly. Their lateral branches, thick with tiny buds, seemed to reach out to me. They were at once just weeds and then again they were like no other plants in the forest. Just little trees maybe, but charged with magic ... they stood for so much. It was more than finding treasure. Some sticky heart of darkness. More than the money. More than the mind-bending power. They represented a promise that everything was going to be different. No longer were we a couple of no-account guys harassed by the cops, given all the bum jobs and tolerated as tame fools. We had position now. We had arrived.

# CHAPTER TEN

ROUND THE BASE of each tree there was a black bag a bit like a hot water bottle. A sort of watering bag, keeping a small forest of dak in peak condition. Just one of these fairy trees would yield more dry weed than the two of us could buy in five years. In awed silence we squeezed through the plantation. The sticky buds tickled my face and caught in my hair. Greeted me. Stroked me. I looked at Devon. He was grinning like a fool. I reckon we had taken on a small fix by just moving through the throng.

I tried to count them, just to get my head around how many plants we were dealing with. It was impossible: the stand was too thick, too chaotic. At one end there were some felled plants, ready for hauling out. It seemed a crime to have cut them and just left them there. A violation. We would soon fix that.

Devon's face appeared through a gap ten metres away; he was holding a torch under his chin. His head looked like a Halloween pumpkin. 'Fucking amazing man!' I was pleased he was blown away too ... for once I felt that we were reacting on the same level. I wasn't the dumb, small-town boy.

'That says they're coming back soon. Tonight maybe,' Devon said, pointing at the fallen plants. 'We better move fast. I reckon they'll have stashed axes and stuff around here, there's got to be a little shelter or something.'

We set off in different directions, circling the patch, peering into the gloom for something that resembled a shed. There was a sudden clank and I felt a jolt of pain shoot up my leg as I fell down. Feeling tentatively around my heel I found I had stepped on a possum trap. I flicked the torch on again to see a whole line of them glinting off into the distance. Devon almost stood on one as he ran over to me.

'You OK?'

'Great. Just thought I would sit down for a moment.' I shone my torch on the trap.

'Jesus! Possum traps, we should have thought. Possums, the dope grower's second biggest enemy.'

Devon held the torch while I levered the jaws of the gin trap open with my knife. It was an old trap, the teeth blunted by rust ... just as well, because there was still plenty of bite left in the spring.

As we had suspected, there was a little ponga bivouac about the size of a pup tent. In it was a sleeping bag, camp stove, tins of food. Someone had been living there. And recently too: there was a carton of milk. under the low part, below head height, were shovels, saws, axes as well as fertiliser and aphid sprays ... all the clobber you would expect from a serious horticulturist. The most useful tool was a pruning saw: long-handled with a hooked end.

'How many do we take?' 'The lot.'

'We can't fit that many on the Ford.'

'Then we'll hide them and make a second trip.' 'Jesus man! Risky.'

Devon had that snappy tone that made me take notice. 'It's all or nothing. Our one big chance ... look at this ... they're harvesting, they'll be gone by tomorrow. It's a fluke we made it at all.'

He looked at me. There was no humour now, no touch of irony. I was impressed ... he had a core of seriousness I had rarely seen.

'How shall we do it? Chop them up and put them in bags?' 'No. Just cut them down, bind the stems ... the trunks I guess... and drag out as many as we can. We'll stash them on the side of the road and come back for more.'

Despite the thickness of the stems they cut very easily. I had felled half the patch by the time Devon had made up two bundles to drag out.

The moon was up high now and I was able to note a few landmarks as we dragged the bundles through the dense bush. We didn't speak; there was no stopping. The sweat poured down my back inside my nylon jacket. Just when I was about to call for a stop, there was the road glowing dully through the thick canopy.

Devon dragged his pile to the far side and laid it in the gorse. 'We want it handy,' he said, 'but not too obvious. Anything for a quick pick-up and get away.'

It was six trips before we had the last of the plants out. We scarcely spoke. The route became worn and familiar but the last hill felt bigger and steeper each time we approached it. I could see Devon begin to sag ... he had nothing left in reserve when we made the last run.

Halfway back I said, 'Sit down man. I'll dump these and come back and give you a hand.'

He just shook his head, too exhausted to say a word, and plodded on. Honour. It must have been some honour deal.

I looked at my watch. Five-fifteen. It was lightening rapidly. We both tried to run up the road to the paddock where the pick-up was parked but we were so stiff and sore we could barely stumble. The cows were all standing by the gateway waiting to be let out for milking. Surely any minute now we would hear the sound of the farm-bike. We had to move fast. Devon ran for the Ford and I tried to shoo the dumb beasts back. I was fierce but they stood their ground. They knew the routine; it was time to come out the gate. Devon brought the ute up behind them but they wouldn't budge.

'Fuck it. Trace, just let them out.'

So I did. I threw the gate wide and the cows made their unhurried journey down the road. You could almost hear them sighing with relief as they shuffled past. Devon followed them through. I jumped on the back of the pick-up. We really sprayed gravel as our red truck rocketed down the road to where the plants lay hidden.

The bundles quickly made a giant-sized mound on the back of the truck. You couldn't drive anywhere like this, let alone on the main road. You'd get stopped for overloading. I climbed right to the top and tried to smash them by jumping up and down on them. They were springy and refused to break.

As we were squeezing on the last ones we could hear the sound of the farm-bike. We swapped looks. We were never going to make it.

'Better call it quits,' Devon said. 'We'll try another load later.' I lashed the load down as tightly as I could but it still spewed out the back in all directions. How could we drive down the main road like this? Reluctantly I hauled the four extra bundles deep into the scrub. Normally you pick your way carefully through gorse but this time I strode into it like it was soft as emu feathers. I saw blood but felt no pain. Fatigue or T.H.C.?

It was unreal.

'Let's get out of here!' Devon screamed, his voice cutting through my stupor.

We were both too tense to talk on the road back to the highway. We passed the herd of cows blocking the farmer from getting out his gate. His stare followed us as we shot past. I tried to shrink down into the cab. By the time we hit the state highway the sun was up and the cars we met no longer had their lights on. Devon drove tentatively, like a learner, sometimes so slow that the cars built up behind him and then too fast so we closed in on the slower traffic. He couldn't get it right.

'Are you trying to get stopped?' I asked.

'No. I'm trying to be inconspicuous, actually!' He hated any criticism of his driving. I remembered thinking how hard it was to tell when Devon was stressed. He had so many faces, so many layers of irony and play-acting. Just when you thought you had scoped the real Devon, some new incarnation would appear. I wondered whether he would ever completely emerge. Whether I would ever be able to say I knew him.

# CHAPTER
# ELEVEN

THE JOURNEY MIGHT have taken 20 minutes, it might have taken two hours. We just stared at the road ahead with such intensity the truck seemed to be propelled by will power alone. For a while we existed in a realm where time had a charged reality its passage was registered in heartbeats, sweat and hope.

As we approached the outskirts of Warkworth, Devon swung the truck down a side road. Suddenly there were no other cars. Few houses. Dust. The sky seemed bluer. We coasted quietly down the hills and I could feel the tension lifting from my body ... it was like being released from ropes. I fired a glance at Devon.

He grinned and shook a smoke out of its packet. 'Better than sex.'

'Jesus! You don't just do this for the buzz!'

'Course you do.'

We came to a gateway where a bunch of axles and cogs had been welded together to resemble a figure with its hands on its hips. Next to it was an old wooden letterbox leaning on a crazy angle. It had been hard yakka and over 24 hours since I'd slept. I had that spaced-out feeling you get when you are no longer completely connecting with the earth: a balloon attached by a thin, cotton strand.

The driveway was lined with macrocarpa trees, tall and thick and old. At the end of it there was a gate. Beyond it I could see the house and all these old vehicles. There must have been 30 or 40 rusty old cars and trucks. Even a couple of housetrucks. A dog stood at the gate barking and two or three others arrived.

'Get the gate, man!' Devon yelled, waking me out of my inertia.

'Shit! I'm not going to tangle with those hounds.'

He jammed on the handbrake angrily and swung down. The dogs seemed to recognise him and quietened down as he opened it. Behind the macrocarpas there was a cluster of ramshackle buildings all leaning against each other. There were cars everywhere. Weird old American ones.

'Is this guy a wrecker?' I asked Devon.

'No, a collector. He collects Studebakers. He's got over fifty.'

This man appeared on the verandah of the huge old villa. He was carrying a shotgun and several more dogs had materialised. We cruised slowly down the hill across the rough lawn and parked in front of the house.

I could see a wide scar running down the left-hand side of the guy's face. It began at the hairline, went down across his eye and cheek and finished on the jawbone. His whole face was lopsided and the eye looked lazy or maybe made of glass. There were thick burn scars on his neck and God knows what lay hidden behind his clothes.

'Hey, Johnno...' Devon yelled as they pulled up.

The man immediately lightened up. 'Devon the Dealer! I thought it was next weekend.' His voice was thin and produced with great effort.

'It was, but everything had to be moved forward.' Devon put his hand and head on the other man's shoulder and pretended to cry, 'God knows, I should have written, forgive me Father for I have sinned.'

Johnno laughed and pushed him away. 'Back off ya homo.

This your off-sider?'

I stepped forward and offered a hand. 'I'm Trace Dixon.'

'So you're the one who keeps him on the straight and narrow eh?'

'I try … that's why I'm here.'

Devon said, 'Hey I'm kind of anxious to unload.' 'You don't want a cup of tea first?'

Devon looked at me and said, 'If I look anything like you Trace, I *need* a cup of tea.'

We all went into the house, accompanied on all sides by a pack of excited dogs.

'Our gear OK there?' said Devon pointing at the back of the truck. It was a pretty outrageous load to have parked on your front lawn.

'The dogs are on duty,' Johnno replied.

It was a big house and every room was full of junk: engines, books, machinery. We eventually came to a large kitchen where it seemed Johnno lived. His bed was in one corner with piles of books all around it: mostly oil-stained car manuals. A wood-burning range was being fired up and near the ceiling was a drying rack, suspended by sash ropes and pulleys. It seemed to hold all of Johnno's clothing, including a couple of pairs of boots. All in all it looked like a bad day's collection for the Salvation Army.

Johnno saw me staring.

'Admiring my wardrobe are we? Envious of my apparel are we?' He laughed. 'So tell me Trace, what's it like being a big wheel in the drug world?'

'Hard work … look at my hands.' I held out my palms, which were bloodstained and ragged. The blisters had ruptured and torn.

'Better put some alcohol on those. How about yours, Devon?' Devon's were OK.

Johnno winked at him. 'Ah Devon, Devon. Nothing changes eh? Did you do anything besides drive?'

'My hands are tougher, that's all. Eh Trace?'

I was dabbing meths on the palms of my hands with the front of my T-shirt. The sting was reassuring.

After the tea, Johnno took us out into the yard to show us where to unload. The buildings seemed to have grown on the earth like a scab. All of the old implement sheds or barns had lean-to structures on each side, and they in turn had canopies adjoining. They were all full. Every one contained some vehicle or at least a collection – a couple of chassis, or maybe a pile of engines. This was as well as the cars and old trucks we had passed on the way in.

'Are they all yours?' I asked.

'Mate, this is only some of it. The best ones are stored under cover at my mates' places around the district. I've been collecting for years now. It mounts up.'

Behind the row of sheds was what at first appeared to be another long narrow shed. It was actually an ancient bus converted into a camping truck with a full-scale corrugated roof on the top.

Johnno left us to it and after Devon backed the pick-up closer we began to hang the plants upside-down from the old chromed luggage racks in the bus. By the time we had finished, the central walkway was filled right to where the driver once sat. Our hands were sticky with sap and the smell of the plants was pungent and heady. We both sat on the old dashboard to have a smoke and admire our handiwork.

'What do you think all that would be worth?' I asked Devon. 'Six, maybe seven numbers in the long run, but we'll lose heaps of it, long before that. Trade-offs and pay-offs … Johnno's the first.'

'Hell, Johnno … what's the matter with his face?'

'He was a courier for a parcel company in Aussie. He was doing this run up to Newcastle in the middle of the night, when the front wheel came off his van. He hit a power pole doing a hundred. He was wearing a belt, but some of the steering column still got stuck in his face and neck. Lost an eye, and an ear too, although they sewed it back on… '

'When was this?'

'A while back. He did all right, eventually the insurance companies paid up, that's how he bought this set-up.'

'He spent it all on old Studebakers?'

'And other old yank tanks … some of them are worth a packet though. I did an article on him for the paper when I was up North. He's a good guy, quite lonely but not … you know, bent.' We closed the door of the bus and walked back to the house.

The dogs seemed used to us now and followed us around at a distance.

Back in the house we smelled bacon cooking as soon as we opened the front door. There was a shotgun leaning up against the wall just inside.

I nudged Devon. 'Ready for armed response?'

'You have to be around here. The whole area is full of whacked-out growers who think you're after their patch. You wouldn't believe how many shootings around here never get reported.'

'Is it loaded?'

Devon broke it and showed the brass ends of two cases. 'of course. You'd look pretty stupid waving an unloaded gun at someone. That's asking for trouble.' He sounded authoritative, like he'd done it himself. He passed the gun to me. It was the first time I had ever held one. It was heavy and awkward. I tried to imagine myself threatening someone with it – but I couldn't. That was just cowboy fantasy stuff.

Johnno appeared at the end of the hall. 'Come on you two.'

He took the shotgun off me and leaned it against the wall next to the wood stove.

We sat in the kitchen and ate our breakfasts. Johnno, who had already eaten, sat on a stool and watched.

After a while he left and came back with a .22 rifle. It had a burst barrel.

'What do you make of this?' he said, handing it to me.

I examined it. The violence of the explosion had ripped open the steel barrel like plastic and left frayed sharp metal spines radiating out. Quite beautiful in its own way.

'I bet that made a hell of a bang.'

Johnno began a long account of how it had happened when he was in Aussie opal grubbing at Lightning Ridge. I had my head against the wall, and as Johnno finished his yarn I was just beginning to nod off when Devon said, 'You're going to hate me, Trace, but we have to go back.'

'What?' I said.

'We've got to go back and get those last bundles.'

'Devon, we're home free … all that skin of our teeth stuff … and you want to go back?'

'Don't worry man, I know you're knackered. I can do it by myself. I'll be in and out in about two minutes, I reckon, and then I'll know the job is done properly.'

'We've already pulled an unbelievable pile. This could sink us.'

Devon seemed to agree. 'I guess you're right. It doesn't matter.' And then he walked out.

I couldn't believe Devon. What a dumb idea. There is a point where you've got to back off. Good gamblers know where it is. Bad ones keep going and start to lose. I leaned back and felt the warm sunshine pouring life into my aching body through the kitchen window. Johnno's place was such a sanctuary, a life lived exactly the way he wanted it. I wondered what sort of place I would end up in if I had the money and time to do it. There wasn't a lot around here that I'd change. The food, the warmth, the weary bones drained to their marrow … I slid into unconsciousness. The delicious luxury of it: like sliding into a warm bath on a rainy day … it was too hard to fight.

# CHAPTER
# TWELVE

S OMEWHERE IN THE dreamy euphoria of aching sleep a noise
kept registering. Deep. Throbbing. Felt rather than heard.
It spoke to me: the thrum of the V8 being fired up. The
realisation came as suddenly as a slap on the face. I jumped up
and ran to the front door to see Devon stopping at the front gate.
'Stupid, stupid bastard!' I yelled, as I bolted after him.

'You were going without me, you prick,' I swore as I slid in the cab.

'It's not your deal, Trace. This is my thing, honest. I shouldn't've
told you. This is a one man op … I just wanted some company.'

'I can't believe you, Devon. We're a team now. You can't just run
off, man.'

I took my jumper off and bunched it up behind my head. 'I know
it seems mad, but those bundles, lying in the gorse… it was such hard,
fucking work hauling them out. It's been pissing me off … I tried but
I can't leave them. There's something nagging at me, "Finish the job!" '

He drove on. 'Anyway, now you're here, just get some sleep.
I'm not too bad but you look rat-shit.'

My head kept bouncing off the window so I put my jumper on the seat and curled up as best I could. Sleep closed in on me.

I COULD HEAR someone talking and it wasn't Devon. The truck was still. I opened my eyes to a blinding square of yellow sun and I lay watching the dust motes slowly floating through it. The cab was filled with the smell of fresh cut hay. I slowly eased up and looked out the windscreen. We were on the side of the road and Devon was nowhere to be seen. There was this humungus trailer-load of haybales, right in front of us. Through the driver's window I could see the forest. A bit further up I could see a ute under the trees. It looked all too familiar.

Where was Devon? I slid silently out of the cab and crept around the trailer of hay. Someone was talking. Just past the tractor was a man using a cellphone. He had a shotgun, the butt resting against his hip, his finger on the trigger. It was pointing into the long grass at his feet. I couldn't see Devon. Then I recognised the guy on the phone. It was the farmer I had seen that morning, in the same black and orange swanndri. He seemed relaxed, almost pleased with himself, lost in his conversation.

We were stuck. Out-gunned, out-manoeuvred. There were no houses, it was a dead-end road, and we were at the end of it. Little chance of being disturbed. I tried to control my panic. Everything depended on it. There were two of us but the farmer had a gun and there was too much clear space for me to sneak up and jump him. 'Devon, you dumb bastard,' I thought. 'After all our luck, all our work, now we lose the lot.' For a moment I thought of throwing it all in, seeing if I could talk our way out of it. If we gave him back the dope would he call it quits?

I crept back to the truck. Was there something, anything, I could use as a weapon? Nothing. Not even a tyre iron. I edged forward again to the front of the trailer. The phone was gone now and the guy was talking to someone in the grass. He gave a kick and I heard a voice yell, 'Fuck you!' It was Devon. There was no talking our way out of this one. I needed to do something, and fast. One fuck-up now and it would be two of us lying face down in the grass, waiting for God-knows-who to walk out of the forest.

All I had in my pocket was my Swiss Army knife, my smokes and my lighter. The keys were in the ignition. That was something. Heart pounding, I lit a tuft of hay sticking out from the bales on the back of the trailer. It wasn't the driest, and took a bit to get going. Just to make sure it'd take, I lit it in four other places as I snuck back to the cab. I could see the farmer now but his attention was all on Devon in the long grass and he had his back to me. He wouldn't see the smoke. After a slow start the fire passed some critical point. It was as though it had hit a cache of petrol. There was a crackling roar, a burst of flames, and then masses of billowing, pungent white smoke.

The guy yelled, I revved the truck, and slipped it into gear. Surprise was my only weapon. The farmer was in the middle of the road now, paralysed with indecision. His gun was trained on Devon, now sitting up, while the hay incinerated before his eyes. Time to add another factor. I dropped the clutch and hammered the accelerator. The truck slewed wildly, fighting for traction on the gravel road and then shot forward. Smoke and sparks poured in through the passenger's window as we brushed the load.

The figure in the tartan swanndri was barely visible in the billowing smoke. I glimpsed his anguished face as I bore down on him, his hay now a ten metre fireball. He dived clear but I managed to clip him with the front guard as I roared past. The gun flew high in the air as he rolled over and over down the dusty road. Devon was up in a moment, sprinting towards the cab.

'Get the gun, Devon!' I yelled as he opened the door.

He plunged back, scooping up the shotgun, but then turned to where the man lay, doubled up, holding his knee. Devon crouched over him, the gun barrel boring deep into his cheek. He looked like he was going to kill him.

I leaned on the horn and screamed, 'No!'

Devon turned to me, his face radiating pure hatred. Slowly, reluctantly, he stood up, withdrawing the gun. I felt waves of relief as he came towards me and then, almost as an afterthought, turned back and gave the man a hard kick on his injured knee.

Once Devon was back in the cab, I booted, it making the truck spin in a tight circle, gravel spraying in all directions.

Devon was too strung out to utter a word.

We stopped at the end of the straight to look back. The last glimpse showed a tall column of white smoke and the small figure of the farmer dragging himself away from the orange flames.

'What was that about?' I asked. 'Were you going to shoot him?'

'I don't know,' he said, his voice stripped of emotion. He squinted as he lit up a smoke. 'Didn't you see what he did to me?'

'What do you mean?'

'In the grass.'

'No.'

'Good.'

There was something about Devon's manner that I hadn't seen before, a sort of sadness. I felt it too. As we drove back to Johnno's I tried to work out why. Eventually I asked him.

He explained. 'We've turned a corner, Trace. Maybe we'd already done it, I'm not sure. But now, there's no going back eh? I guess it's not a game any more.'

He looked haggard and done in. The easy pick-up job had turned into a disaster. He knew it. He had put everything in jeopardy – including our lives.

WHEN WE MADE it back to Johnno's car farm Devon said 'Stop here' just before we reached the gate, so I pulled over. I noticed that his eyes were red. 'What's the matter?'

'I'm sorry, Trace, I blew it. I reckon if you hadn't come along I'd be in a hole in the forest.'

'Doubt it. It was worth a go. And hey, we came through.' I tried to sound light. 'Don't worry about it.'

'I won't forget this, Trace. I'm in your debt now.' 'Bullshit.'

He smiled and slid out of the truck to open the gate. As we drove down the driveway he added, 'Don't mention it to Johnno. He doesn't need to know.'


WHEN WE WALKED in, Johnno was cooking a stew in the kitchen. The smell of it filled the whole house. Rich and strange. Neither of us had eaten a proper meal for ages and we ate until our stomachs were stuffed tight. Later that evening Johnno let slip that it had been possum. I immediately felt a bit nauseous. It must have been the stress of the day. I slept on the couch and Devon dossed on a foam squab on the floor. Even though we were dead-beat neither of us seemed to sleep very soundly. Every time a dog barked I was sure we were under attack and stumbled over to look out the window. Devon was awake but we never spoke. When morning came, he was gone. Johnno was nowhere to be seen either.

I wandered around the yard, thinking Johnno might be tinkering with one of the cars. None of them looked as if they had been touched for years. Grass up through the wheels, lichen on the roofs of some. It made me wonder why people bother to collect things. Finally, I heard a noise coming from the other side of the buildings. It was Johnno on a farm-bike. It was a great sight: a dog on the tank, the rest of the posse swarming about, bunches of possums and rabbits hanging off the bike from all angles. It had obviously been a busy morning. He waved as he cleared the edge of the shed then rolled to a stop.

'Dinner or dog tucker?'

'Bit of both.'

'Where's Devon?'

'He was here when I left at five.' Johnno rode off down the back of the lot where he had his skinning table. I headed to where the old bus was parked. As soon as the door was opened the smell almost knocked you over. Essence of skunk. I wouldn't have believed you could fit so much greenery into such a small space. It had looked magical in the forest. Sort of 'lost treasure of the Incas'. But here it seemed ominous. Like it had changed from the innocent weed to an evil narcotic. How would we ever sell this much dope? Who could afford to buy it? It was overwhelming. Gathering it up might have been the easy part.

A stocky pit bull barged down the aisle thumping my leg with its weighty shoulder. At the bottom of the stairs a big striped dog stared silently. Devon and Johnno appeared at the doorway a moment later.

'Where've you been?'

'Out driving.'

'Where?'

'Here and there.'

'You didn't go back to the patch?'

'I'm not that mad, I couldn't sleep so I got up and drove towards the sea. After about an hour it was like I had to put more miles between me and … you know … stuff.'

He had a wistful, faraway look on his face. He leaned in and looked into the body of the bus. 'What are you doing here?'

'Just taking it all in. It's scary vegetation. What happens now?'

'We leave it for three or four weeks. We keep it really quiet and then we come back and clip it and dry it and bag it…'

'… and mark it with T.' Johnno added.

'Then we're high rollers?'

'You guessed it, Trace. A chance to flash it about. Fast cars, and I mean really fast.'

'I reckon a new Evo, twin turbo.'

'Godzilla!'

'Nitro boosting.'

'Yeah, nitro, that'd do the damage.'

'Thunder Road will have a new king. Move over Sloane. And there'll be women. Man! Wall to wall women.'

'I can picture that. I reckon it's a lifestyle I could get to like.' 'Better gather some samples,' Devon said, clipping the buds off a Christmas tree-sized plant hanging in the central aisle of the bus.

'For promotional purposes only,' he claimed later, waving a big bag of primo dak.


As SOON AS we arrived back at Mrs Jacques', Devon went off in the truck and I took a long shower. I seemed to be clogged with the accumulation of days of fear and tension. It was almost comforting to be smelling Mrs Jacques' cooking and hearing Sergei thrashing away at the piano with August. Mrs Jacques seemed tetchy though. The least thing brought on one of her long-suffering, loudly voiced complaints. 'Oh, so I've got nothing better to do than fetch your cups from the verandah?' Or 'Someone has been dribbling on the floor of the toilet again, and it certainly wasn't me.'

When I heard an unfamiliar burble through the window, I looked out to see Devon returning with the Subaru.

'What happened to the pick-up? I liked the beast. It was trusty.' 'I had to get rid of it,' he said. 'It's a marked vehicle now. I want our profile to be so flat for the next few weeks that we're practically below ground level.' 'The earthworm profile.'

He nodded.

'Where's the truck? Rebel got it?'

He looked furtive for a moment. 'No. I've done another deal, I'll tell you about it later. It's like ... it's still going down.'

'Oh yeah, your deals.'

'No, it's a good one. It's going to mean a few changes for you and me.'

'I've had almost enough changes lately. I sort of wanted the quiet life.'

'Keep that for when you're old and dead.' 'Better than being young and dead.'

'I wonder.'

At dinner that night I sensed a tension. Mrs Jacques wasn't her usual nosy self. She dished up the casserole and mashed spud, banging it on our plates, spoon-load by noisy spoon-load. After that she ate with slow deliberate mouthfuls. There was an angry energy in the air.

'Trace, this dinner would have been on the table an hour ago, but I was held up.'

'Don't worry about it, Mrs Jacques.'

'Our routines are all over the place when August's here for his lesson.'

I said nothing, but noticed that Sergei had stopped eating. 'We used to have a seven o'clock deadline... .' Her voice trailed off. We all looked at Sergei: his face reddened and his eyes bulged. He squeezed his knife and fork so tightly his knuckles went white. Me and Devon exchanged glances; it was as though a bomb were about to explode. Sergei began to talk, so softly at first, I couldn't hear it.

'About your routines. A gifted ear is something that is nurtured, coaxed ... Oh, what is the point...' He sat there, staring at his dinner for a few moments and then muttered, 'Excusez-moi. Je me retirerai,' and surged off to his room.

'Excusez my French,' quipped Devon, 'but oui!'

After he had gone Mrs Jacques seemed to relax a little, but said nothing beyond pass this, pass that. I kept waiting for her to ask us to give an account of ourselves, or at least to ask why I had skipped work, but it didn't happen.

Back in our room I asked, 'What's up with Mrs J.?'

Devon claimed she was jealous of the Boy Wonder. I hadn't thought of that. When your own life fills out, other people's stuff disappears into the background. In Sergei's room there was some big piano piece being hammered out. Too much music for one pair of hands, it must have been a duet.

# CHAPTER
# THIRTEEN

**M**AYBE SOMETHING HAD changed between Sergei and Mrs Jacques, but compared with how our lives had moved on, it was minor. For the next month or so going to work seemed pointless. It had been going downhill ever since Karen left. When I found out that I couldn't be forced to work weekends, I stopped doing that too. Even old Bob's rebuke: 'I thought you were going places with this firm,' had no effect.

Going places? More like crawling along in the slow lane. With Devon I was turbo-charged and Bob and his mates were just specks in my rear-view mirror. Not for me the life of work and save, and work some more. It was all I could do just to set off in the morning. Arriving late became a habit and every Thursday I barely noticed that my pay had been docked.

The first thing Devon did, though, was quit his job with the paper. He was now freelance. So he said. He sure was free. Free to spend a lot of time just hanging out. He claimed he wanted to become independent, subsidising his writing from 'other income'. He had these cards printed. Business cards with the words 'Euphoric Enterprises' in embossed script. Below this was a logo of a smoking joint and the words 'Happiness is only a phone call away'. The prepaid mobile phone, he claimed, had been invented with the dealer in mind. I thought the cards were a loony idea, like a boast, bound to cause trouble.

Devon, being Devon, didn't stop there. He had press passes printed too. There was nothing about the card that ensured any right of entry, yet in Devon's hands they were a magic key to go everywhere and do anything. All it took was the enchantment of limitless confidence.

Getting into places without paying, without invitation, started off almost casually. It wasn't that we were short of money; we did it just because we could. It grew into getting into functions and parties where not only were we not invited, we were definitely not wanted. There would be a rock concert at Western Springs stadium. We'd cruise down. Devon would flash the pass at some old dude in a white coat who would blink at it a few times and then wave us over to where the roadies' trucks were parked. The next step would take a bit more nerve, usually because it meant persuading a couple of two-metre tall, Samoan security guards. Like this one time.… .

'What are you boys trying to pull?'

'Press, man, here's the card.'

They examined it for a regulation period of time and then handed it back.

'That card's crap,' said the one with the little chin beard. 'Bullshit it's crap. You want a show with no review in tomorrow's paper? OK. Great. I'll write an article about the security guards instead. How they blocked New Zealand's biggest newspaper from attending.'

They started to seem a bit unsure of themselves, looking around to see if there was anyone else to check it with.

'Take his picture, Trace. He's going to be the star of the article. I reckon his boss will be pleased with the publicity.'

'You take my photo and I'll smash ya fucken camera.' The beard pointed at the security office. 'See that box up there? You go there, run it by those fullas. If it's OK by them, then it's cool by me.'

We walked through the gates up to the little portable office.

The bouncers were watching all the way.

Devon waved back as we walked in. Inside were three of the biggest guys I have ever seen. What is it with Islanders that they get so big? They were playing cards. They all froze and looked towards us. One, the boss I guess, asked with a voice that seemed to come from the bowels of the earth, 'Can I help you?'

I remember thinking, 'We are going to get seriously done over here.'

Devon said, without a moment's hesitation, 'We were sent here by your mates at the front gate.' They all looked out the window to where the other guys were watching. 'They want to know when you're going to deal them in.'

The three men erupted with laughter, the biggest one giving the 'fuck you' sign to his mates down at the gate. We were in. It seemed almost too easy.

We pushed this magic card to the limit. It worked for clubs too, sometimes even for drinks at the bar. Other times it got us into venues, like corporate boxes, and members' enclosures at the races. I would shrink at how our clothes didn't cut it, like nowhere near cut it. We always won through, held aloft by Devon's unsinkable confidence. He would push on in, with me floating tentatively in his slipstream. It was definitely more than just the press pass. There was a sort of aura about Devon, that allowed these two 19-year-olds to go places where everyone else was pushing 50 and holding down half a mill.

IN JANUARY, WHEN the weather warmed and the days lengthened, I'd often skip work and we'd head for Piha Beach on the Norton. We hooned past the crawling lines of family cars: the white line was a highway made just for us.

After a day surfing and sunbathing we would get into the serious business of hunting down girls. Making contacts. And our real jobs: finding out where the parties were. There were always parties, and free doobies were an absolute guarantee that we wouldn't be turned away even from the snooty Ponsonby crowds, where everyone stood around chatting, guarding some expensive bottle of wine, and all the while trying to sound intelligent. They were the best and easiest places to unload dak.

Sometimes we'd head south and hang out at the funky hip-hop clubs in Manukau City and Papakura. Or, if we were hungry for something extreme, it was the gang bashes in South Auckland: hundreds of people watching dogs fighting in a warehouse, liquor so cheap it had to be stolen. With each new fight everyone pressed in close to the ring to watch their bets or satisfy their hunger for blood and pain. Minutes later most of them pulled away as one ugly, brindled mutt locked its teeth into the other one's throat.

ONE NIGHT, AT a rage in Mangere, one of the fighting dogs was killed. usually the losing dog's owner pulled him out of the fight, but this time a group of men blocked him. A huge fight broke out. It was like the tension had been building up all night, and everyone became fighting dogs themselves. There was no core, no structure, just a seething mass of people kicking the shit out of each other. At some invisible signal, fists flew, along with nearly every moveable object in the building. We just made the back door as someone took out the fluorescent lights with a shotgun. We were showered with tiny splinters falling like snow. Devon's head and shoulders were sparkling and he was laughing in the greenish light.

'Time to make like the good shepherd – let's get the flock out of here.'

We jumped into the WRX and were clear of the fray as the first of the cop cars showed. Because it wasn't even midnight, Devon said we should chill out on Thunder Road.

Things were buzzing on the strip. We could hear the roar of cars well before we arrived. This time it was different. We were real players in a beasty car. For Devon the Escort was history, as soon as it had been burned off by that yellow Skyline. We were late and had to find a place right at the bottom of the strip, down among the school kids in the D.C.s. We only saw the tail end of the burn-offs which was boring compared with the first 50 metres where it all happened. Devon went off on foot, hunting for the Skyline. He had something to prove.

I was just happy to sit back and drink it all in: the cars, the smell of petrol and rubber, the skittery lights of grunty cars weaving their way down Thunder Road.

Just as we were about to pack it in, Devon sighted the car he had been searching for all night. It was just ten cars up the strip, tucked in behind a Big Foot.

'Buckle up Trace, we are in business.'

We cruised down the row of cars during a break in the races. There were all these little gangs parked side by side: three Asian guys with long bleached hair gathering around their matching Preludes and drinking beer; a whole row of Toranas with super-chargers poking out through the bonnets; a team of matched Mazda Rotarys and finally the lone yellow Skyline. It was the guy from Huapai who had done the business on Devon. We backed in next to it and Devon leaned across my seat.

'This for show or for go?'

The guy in the other car had his girlfriend on board and seemed a bit unimpressed by the grey WRX.

'Who wants to know?'

'I used to have the orange Escort, but now I got this. You got what it takes, or are you just here to watch?'

This seemed to get the response he was after. The other guy turned to his girlfriend, they kissed, then she leapt out of the car and hurried back up the line.

Two more seventies rockets roared past, only a few metres from where we waited. Their deep honest exhaust note was opera to my ears, a reminder of how cars were before new age rocket technology took over. The laptop had replaced the screwdriver and the guy with an ear tuned for engine music. It was sad really. Some of the beauty had gone.

At the top of the run Devon dropped me off. I sidled up near the big black Mercedes which, I guessed, contained Sloane, self-elected King of the Strip. The massive figure of his minder, Mark, was visible only by outline and glowing cigarette tip somewhere in the gloom behind. I wondered what dubious activity was going down.

Then it happened. Devon's plain-Jane, grey WRX toed the line next to the gaudy Skyline. This time his car was understated. A real wolf in sheep's clothing. The cars cackled and snarled, perched there like sprinters, pumped up and waiting for the jump. Devon missed the start by moments and had to make up two car lengths. The little car screamed as all four wheels tore away at the tarmac.

From where I stood the two cars were instantly buried in the thick white smoke of burning tyres, their tail lights just a fuzzy, weaving glow, the weird whistle of the turbos punctuated by the kishhh, kishhh, kishhh of the blow-off valves. Even watching from the back you could tell that a moment later it was all over. The Skyline's round tail lights a lonely sight, hopelessly out-gunned. Devon was way clear! A flood of relief washed through me. He could hang out on Thunder Road with his rep intact again. He had found redemption in a nine second burst.

DEVON TOOLED BACK up the strip, drinking in the glory. He paused in front of Sloane to make the slightest of waves to the darkened windows. I jumped in and we headed off. He had no interest in staying now, nothing further to prove. Once we were clear of the line of cars, he threw the WRX into a series of doughnuts, just for the sheer joy of it. When he straightened out, allowing the tyres to once more bite the road, we shot forward as though kicked by a giant boot. Our heads snapped back and forth in time with the gear changes. Our bodies were jammed back into the bucket seats by the G-forces. What a buzz! Better than any drug. We touched 160 ks by the end of Thunder Road.

Out of nowhere, a siren and lights forced their way into my brain. It was like being woken from a delicious dream. They had been waiting for us … for Devon. I felt a rage rising in my body. We stopped and looked back. A young cop was getting out of the patrol car, torch and note-pad in hand. I could see him adjusting his uniform, putting on his authority. He ambled over, a smug look on his face. He was nothing. What made him think he could stop us? The uniform? Some piece of paper from cop school?

I looked at Devon, straining to contain my anger and frustration.

'He's by himself, let's take the bastard … we can do it.'

'No,' said Devon, holding up his hand, 'It's Carmody, he used to be one of us. These are the rules. We race. He chases.'

As he drew level with the back of the car, Devon floored it. We were off again fast but steady. This would be no 400 metre burn-off. We were around the corner before the other car even started up.

'Go on the motorway,' I said. 'He'll never catch us.'

Devon stuck to the side streets. 'He can't catch this car but he'll be radioing ahead. Motorways are too easy to intercept.' So instead we wound our way back to the used car yards of Otahuhu till Devon said it was time to hide. After reversing onto the end of a row of cars we slouched down low. Sure enough, two or three police cars flew by, lights ablaze, before we even had our smokes lit.

He turned to me. 'What fun would there be in a world without rules?'

# CHAPTER
# FOURTEEN

IT WAS LATE summer when Karen came back into my life.

Devon had persuaded me to skip work for the day. 'It's a crime to work on a day as nice as this … a crime against the soul.'

We both threw a bit of gear into a backpack and headed off on the Norton for a day on the black sand of Piha. The beach was quiet: being mid-week most people were sweating it out in the work place. There was that freshness in the air, the water was thick and glassy and the sunlight took on a golden tinge as it found its way through the spray. We lay near the high tide mark savouring every moment.

Down the beach a small crowd emerged from behind the rocky outcrop that cut off the next bay. Their clothes were mottled and fragmented in the heat haze. I lay back with my towel over my face. Sometime later the quiet was broken by Devon hissing, 'Chick alert!'

I sat up. There were about 30 girls and a couple of older people. They were obviously some sort of school expedition. Everyone was wearing a dinky little day pack and carrying a water bottle.

Even a hundred metres away I could hear them laughing and talking over the roll and thump of the surf. 'Girls en masse. What happens?' Part of the group broke away from their controllers and walked our way to check us out. Devon lay quiet and still, watching their approach with a hunter's calm. I felt a bit outnumbered. About eight of them walked past quite close – not paying any direct attention – using the group to scope us out. Karen was one of them. We looked at each other for a moment and then she moved on, saying nothing.

She was a vision to me. Tanned, elegant even in shorts and T-shirt, her feet seemed to hardly dent the sand.

When they had passed Devon said, 'School girls! Give me a break.' Then he lay back and I guess resumed mulling over mysterious schemes and obsessions.

I replayed the little movie of Karen walking towards me again and again in my mind. The same nine steps. It wouldn't go away.

The next day, back at work after my day bunking off, I was given a note asking me to ring her. What was this about? Perhaps her parents had reconsidered. I would be allowed a second chance. Why should I ring her? I was the one who was rejected. The one who wasn't good enough. But I knew I'd call her no matter what my head tried to tell me.

The phone was answered by a strange girl with the ponciest accent I have ever heard. When I asked for Karen there was some muffled remark followed by giggling before Karen came on.

It was awkward at first. Neither of us were sure quite how to get started on all that 'what's up' stuff but then we were into it. She was sorry about what had happened. So was I. Her parents had seemed so *modern and liberal*; she now realised that this *modern and liberal* didn't apply to her, their prized possession. I told her that I was no one to talk about fitting in with parents. I had walked the first chance I got … and never looked back. She wanted me to come to a particular address because there was something she wanted to ask me.

I was blown away. All my anger and hurt melted in a moment. Without Devon around, my attitudes to the stuck-up middle class doctor types seemed to vanish at the same time. The straight world still had some appeal. I scribbled the address on a piece of paper and told her that I'd be there.

The address led me to a street of stone walls and grand entrances: a quiet oasis in the busiest part of Auckland. There was this big wooden house stuck on the side of Mount Eden by some shrewd settler a hundred years ago. It was two storeys high with this dinky little room like a lookout stuck on top.

I parked the Norton out on the road and walked up the curving tar-seal driveway to the front door. It had a stained glass version of a kowhai tree on the door and a sort of twisted rope pattern down each side, all panelled with fancy wood. My knock was answered by a pretty blonde girl. She was puffing on a cigarette and had that sort of over-the-top confidence you get when you are playing dares. I could tell that there was no adult at home. The next thing I expected was that we'd all raid Daddy's liquor cabinet.

Karen appeared and the three of us sat in the kitchen. She was wearing jeans and a T-shirt with a brand name on it. To anyone else she probably would have seemed like any other well-groomed private school girl but to me she was a vision, golden and shimmering. Her heavy hair, flawless skin, clear eyes reminded me of a world left far behind: a world I knew when I was nine years old. A world of purity, of virgin beauty.

We sat around for a while. It was like I had walked in on a conversation and had no place there.

'Trace, this is Angela.'

'Hi.'

'It's her place.'

'Me and my dad live here … but mostly, it's just me.'

'Her dad's an airline captain.'

'Cool job!'

'I guess … it means he's never here. This place is just a stop-over.'

I could tell that this was a topic not to get started on. 'Parents eh!' I offered. 'Can't train 'em. Can't tame 'em.' They laughed.

'I thought mine were trained,' said Karen. She sounded serious. 'or my mother, at least, but I was wrong.'

I made like it didn't matter. That I understood. But it did matter. I had been prepared to like her parents. To make the big effort to be something I wasn't – but it hadn't worked. They'd reminded me that I was someone you invite around only once to prove how reasonable you are … how accepting. Finally, though, I had to be reminded: I was a nobody from nowhere. I imagined one of those dry little stories being told at the bridge club, or by the photocopier at work.

*This rough boy from Karen's work … language of the streets … showed unusual gallantry … we thought it would be nice if … it was quite funny really … shouldn't have been surprised … drunk and rowdy…. I suppose one could say it was an interesting experiment … what do they say? … oil and water….*

Karen explained everything rapidly, as if it had all been rehearsed a few times before I arrived. She wanted me to take her to a school ball. She wouldn't tell her parents. Then there was this big story that I couldn't follow: some sort of cunning plan. It involved taking Richard but actually he was going with Angela, and Jason fitted in there too or something. I couldn't follow all the complicated scheming. I just blissed out on the way Karen kept flicking her hair off her forehead and how clear and bright the whites of her eyes were. She was such a picture, prattling on, enjoying her own deviousness.

I guess after Euphoric Enterprises it all seemed like school-girly high jinks. The only danger was that it would turn into one of those boring, awkward, social traps, like the dinner at her parents' place. With me ending up shaming myself in front her twitty friends. But it was a while away yet. Plenty of time to pull out if something better turned up. And anyway, there was Karen, flowing like warm water into my life. Every moment, every gesture, fed the lonely places.

Angela made herself scarce and Karen's giggly girl stuff gave way to a quiet seriousness that I liked. We went out and sat on the front steps. I had to invent stories about what I had been doing, because the truth would have scared her to death. She picked up my hands and spotted the spider's web of little scars, reminders of our mad midnight scramble in the bush up north.

'What are these from?'

'Me and Devon did a bit of farm work a while back.'

'What sort of farm work?'

'Harvesting.'

For a moment we sat there on the step. We held each other's hands and the sun dipped low over the city beneath us, clothing it in hazy light. From somewhere there came the soft whoosh of cars and the smell of freshly cut lawns. It was all a bit too perfect, too brittle to last. Like that time you have in a warm bed last thing in the morning before the alarm rings telling you it's time to get up and go for it. We both stopped talking and sat there, enjoying just being there. Being alive.

Karen's dad was picking her up on the way home from the surgery so I left early to avoid crossing his path. Even his intrusion couldn't dent my bullet-proof happiness. I rode aimlessly for an hour, through the endless streets, feeding on the feeling. It was still there when I decided I definitely needed to return to Mrs Jacques'. Sergei had snibbed the front door for some reason and had to let me in. 'Ah!' he said 'The Valkyrie returns!' and disappeared into his room, wreathed in his own laughter. Mrs Jacques appeared momentarily in the hallway, stared at me and then returned to the lounge. Devon wanted to know where I had been but I was in no mood to tell him. I knew his attitude to Karen. Any news of our reconnection would only start him on his favourite topic, *The Glass Dome, Chapter One: The Hypocrisy of Rich Doctors*. I had no answer to that. After years of brooding, his bitterness went too deep.

I felt stink because he was so open and here was I, nurturing a guilty secret; it was as if we'd agreed to pool all our money, but I still had this big stash hidden in my back pocket. A stoolie, holding out on him.

# CHAPTER FIFTEEN

I READ SOMEWHERE that animals can tell when an earthquake's coming. That they can pick up on stuff that we don't know about. It would have been good to have had some sort of animal warning about the next quake headed my way.

I had worked late on a Thursday because a load of paint had arrived five minutes before the place closed. Instead of telling the driver to come back tomorrow as I would have done, Bob insisted that we unload the order. Everyone else had gone except him and me, so we spent 25 sweaty minutes getting the stuff off the truck.

By the time I hung a right off Dominion Road it was after six o'clock. In the distance I could see a green Holden outside Mrs Jacques' house. There is some little alarm bell that rings when I think I'm near cops. I chopped back a gear and cruised past. Sure enough the Holden had those little blue pursuit lights buried in the grille. My mind was racing. Had they busted the place? How could they prove who the dope belonged to? It had to be either mine or Devon's. It would hardly be Mrs Jacques' or Sergei's. I had no idea how much was stashed. Devon hadn't told me and I hadn't asked. I knew where it was though: stuffed into a disused food safe attached to the outside of the house.

I drove a block and then pulled in behind a van about a hundred metres short of the house. There was nothing to do but hang back in the shadows and wait for the Ds to go. I needed to think long and hard about my next step. A lot depended on it.

What was going on? Would Devon nark? After 20 agonising minutes I couldn't bear it any longer: I had to sneak closer. I was two houses away when three figures emerged. I flattened out against a hedge, too late to hide in a driveway. I pushed hard until I was mostly enveloped in its spiky foliage. The doors slammed then the car started. It powered off like there was no time to lose. I had to act fast. Every light in the house was blazing … something strictly against house rules. That was a sign.

I snuck up through the long grass and junk which filled the gap between the house and the hedge. There might be a cop left behind, waiting to pick me up. Why hadn't they come for me at work?

I could hear a strange snuffling noise. It came from the kitchen. There was Mrs Jacques at the dining room table, her head in her hands, crying. I felt this stab of guilt, like I had brought dishonour on her house. Had violated it. I circled the property, checking the other rooms. There was no one there. Back at the kitchen window again, I saw something that completely threw me. It was Devon. He came in from somewhere, pulled up a chair and sat next to her, his arm around her heaving shoulders. His radar must have been working because he looked up and locked eyes with me. I walked forward into the light and waved. He signalled me in.

I went around to the the front door and walked into the house like everything was normal: dropped my bag in the bedroom and went to the kitchen. I wanted to go and ask what had happened but I knew I couldn't. It was all too tense. After a time Mrs Jacques raised her head and looked at me with reddened eyes. She gathered up a sponge and after a frantic wipe of the surfaces announced that it had been a long day and if we wanted any tea tonight we would be getting it ourselves because she was *off duty*.

At this point she left so fast she almost ran to her bedroom. Devon leaned back and put his feet up on the table.

'Do you believe in omens?' I stared at him blankly.

'That could have been us, man. Whew!'

Devon had lost his cool this time – his face was frozen and he looked really scared.

'What's the story? What happened?'

'It seems our Sergei is more than just a bit *artistic*. He's the real thing.'

'What do you mean?' Then I knew from the way Devon gestured. 'He's gay? That's not against the law is it?'

'August's a minor. It's called molestation.' 'Sergei's a molester?'

'Is, was, will be.' He began to recapture his old confidence and turn it into a story. 'Look, it's like this. Musos are horny bastards, right?' He paused, waiting for agreement. 'Well, it seems he'd been playing with August's little willy as he ran up and down the scales of the pee-anna fortie.'

'True?'

He nodded.

'You sound like you knew all the time.'

'I used to wonder … he's such a weird bastard, but then I thought, "No! He's a musician, a foreigner," and anyway, you know my motto. "Live and let live." '

This amused me a bit. I'd never seen Devon as a tolerant person.

'Anyway, Augie told his big brother – who it seems had enjoyed the same finger exercises when he was learning.'

'So big brother thought, "enough is enough."'

'Got it.' Devon had an almost smug look on his face.

'What an evil bastard. August is just a little kid. I tell you. I would have beat his head in.'

'I was sitting here in the bedroom, doing my homework… organising some foils … when they came. Mr Plod and his friends knock at the door and I think, "It's probably just the Mormons … who else calls here wearing a suit?" I open the door and there we have it, two police dudes in mufti asking me if my name was Sergei Hakanakaoff.'

'Sergei what?'

'Sergei something absolutely unpronounceable. He *is* a Pole for God's sake.'

'How did you know they were cops?'

'There's something about cops, you can spot them a mile away. They might as well have had revolving red lights screwed on their heads. My first reaction was, "That bastard, he's dobbed us in".'

'He doesn't know about the dope.'

Devon looked around anxiously. 'Not so loud man, Mrs Jacques is just through the wall … on her bed of sorrow.'

'Well he doesn't, does he?'

'Who knows what Sergei knows? But he's not dumb. He knows we smoke it. He's not like Mrs Jacques. He doesn't buy the "herbal tobacco" line.'

'Yeah, but that's no reason for him to dob us in.'

'Listen man, he's been collared for the big one. Nothing good's going to happen to our Serge for a long, long time. He'll do anything to buy favour. It's all he's got.'

'But he didn't.'

'He hasn't *yet*. He had his hands pretty full. But like I said, it's an omen. We ought to get out of here.'

'Mrs Jacques seems pretty cut up.'

'Ah well, there is a reason for that. He's definitely been slipping her one from time to time.'

'What bullshit!'

'True. As a means of avoiding his rent.' 'How do you know?'

'I've heard their sighs and grunts when I've been having a midnight dump in the back toilet.'

'Man. I thought he'd been stringing her along getting her hopes up. You reckon he hasn't paid any board for a while? Maybe she thought he was going to be the third Mr Jacques.'

'After what happened to the other two I reckon he chose the easy way out. Anyway, Trace, it's a sign.'

'A sign?'

'Yeah man. A sign that….' then he began to sing, 'We've Gotta Get Outta This Place'.

'Time to get a flat?'

'We can do better than that.' He paused, as if he had been planning this for a while. 'I've taken possession of a cosy little cottage in snooty Parnell. Something more fitting for our new status.'

'When?'

'A week or two ago.'

'Parnell? Are you planning to deal in smack? How can we afford that?'

'Remember Wes, the big property guy? We'll stay in one of his places.'

'What'll that cost?'

'Nothing … much, maybe a few bullets from time to time.' 'He imbibes?'

'They all do, Trace, it's the thing for richies. They like to play at being one of the cool guys when all the time they're still one of the stiffs.'

So there it was. Proof. Proof that every action causes a reaction. We were all in for a change of scene. Me and Devon were going up in the world. Mrs Jacques was left to potter around in the ruins of her tidy little life. And Sergei? We never saw or heard of Sergei again, but I'd say he's got plenty of time to reflect on how sweet he had it at Mrs Jacques', because I reckon he won't be getting first shower where he is.

# CHAPTER SIXTEEN

**A** DAY OR SO later, we fired all our stuff into the back of the Subaru and moved out. Devon promised to give Mrs Jacques a forwarding address in a few days but I knew he never would. Being untraceable was the whole reason for moving.

I was pleased to go. I had felt really sorry for Mrs Jacques since Sergei had been taken away: but the whole scene became a miserable one and there was nothing we could do. The cops had been back a couple of times trying to get statements from us, but we were no use to them.

The real surprise was the house we moved into. I should have guessed. It was where Big Martin, Gail and Little Martin had lived. They had been the ones Wes had wanted Devon to move out. Quite a lot of their furniture was still there. The whole thing struck me as a lousy stunt to pull.

'What's the story, Devon?' I was almost afraid to hear what he had done. They were, after all, his friends.

'Oh, it's cool. I gave them the truck and some buds.' 'They were a family, man.' It still didn't seem right.

Devon looked a bit pissed off. 'Yeah, they still are, Trace. They're a family with a Ford F100 and a good stash. Jesus! *A family*! Where do you get off with that stuff? What's so great about a *family*?'

I was taken aback by the anger of his answer. 'Where are they now?'

'They've moved out into the Waitaks. They were going to go anyway. This was just the thing they needed. Everyone's happy. It's cool.'

That was an end to the matter as far as Devon was concerned.

I could tell it was a no-go topic.

The little wooden house was sandwiched in between massive blocks of apartments which were all balconies and German cars. Most of Martin's vehicles had gone from the driveway but there were still the carcasses of dead cars scattered around, sticking up here and there in the long grass. It had a decent chunk of land which backed onto a sort of wilderness next to the railway line.

Beyond the railway line was the Auckland Domain with its hundreds of acres of mown grass, a good dense perimeter of trees and the huge stone museum sited on the top. Pretty idyllic. It had something you don't get often in the city. Space.

The house itself was old and rotten; no one had fixed anything properly for years. It was all black tape and four inch nails. There was the slight stink of piss in every room. I assumed that had been the work of Little Martin. Gail's art leered out creepily from the walls, with its figures of death and virginal angels. Every now and then Martin had scrawled a line or two of his verse – I assumed it was his – in black vivid marker alongside them.

*I went to the preacher,*
*He asked for my soul,*
*Preacher man said*
*'Sin has taken its toll.*
*On life's great beach*

*You're just a grain of sand
A lonely speck,
Between sea and land.'*

This was beside one of Gail's paintings of a huge bearded figure, like an old testament prophet in robes, with his hand reaching out towards you.

'What do you make of that, Trace? I reckon a few acid tabs have been dropped in this room.' Devon appeared behind me. 'Gives me the creeps. I reckon the first thing we do is paint the whole place. It's too much like a shrine to Gail and the Martins.'

'It might get rid of the smell of piss, too.'

There were two bedrooms: one looked out on the gully and the other on the carport. It had to be mine because Devon claimed first pick. After we had moved our gear in I had this real cosy buzz. Our own place, I thought: we don't have to consider anybody else. It's old and it's shitty, but it's ours.

'How long have we got this?' I asked Devon.

'As long as we want, I reckon. Wes likes to sit on property and wait until someone *really* wants it.'

This house was our last step towards complete freedom. What a feeling. Like we had opened a door and instead of a room we had discovered a whole new world.

We both sat on the back deck staring out over the gully towards the Domain and the glow of the city lights. Devon pushed a joint at me. I took it.

'It's like a home eh?' Devon said, voice soft and dreamy. 'Better than a home ... it's somewhere where we can be us.'

'What do you mean?'

I tried to explain.

'When I was little my father used to say, "Trace, there is a right and a wrong way of doing anything." I could live with that. When I was about thirteen or fourteen it changed to, "Trace, there is my way and the wrong way". I couldn't live with that.'

He looked at me sort of funny and then nodded.

I carried on. 'There's something in me that hates being told to do stuff. Maybe there's a pay-off. My house, my rules - I don't know. But you reach an age where you won't take it… so you split.'

Devon stretched out on the verandah floor, the light catching his eyes and teeth.

'At least your old man gave a shit. Mine shot through when I was about ten centimetres tall.' There was pain in his voice. Neither of us wanted to go there.


I DELIBERATELY MIS-TINTED a whole lot of paint colours so that they were useless to anyone else, then I took them home and for the next few days we painted every wall. My room was dark so I painted the walls, floor and ceiling white. Devon's room had big windows and plenty of light so he chose deep purple, which took ten litres of a colour called heliotrope. It looked so cool that we painted the lounge and the kitchen the same colour. We were going to finish off all the other rooms with it too but our redecorator enthusiasm ran out.

Next we gathered a few sticks of furniture to make the place truly habitable. A huge old couch from the auctions. Table and chairs from the St Vincent de Paul Society. A tall lamp from the inorganic rubbish collection. It didn't take much.

It took an extra ten minutes to get to my work from the flat, which meant my attendance began to drop off. I was ready to get the sack. I was even looking forward to it: it'd take away the need to make a decision. But it didn't happen. Whether I liked it or not I was a regular there now and they were tolerant. Devon claimed that I was 'evolving away from the straight currency'. Which meant Devon's dope dealing covered most of the expenses. All I needed work for was spending money. It was a front: just a way of *appearing normal* to the outside world. But with all the cash coming in, appearing normal was really tough.

A few weeks later we went out to see Wes at his cliff-side mansion. Devon felt it was time we paid him a social call to tell him where things stood. Although there were a couple of cool old Brit sports cars in the drive, Wes wasn't home. Joey, Wes' slick houseboy, opened the door a crack when we knocked. Devon tried to get him to loosen up but he was as jumpy as a cat. He kept saying, 'Wes onna root. Wes onna root,' all the time, in a high voice. He was scared.

'What the hell does that mean?' I asked Devon. 'En route, man. On his way home.'

Devon reached in and put his hand on Joey's left shoulder near his neck – 'It's cool Joey … it's cool,' calming him down like you would an over-excited animal. His voice soft and gentle. After a brief pause we were in.

It was good to have a look around during the daytime, before Wes' huge presence began to fill every crack. Joey tried to keep us in the sitting room but one or other of us compulsively shot off down the various passages looking for I don't know what: evidence of humanity, perhaps. There was none. No photos or knick-knacks. No little signs that Wes might have come from a family, that he had people somewhere who cared about him. No. He might just as easily have been hatched from some alien egg, fully grown: past programmed in. The house was a cover. Wes was a monster.

AT THE SOUND of the V8 burbling up the driveway we quickly regrouped in the lounge and tried to look as casual as we could in the space of 15 seconds. Wes entered, appearing not to even notice us. He presented his cheek to Joey for a kiss then headed for the drinks' cabinet.

'So boys, what's the news? What do you have to tell me?' He had his back to us. Me and Devon exchanged looks.

'We have moved into the Parnell pad.'

'And?'

'And it's great. Thanks very much.'

'Is that all?'

'What else do you want, Wes, the twelve prostrations?'

'No, I don't Devon. What I want … what I *expect* from you … is a degree of candour.' The tone was icy.

'Sorry, Wes. I can't think what you're getting at.'

'You can't?' He was leaning against the bar glaring at us. Waiting for an answer. 'Perhaps you should come back when you can.'

He and Devon stared at each other for a while, silently. Buried in that intense face-off some ferocious, unspoken debate raged and then slowly died to a sulky stalemate.

We left.

'What was that all about?' I asked as we drove off.

'Something's up, that's for sure. He's had some sort of info, but it's incomplete.'


I HAD THE uneasy feeling that Devon knew a hell of a lot more than he was telling me. But I didn't push. I knew he'd tell me when he was ready – when he felt I needed to know.

# CHAPTER
# SEVENTEEN

**W**E KEPT AWAY from Wes after that. I was glad. Those watery eyes, his smooth, hairless face, his cold, blank manner all gave me the creeps. Devon was drawn to him – like he needed his approval. I couldn't figure out why, but anyway, at the time I had plenty of other things to think about. I was leading this double life of straight guy and dealer. Even though Devon was sure I had left all that stuff behind, I still had one tie to the old world: Karen.

The one thing that Karen's parents and Devon had in common was that neither party wanted us together. We had this life of secret meetings. She would claim to be studying late at the school library, and I would leave work early – I told Bob Bryant that I was doing some Small Business course at the polytech, which got his approval, no worries. Karen and I would meet at Angela's two or three times a week to talk or drink coffee, but mostly to keep alive that little part of ourselves that had its own demands. The small insistent voice that says, 'This is how it is meant to be … this is important.' The words of an old song, 'Crazy He Calls Me', kept coming back to me, about the difficult things being done straight away but the impossible taking longer.

Most evenings, though, me and Devon would go out together on the Norton. He figured the bike was the ideal inner-city escape vehicle if we got into trouble making a deal. Although Devon hadn't met anyone who could handle a kilo at a time, the money still stacked up. We were only starting out, but each night we unloaded more money than I could earn in a month. Wes had claimed that losing his fear had taken the meaning from his life; the drug money took all the meaning from my work. It also messed with the idea of ownership. Nothing belonged to anyone any more. Everything was just stuff: cars that came and went, things we bought, even the money itself.

It was like nothing was worth anything.

Saturdays were special, though. They were when we would both pile into the Subaru and head for Thunder Road: a priority, no matter what else we both had organised for the night. But now, the need to race had lost its importance. Gone were the stare-downs and the challenges. We were there to deal.

We'd get to the strip early. Devon would wander down the lines of cars, swapping money for smoke, while I sat on the wads like the banker in a game of cards. I didn't like being stuck in the car but the job had to be done.

One night, this figure loomed out of the dark: huge and glistening in his black leathers. It was Mark, Sloane's side-kick: his tattooed face filling the entire window of Devon's low-slung WRX.

'Where's Devon?' 'Out walking.'

'I've got a message for him.' His face was inches away from my own. Huge and impassive. The whites of his eyes glowed but his moko made it hard to read any emotion. 'We know how much shit he's moving.'

I nodded. I didn't know what else to do. Denial was pointless. 'Dak's never been part of our operation here. We leave it to the kids. But now we want in.' 'OK,' I said, hesitantly.

'I've got a block here.' I could see a cube buried in his massive hand.

'Two things.' He reached in and touched the end of my nose with his forefinger. 'Listening?' His finger was feather-light, but it seemed to carry a million volts.

I nodded.

'He does his dealing somewhere else. You got that?' 'What's the other thing?'

'We're in for a block. Bring it tomorrow. Tell him to be generous. Think of it like a ...' he paused, '... a goodwill gift.'

He grinned and slowly stood up. For a while he sat on the bonnet, waiting. His back filled my view, and his weight made the front of the car dip. Just when I thought he'd become a fixture, he stood up and ambled off into the night.

When he had gone I felt the overwhelming desire to pee. I hoisted myself out the door and found there was no strength in my legs: they bent like rubber. I had to support myself on the side of the car as I pissed on the tyre. The air was warm and filled with the residue of burnt rubber. I felt light-headed, as though I'd had a brush with death and had lived to tell the tale. Through the smoke I could see Devon approaching.

'Good timing,' I said.

'I know,' he replied. 'I saw Mark so I hung back.'

'Thanks.'

'He was looking for me, right?'

'Yep.'

'What did he want?'

'He wants to use your skin as a seat cover for the Merc.'

'There'd only be enough of it to cover the steering wheel.' 'The gear knob.'

We both laughed.

'Do you want the bad news or the worse news?'

'Does it make much difference?'

'Well, he's got a block for you.'

Devon grinned, and reached for his smokes. 'That's cool. A block is a big lump of money.'

'I thought it was a block of wood.'

'No, it's usually ten thousand in twenties.'

'How do you know all this?'

He tapped the side of his nose with his forefinger. He leaned back casually on the driver's door while he lit up. He always played these mentor moments up. 'I learned it all from the feds up north. It was a real tertiary education. When Charlie Crim exchanges money for services,' he put on this phoney policeman's voice, 'he has neither the time nor the inclination to count it. He feels a little … vulnerable.' He made a sympathetic face. 'So he uses the trusty block. Fat blocks of bank notes folded in half, all in ten grand lots. They're passed from hand to hand, never opened, just exchanged. It's an honour thing.'

'Here's five blocks. Gimme your house,' I suggested. 'A bit like that. What was the other thing?'

'Oh, the other thing. He wants us to come back tomorrow with a big bag of product.'

'And?'

'And no more dealing on the strip.'

His 'don't give a damn' manner melted away instantly. He turned away, as if to hide his face.

'I guess we've done too well, Devon. He's starting to lose some customers.'

'Yeah. It's the same everywhere, eh. "Go for your life man" and "No worries", until it starts to affect them and then it's "Oh no, you can't do that." '

'He wants you back tomorrow.'

'A final big kiss-off.'

'A big fuck-off more like it.'

'Let's get out of here. I've had a gutsful of this place.'

We slid into the WRX and blitzed it down the strip in the wrong direction. Frenzied runners cleared a path for us like startled animals in the headlights. This was Devon's final 'up- you' gesture to Sloane. And he did it with style.

# CHAPTER
# EIGHTEEN

I N THE MORNING we decided to do a stock take and money-count. There was money under the bed, in the toilet cistern, rolled up and stuck in shoes; there were plastic bags of it in the freezer and stuck in the guts of the TV. It was coming at us from everywhere. Each time we located a new wad, we threw it on the kitchen table. Devon retrieved the dak from places only he knew of. We had been selling and spending without a clue where all the crop and cash were going.

All totalled, our stash came to about eight thousand bucks and less than a kilo of buds. The rest was cabbage and Devon refused to sell that (bad for the rep).

I put it all in a Foodtown bag and weighed it in my hands. 'Does this look like ten grand?' I asked.

Devon looked at it sceptically and shook his head. 'I could get it by cutting in cabbage and shoving it into one ounce bags but I don't think Sloane will see it that way.'

'Why don't we just say "fuck him" and do it our own way in other places?'

'I liked the Thunder Road scene. There were no narcs, and it was more like fun than hard-out dealing.' He paused, thinking. 'But that's all gone now. Why should I supply Sloane if I can't deal on the strip? What does that say? That says you and I are bum boys. That says "Fuck us over, Sloane!" and then "Thank you, sir." That's not us, Trace. That's like the end of the line. That's where you accept you're just a nobody, and pleased to be one.'

I could tell where he was going with this, but I wasn't sure whether to be pleased or worried because from the beginning it was Devon who called the shots. I liked it that way. I've always found decisions hard.

'There are a lot of scenes in this town, Trace, and the street racer scene is just one of them.'

'Yeah, and it's sewn up.'

'Yeah. So we look for new ones. A friend of mine hangs out in the Viaduct Basin with the yachties. I reckon there's money there.' Devon leaned against the kitchen cupboards, arms crossed.

'No way, man! Poncey guys in shorts and those crappy little shoes without socks. Dev, I've got my standards.'

'Yeah, and one of those crappy little forty foot yachts.'

'OK so I could go that. What about the clubs and the uni students?'

Devon thought it over for a moment. 'There are heaps of people there dealing already … and narcs too. I reckon it's tricky. Still, worth a go.'

'At least it wouldn't mean an image change.'

'Trace, just see threads as costumes. Something we can slip off and on for effect, so we don't look like foreigners.'

I considered that. I could live with it if I saw it that way. Part of an act. Not the real me.

'There's another reason for changing scenes.' Devon straddled a kitchen chair. He seemed reluctant to go on.

'What's that?' I asked.

'Sloane will be looking for us now. We've got to keep a low profile. The Subaru will have to go. Maybe your bike too.'

'No way. I'm keeping the Norton.'

He looked at me sadly, shaking his head and smiling. 'Trace, it's only a bit of metal. We can get a new one when the heat comes off.'

'Nope.' I zipped my lip and grabbed the old *Trade and Exchange* from the kitchen table. Devon watched me, as I stared at blurry hardware advertisements. He must have guessed I couldn't be moved on this one.

'Keep the bike then, but don't use it during the day time.

It's too unusual, it's like your trademark.'

After we'd agreed to this compromise, we headed off into town to look for new outfits. It was fun really, because we bought the stupidest most over-the-top clothes we could find. We didn't care. Big baggy shorts. Hawaiian shirts, nautical jackets and dumb little brown slip-on shoes. I couldn't believe how much they cost. Devon wore his home but there was no way I could do that. I had to practise wearing them around the house first. One item at a time. First the shirt then the shorts and last of all those shoes. It was going to be tough. Devon thought it was so funny. He looked it too. I never realised how skinny he was. The big shorts made his legs look like broomsticks, and the shirt flapped around on his chest as if it belonged to some big Island dude and he had borrowed it for the afternoon.

As CAMOUFLAGE THOUGH, the clothes worked. We went to this bar, the Salty Pig. Devon's mate Travis was meant to hang there. It was all done out with boat stuff, old divers' helmets, rope, a harpoon ... other junk I'd never seen before but which looked like it came off a boat. We really stuck out at first because it was mostly full of suits, the BMW crowd dropping in after work. The mysterious Travis never showed up at all.

Some time after nine the suits gave way to boat people. We hooked onto a bunch of Swiss who were sailing around the world. They were desperate for dope. They took us back to their yacht so they could try a sample smoke; there were six of them, four guys and two girls. With their strong accents it was hard to catch their names but there was one girl who was a stunner. Thick blonde plaits like rope and bright blue eyes that lit up her tanned face. She was called Heidi, like the girl in the story. I guess most Swiss girls are called Heidi. It's probably the Jane or Liz of Switzerland, but I thought it was a cute name.

Their boat was tiny. They had been in it for over a year and it sure smelt like it. No wonder they wanted to buy some smoke. All that time staring at each other across the little cabin. They had money, though. Between the six of them they bought nearly all we were carrying. The next day they planned to sail off down the coast heading for the South Island.

I tried not to smoke too much – that's important when you're working – but still I was pretty whacked by the time we squeezed out onto the wharf. Devon was worse; he banged the little WRX three times trying to move it out of the parking space, so I made him get out and drove home myself. On the way back we both had a paranoid spell. We thought we were being followed. It gave me the excuse to blat down a couple of one-way streets the wrong way, stonewalling past the tooting horns and outraged yells of drivers we met coming the other way.

For Devon, though, I guess the paranoia went even deeper. The following day the rally car was gone and he came back with a Holden. I wasn't impressed. It was like he had sold his soul for the dope: renounced the great petrol god who infuses us all.

'Devon, what's happening to you, man? Not even an HSV. It's a mum and dad car.'

He grinned, jumped out and leaned against the mudguard while he lit a smoke. 'I thought you might say that, Trace, and I'm pleased. It confirms my theory.' 'What theory?'

'That this humble Holden is the last sort of car anyone would expect to see Devon driving around in. It's part of going underground. You see how far I'm prepared to go? And the fuss you made about ditching the Norton. You should be ashamed of yourself, man.'

Although his tone of voice said he was only joking I could tell that part of him meant it, and I was a bit defensive.

'You don't really care about these cars though, that's the difference. For you it's just about going fast and beating the other guy. For me it's different. It's sorta … emotional.'

He smiled. 'I know that, Trace. I was just stirring.'

THE NEXT NIGHT at the Viaduct, Devon's mate Travis showed up. He was with about eight or nine other guys and they were drinking beer like it was some sort of contest. Maybe it was. This time, though we had the clothes right, it was obvious we didn't fit in. They had all been match-racing … that's what it took to be part of their group. That and a big capacity for beer.

They were all about the same age, so I guess they had all been to the same school, but no matter how well they knew each other, everything still seemed to be about competition. Whenever anyone finished a can he would crush it on the head of the person next him. Everyone thought this was really funny. Even Devon.

The guy next to me, Greg, made to squash a can on my head. I stood up and faced him. It was suddenly all a bit tense. The talking stopped. Everyone sat, waiting to see what was going to happen. I had that 'here we go again' feeling. Then he turned and banged the guy on the other side, who seemed so wasted he didn't notice. When the talking resumed it didn't include me. Devon and Travis went outside for a bit and I was stuck there by myself.

After a while some guy said to me, 'You sail, Trace?'

I thought for a minute and decided against bull-shitting. 'I've never been on a boat, well, a yacht that is. My uncle used to take me out in a fourteen foot Fyran. Fishing on Lake Taupo.'

This didn't seem to cut it.

'A fry pan? Stink boats, we call them. You should try match-racing some time.'

Then he turned away. I thought, 'Too fake for me. I'm not up to it'.

I looked for a chance to slip away. People kept buying a round: ten cans at a time. The pile of full and squashed cans was building up rapidly. I know enough about drinking to know that you can't pull out until you've bought your round. My turn was still about four rounds away. I couldn't stand it for that long. Greg went over to the bar and ordered. As he was about to pay I reached past him with a fistful of twenties and said, 'I'll get these.' He wasn't expecting this. For the first time since we came in,

I felt I had wrestled back some control. As he staggered to the table with an armload of cans I slipped out the door.

The air outside was at last clear and salty. Devon and Travis sat over by the edge of the wharf, talking. Devon, always super alert, spotted me at once and made a 'stay' gesture with his hand that Travis didn't notice. I sat on some steps behind a row of parked cars, trying to blend in without actually hiding. After a while they stood up and went back inside. Past the bar there was this block of ritzy looking America's Cup apartments, so new it was hard to believe anyone lived in them. It was like one of those model villages for rich people. Everything perfect, secure and clean. In front of it was this mint Falcon ute. An xR8. Quite a rare beast. Someone lit up a smoke in it. The glimpse of face was vaguely familiar. I couldn't get any closer for a snoop without passing open ground so I walked a whole block to come up behind them. I guessed from the matching red mullets who it was. It was the Taylor Twins. Rebel's sidekicks. What were they doing there? Nightshift for Midnight Autos? Something caught their attention because they slid low in their seats, so they wouldn't be spotted.

Devon had come out of the bar and was looking around for me. I stayed down. He headed off towards the car. I had to run for it, back the way I had come. He was already pulling out when I finally made it. I flagged him down.

'There you are. I thought you'd shot through.'

'It doesn't suit me, that stuff. I can't do it like you.'

'You just relax into it. See it like a game. That makes it fun. Sure they're wankers,' he said as he drove out into the traffic, 'but what does it matter? We're not there to make life-long buddies. Lighten up, man.' He gave a little laugh. 'You wouldn't even let him squash a can on your head. How do you expect to get on in the world, Trace? It's a bonding thing.' He was only half joking.

As we pulled up at the lights I looked back, and sure enough, a couple of cars behind us – was the ute.

'Do you see anyone trailing us?' I asked.

Devon glanced in the rear vision mirror. 'Uh uh.' 'A few cars back. The xR8.'

'So?'

'So it's the Taylors. They were spying on you at the Salty Sow … whatever that bar was called.'

'Bullshit. This is not Taylor Twin territory.'

That pissed me off. 'They were there, and now they're following us,' I said with more emphasis

Devon turned into a side street and made his way back the way we had come. The ute did the same. Now they knew that we knew – the surprise had gone. We drove for a while in silence, both a bit spooked.

Devon turned to me. 'OK. So they're following us, what now?' 'I reckon we either outrun them or stop and have it out with them.'

'What do you mean, give them some fist?'

'No. Be straight. Ask them what the hell they want.'

'The old direct approach,' he said in a silly cartoon voice. 'It might be worth a try. One thing's for sure – we can't burn them off in this crate.'

We pulled over and the Taylors drove on past pretending not to see us, and they turned off a little way down the road.

'Jesus. Cat and mouse stuff.' Devon did a u-turn and once more headed off home. I kept a look-out and saw nothing. Neither of us talked until we had nosed the car into the carport back at the house.

We made some tea and sat out on the verandah in the dark, smoking. It was our evening routine.

'I wonder what that was all about?' Devon mused. He seemed a bit shaken.

'God knows, but I reckon it's not good. Do they know where you live? Rebel or any of that crowd?'

He shook his head. 'They know I've moved out of the old place, but they don't know where I am now. They've asked but I've made a point of not telling them.'

'Well, I reckon that's what they're trying to find out.' 'A rip-off you reckon?'

'Don't you?'

'It makes sense. Those Taylors would be up for it. They don't like me.'

'How about Rebel?'

'Doubt it. We've too much joint business and I don't just mean dope.'

'You reckon he wouldn't pull a double-cross?'

Devon sat there, burning the hair on his wrist with the tip of his cigarette. I could see this was an angle he hadn't given much thought to. 'Buggered if I know. Anyway, it's been a good night. Travis wants a kilo.'

'Shit, he must have some money.' 'Half now, half when it's sold.' 'You'll be waiting forever.'

'He reckons three days. Yeah, there's money in them there boat boys. Not that Travis has got any, he's just a try-hard hanger-on.'

'Yeah, I picked that.'

'I'll get Johnno to bring down a pile tomorrow. It'll do him good to come to town. Stop him talking to his dogs for a while.'

# CHAPTER
# NINETEEN

THE FOLLOWING DAY was Saturday: the day that I had agreed to take Karen to the ball. I had still managed to keep my relationship with her a secret from Devon – it was not easy. I reckon there was a bit of jealousy there – he wanted me to himself and any girls we had were strictly short-term – nothing serious. I felt a bit stink, but I needed this piece of myself to be kept Devon-free. The trick was to get away without him tagging along and to avoid telling lies.

Some time that morning there was the clatter of dog claws on the concrete path outside my bedroom window. I got up and saw Johnno arriving surrounded with his posse of pig dogs. He seemed weird and eccentric enough in the country, but here in the city, he was something else. With his old clothes, obviously slept in, the leather hat and the funny mannerisms and noises he made, you could tell at a glance he spent little time with other people.

Devon met him half-way down. Johnno reached out and cupped Devon's chin like you'd do to a four-year-old or a favourite dog. *Devon, everyone's missing son.* I pulled some clothes on and went to the front of the house to meet them.

Johnno said, 'So, this is your hideout, eh? This is where the big deals go down?'

His voice was loud and I noticed Devon looking around anxiously before hustling him inside. We wandered from room to room while he checked things out. 'Where's all ya stuff? You just camping here?' The place didn't seem empty to us but I suppose compared to Johnno's junkyard house it was like a show home.

We had tea and then carried the bags in from his old Studebaker truck. When we opened the haul inside the smell was overpowering. Not the usual dried hedge clipping smell but a thick pungent stink that immediately filled the room.

'Jesus!' I gasped. 'We'll all get ripped just sitting in the same room as this stuff.'

Devon looked at me proudly. 'I'm telling you, it's high grade skunk. Generations of careful breeding. It's like the essence of dope.'

'It smells like a dead body,' I said.

Johnno poured the contents of the bag onto the kitchen table. It was just buds now, all the leaf and stalks had been taken off; hard and dry, it riffled like paper.

Devon picked up a bud and sniffed it. He looked at me significantly.

'Show a bit of respect, Trace, some of the best minds in the country have been working on this. It's connoisseur's dope, not for your run-of-the-mill stoner. This will take you places you've never been.'

'Travelling first class all the way!' Johnno chipped in, as he rolled a joint.

I thought, 'Here goes the day.' It was the last thing I wanted to do, I had too much on. I went off to the toilet but in true doper fashion they couldn't bear the thought of me missing out. When I emerged, there was Devon, waiting for me with the remains of the joint in his hand and an idiot's grin stuck on his face. He could barely speak he was so whacked. I took the joint and made a point of inhaling shallowly, most of the air by-passing the joint and slipping in through the side of my mouth.

There was a rushing in my ears and a blast of hot colour poured through my whole being. It had the fullness and power of a fire hydrant being opened. This was not the weak, gentle stone I was used to. The room rocked and rolled, and the walls ballooned like rubber. Devon and Johnno were no longer people, they were figures in a painting, animated but flat. The house was confusing and difficult to navigate. My mouth was as dry as dust but even getting out of the room was nearly impossible because the floor reared up in front of me. I made it to the bathroom and climbed into the bath. At least here there was water and something to hold on to.

SOME TIME later (my watch claimed about three hours), I was able to prise myself out of the bath and stagger into the shower. It took all my concentration just to swing on the cold tap. At first it was as though the water was falling on someone else. Then slowly, it soaked through the thick narcotic fug I was trapped in. I wriggled through the small opening which led back to the real world: normality. The pleasant familiarity of being cold and uncomfortable. I took off my drenched clothes and towelled down.

It was strangely quiet wandering through the house looking for the others. My feet seemed noisy and I was jumpy. The big pile of skunk weed was lying on the kitchen table, undisturbed. The other bags were on the floor, thankfully unopened. I closed the windows. I reckoned any decent drug dog worth his biscuits would have picked up this stench all the way from Auckland Central Police Station.

Devon had made it to the bedroom and was lying on his back snoring loudly. There was no sign of Johnno or his dogs. Surely he hadn't driven home? That would be unbelievable. I dressed quickly and headed out to look for his truck. As I walked up the path to the front gate I saw him, fast asleep, with the dogs lying under a big rhododendron bush. The pit bull looked up and made a quiet growl, the rest seemed content to wait quietly.

I was to meet Karen in Newmarket at three and hire a suit. From there it was all too complicated to follow, what with getting to Angela's place for drinks, a pre-ball and after-ball party and somewhere in the middle the ball itself. I had this gut feeling it could turn out to be a twelve hour nightmare.

I went back inside to check Devon out. No change. He was lying frozen, in a punched-out position. The picture of a boxer, cleaned out in the first round.

The only paper I could find for a note was toilet paper. It was hard to write on; the pen kept snagging and going through.

*Devon,*
*Gone out with Karen to her school ball.*
*(I know, fraternising with the richies).*
*Don't wait up.*
*Trace.*

That seemed about it. No point in trying to justify myself. I couldn't.

I tried to check out my appearance in the little mirror in the bathroom. I seemed OK except for my fiery red eyes. Trademark skunk eyes. Perhaps no one would notice. I had only 14 dollars in my wallet so I grabbed a bunch of twenties from the top of Devon's chest of drawers. I didn't even bother to count it. Money was not an issue.

# CHAPTER
# TWENTY

MANAGED TO make Broadway, the big shopping street in Newmarket, a few minutes before three. Waiting outside the hire shop, feeling conspicuous and out of place, I was reminded how furtive and uneasy I'd become in public. Like a criminal. I scanned the cars driving past, the people coming towards me: I had my radar out for cops. The street was packed but everybody else seemed part of the scene, unselfconscious participants. Maybe I was invisible to the eyes of innocent passers-by, but I felt as if I stuck out a mile to anyone who knew what to look for.

'There he is!'

I started. It was Karen and Angela.

'Hi,' I said, feeling a bit freaked.

Karen put her arm through mine. 'I knew you'd make it,' she said, sounding like'd she actually been sure that I wouldn't.

'She's been a nervous wreck,' laughed Angela.

'Lies.' Karen hauled me away. 'We'll see you back at your place at about six, Ange.'

As it turned out I was glad I had snatched as much money from

Devon's pile as I had. Hiring suits wasn't cheap. After the deposits had been paid there was only forty dollars left. Did I have enough to get in? Karen must have sensed my anxiety; she told me that her dad had paid ages ago, and not to even think about it. The idea of Raymond funding the evening made me crack up. There was some justice in the world after all.

With Karen at my side I was able to enjoy wandering up and down Broadway, picking up the odd thing that she still needed to complete her outfit. The feeling of being an outsider, having to be constantly on guard, slowly dissipated. We were just two more people thronging this busy street, with every right to be there. Having a girlfriend poured meaning into the silliest and most pointless of activities. At a florist shop the woman said, 'You haven't ordered her a corsage already?' I hadn't. I didn't even know what a corsage was. Another little custom that tied me into the real world. Just being able to buy something for Karen, something pretty, that only lasted one night ... it seemed so right.

Every now and then we would pass girls from her school and she would stop and exchange a few words.

'Are you going?'

'Who with?'

'Whose pre-ball?'

'Whose after-ball?'

And sometimes, 'Who's this?'

'Trace. My partner.' Nothing more. The mysterious boyfriend.

This was part of the whole ball thing. We had started already.

LATER, BACK AT Angela's, the two girls embarked on the serious business of getting ready. Running in and out of bathrooms and bedrooms, sometimes half-dressed, sometimes only in bra and pants. There were other people coming and going. The phones kept ringing for thirty second conversations: checking times and places, and states of readiness.

There were liquor bottles and beer cans all over the place, like it had been used as a party house for some time. All this fancy old furniture, this huge building, and not an adult to be seen.

I had a snoop around. Where were the parents? I knew that the father was an airline pilot, that explained him, but where was the mother?

'In a sanatorium,' Karen whispered. 'What's that?'

She looked around warily. 'A place where alkies dry out.' There was a knock at the door. Angela called from upstairs.

'It's Richard. Let him in.'

I opened the door. He looked very different from the gawky guy at the hardware shop. Not. He was now a gawky guy in a maroon suit, wearing lacquered shoes. He was surprised to see me, but not pleased, and it wasn't just awkwardness. What had I ever done to him? I guess it was just what I was, that's all. What I represented. We had a couple of stabs at conversation which didn't work, so he busied himself with one of the aircraft magazines he found lying around in a designer magazine rack.

Angela came down a few minutes later. She was wearing this full-length dress in midnight blue satin. She looked amazing. All grown-up from giggly schoolgirl to fairy tale princess.

'Just hair and make-up to go and then it's lights, cameras, action!'

She tottered over to Richard in impossibly high heels, and gave him a peck on the cheek. Richard flashed me a look and then blushed. We both watched her mincing out to the bathroom. Maybe the hostility on his part was just shyness. 'Who knows, who cares,' I thought. The idea of him and me being anything more than fellow passengers in the same car was more than unlikely. We were worlds apart.

At last Karen appeared. Her dress was tight and shiny, like Angela's, but its pale blue picked up the colour of her eyes. All her hair was held aloft by a glittering clasp, making her neck seem even longer. My heart ached: she was the most beautiful thing I had ever seen. 'What do you think?'

I was tongue-tied. No words or even sounds would come out.

'You don't like it?'

'I'd like to buy you a sapphire ring. The colour of your eyes.' It came out all croaky. Then it was my turn to feel the blood rushing to my face.

She laughed and gave me a little kiss on the lips before disappearing into the bathroom to work on Angela's hair. I felt so elated. So proud, so knocked out by her transformation it was like I was afloat. Weightless in a blue sky.

There was the sound of a car arriving. It sounded more like a party in full swing. Richard went to check it out. He opened the front door to a blast of noise. I looked out the window. There was this big green Merc full of people singing and moving in time, making the car rock. They all clambered out when the song finished: three guys like a rugby front row, large and beefy; the girls like Barbies. They gathered around the front of their car, the guys stiff and swaggering. Their large upper bodies, exaggerated by the hired suits, told of long hours in the gym. The girls who had the loud, brassy confidence that came with a few tokes, walked up the path, sure of their mission. They passed by Richard like he wasn't even there. He stood indecisively for a moment and then wandered on down to the car to make some sort of contact.

One of the guys, the driver (dark suit, killer shades, shaven head) said, 'Hey Richard, what's happening man?' I could tell from the exchange of little smirks that he was regarded as a loser.

When the guys came up the path I sat down on the couch again and pretended to be reading one of the flight magazines. I could hear one of them say 'Where's the captain?' And Richard reply 'Kuala Lumpur'. Then there were the inevitable mocking echoes from the other two.

Koala lumpier. Torana Roopa. The girls went straight upstairs with Angela and Karen. I was waiting when the guys wandered into the room. They tried to mask their surprise at seeing me, someone unfamiliar and dressed down. I could see all the unvoiced questions.

Who was I?

What I was doing here?

What school did I go to?

My ploy?

Say nothing.

Offer nothing.

Hold the power.

I wasn't going to make them feel better by giving away anything so they could slot me into some category to sneer at.

We staunched it out for while in tense silence until one of them decided he would 'go out for a smoke'. The others were pleased to follow him. Beyond the dope, their confidence was paper-thin.

After Karen had introduced me to the three Barbies (I didn't really listen, just gave them each a cheesey little smile so they wouldn't think I was stuck-up) it was time for me to suit up, like the others. I was sharply aware of what I was giving up to go through with this, wearing a penguin suit. First Devon and the boatie outfits, now this!

As soon as I was dressed, Angela appeared with a big bottle of vodka and a carton of orange juice. Everyone skulled and then took a quick pull on the fruit juice to kill the taste. More people arrived. The rituals were repeated, each time getting a little looser as the vodka did its job.

Someone suggested we better go while we could all walk straight. As we climbed into Richard's dad's Jag I looked back at the house. Not only were all the lights on and the stereo blasting but we had left the front door wide open too. Angela didn't give a stuff about the place. It was weird. All she was interested in was finding a lost joint; she and Karen had evidently stashed one away for the big night and now it couldn't be found. (I suspected the rugby boys from earlier in the evening: they had been sniffing around all the rooms, picking up stuff.) Then Karen turned to me and said, 'Trace, you can get us some can't you?'

I felt really on the spot. It was such a knowing voice. It seemed to hook directly into my other life.

Angela turned to me. 'Please, Trace. Please, Trace. I'm counting on you now.'

The last thing I wanted to do was give them some of the new Northland skunk. They wouldn't be able to get out of the car. I tried to make a joke of it.

'I'm sorry. I don't use drugs. Reality's my trip.'

They weren't amused. This was serious. At least they let the matter drop, Angela holding out, hoping to score in the car park. Richard said nothing but his whole back bristled with disapproval.

The venue was a yacht club down on the waterfront. We had to drive past the same bar where me and Devon had been dealing earlier. The boat harbour was a forest of waving masts. Floating money. Money I could never hope to earn. I thought of the yachties we had spent the night with. Travis' friends. Devon was right. The world was screwed.

It didn't make sense.

None of it did.

# CHAPTER
# TWENTY-ONE

THE CAR PARK turned out to be a scene in itself. There must have been over a hundred people milling about. Delaying final exposure. Angela scored a blast from the daughter of one of the teachers then at last we were able to go in.

In spite of all the fancy frocks, undertaker suits and statement cars, it was no different from the grope-and-stumbles I used to go to when I was at school. It was just a school dance in fancy clothes: everyone struggling to relax, to impress, or just to make it through the night with a smile on their face.

Richard and I spent most of the time sitting together while the girls went off to compare notes with their friends. Every now and then Karen would return and tow me off to meet someone she wanted to impress. New role: the trophy boyfriend. The rough boy.

By eleven I had been thoroughly exhibited so we danced while Richard and Angela waited restlessly at their table. With about half an hour to go Angela wanted out. She had agreed to meet some of the others at a local bar and then go on to an after-ball party. Richard was keen. He would have done anything to escape at this stage, whereas

Karen and I were finally getting to chill and enjoy each other.

THE PUB WE went to was the one me and Devon had been hanging at. I wasn't keen to show my face so I sent the others in ahead while I looked for a toilet. Once they were safely inside I walked around to the bi-fold doors to spy out the scene. There seemed to be no one I knew so I went on in and sat with the others. They were all a bit reluctant to buy drinks, being under age, or, in Richard's case, tight-fisted. I went to the bar, relieved to be through the night with an unscathed rep. I guess I was halfway across the tightly packed room when I spotted Devon on the far side of the bar.

Why does this happen?

Of all the places he could have been, he had to be here, tonight. I felt guilty for the lies and for not including him. Then I felt angry for feeling guilty. There was no end to it.

I snuck back to my seat empty-handed and gave Richard the money to get the drinks. He was pleased to be on his feet, doing something. I guess it had been a long night for him too.

Angela went off to the toilet, so for a while it was just Karen and me, but with Devon around I could feel the distance between us. Her world seemed to revolve around her school and home. I had no interest in either. Whatever we tried to talk about fizzled out and returned to something school-based. She was just mimicking her South African Bio teacher's accent when I saw her eyes light on something over my shoulder. I turned. Angela and Devon were walking towards us.

'Look what Angela's found,' Karen whispered in my ear. I had this sick feeling in my gut.

'Guys, I would like you to meet Diego,' Angela gushed proudly. 'He's from Spain originally but he's stopping here for a while. He's been sailing around the world.'

Devon had a fake accent to go with his fake gestures. 'Ima pleased ta meet yous beautiful women. You two are – a lucky guys,' he said, grabbing my shoulder and pointing at Richard. 'Let me buy you all a drink, a vino, si?'

He swaggered back to the bar … even his way of walking had changed.

'God, Angela, where'd you find him? In the women's toilets?' She laughed and refused to say. Her whole demeanour had changed. She was flushed with excitement. Joyous. I felt for Richard. He was history. What had seemed a pretty bad night had just got a whole lot worse. He sat at the end of the table, in a space inhabited with silence and rejection.

Devon came back with a bottle of wine and some glasses. He was like a one man party. I didn't know how to play it, so I did it by his rules.

'What's that drink, Luigi?' I asked.

'Diego, my friend,' correcting me: a chilly edge crept into his voice, like a warning. 'This drink, it is Lambrusco, nectar of the gods.' He turned the label around. 'See: frizzante, it means sparkling, bubbly, like – a my friend Angela here.' He picked up her hand and kissed the back of it. Richard stood up and walked towards the toilet. No one even asked where he was going. When he neared the door he looked back briefly, catching my eye, and then left.

When I pointed it out to Karen she seemed unworried. 'I was surprised he stayed as long as he did. He hoped something might happen between him and Angela. It was never going to.' She had it sussed. It was a blast of cold air, the way she said that, considering he was a friend of hers. She too was suckered in by Devon in this Spanish incarnation. I looked at her face in repose. Mouth slightly open, ready to laugh, ready to be amused. Ready.

'Where is Ricardo? He hasn't left you … how do you say … up the lurch?'

It was all too easy for Devon. No wonder he was so cynical. Anything was possible. Anyone was available. I wanted to slip off like Richard. My last Devon-free realm was now utterly conquered.

Then I smelt it. The rich smell of decay. Faint but unmistakable even in the smoky bar. There was a small backpack hanging off Devon's chair. It all began to make sense to me. After being stalked by the Taylors I had thought for a moment that Devon might have been stalking me. It was just Devon's incurable habit of spinning and play-acting. I was relieved – cheered up.

'Whereabouts in Spain do you come from, Luigi?' It was about time to put pressure on Devon. This was too easy.

'Are you familiar with Spain, amigo?'

'Oh yes, bullfights, tango.'

'I come from Barcelona. Tis very beautiful, I must take you there.'

'We could go on your yacht … sail away!' Angela. High-pitched.

'Yeah,' I joined in. 'Let's go on your yacht.'

'And you will, my eager young hombre, but first I have a little business.' He turned to Angela, his face close to hers. 'Will you wait for me?'

She nodded silently, her eyes glazed.

Devon leaned forward and kissed her on the forehead and then sprang up and headed for the door. I followed at a distance to see what he was doing. Outside, sure enough, was Travis standing at the door of his car. Devon climbed in the passenger side and they were off without a word. I watched to see whether anyone was following, but saw nothing.

Back in the bar Angela was looking a bit worse for wear. Her eyelids were drooping and she slid down low in her chair. Karen looked a bit lost too.

'I think it's best we push off,' I said. 'That Spanish guy has gone off in a car. And I reckon you're about had it, Angela.'

'You go. I'm staying.'

'Let's get her home, Karen. The party's over I reckon.'

Karen was keen to get out but Angela became stubborn. 'I'm waiting for him. You don't just walk out on guys like Diego.'

It was a line straight out of those afternoon soap operas. 'Angela, he wasn't even Spanish, he just had a good tan. He was more likely from Mangere.'

She looked at me a bit cock-eyed. 'So jealous,' she said. 'What a pity.'

The three of us sat there, stalemated and immobile. Other people powered in from the ball. The crowd swelled so much that movement was difficult and standing up meant immediately losing your seat. Three boisterous girls climbed on to one of the tables and began to do the cancan. The crowd went wild. Karen told me they had been the hit of the school's musical production. Just when they were into their second verse with the full attention of the bar the legs broke off the table they were dancing on and they disappeared among the sea of heads. I turned and discovered that Devon/Diego was back. He was crouched next to Angela with his arm around her. She leaned her head against him.

'All aboard, my land yacht awaits.'

It was good to see him back again but I knew deep down that things could only get worse. All my efforts to be a straight-up guy in Karen's eyes were about to be demolished by some act of outrageousness.

Devon had a taxi waiting for us outside and we all trooped out and sank into the cool quiet interior, a sanctuary from the mayhem in the bar. All the way back Devon regaled us with stories of white-washed buildings and strange local customs. Karen kept dropping off to sleep, with her head against my shoulder. When we got back to Angela's place it was lit up, the door still wide open and the stereo belting out the same music. Devon paid off the taxi man and half-dragged/half-carried the giggling Angela upstairs. I guess what was going to happen next was obvious. I was envious and a bit shocked. Sure, the possibility of sex with Karen had been dancing in the distance ever since I first laid eyes on her, but not when she was zombified with booze and exhaustion. I just knew I couldn't do that.

I sat Karen down on a couch in the sitting room and went off to make coffee. Moments later she was asleep. So much for that. I went upstairs to look for Devon and Angela. Trying to grab back a bit of control. It was all happening too fast. I guess I wasn't prepared for what I saw when I reached the landing. Angela was lying on her father's bed half out of her sleek ball dress: the image of a wilted flower. Devon appeared from a side room and began hauling her out of her clothes. He was rough, like he was angry. Gone was the jokey Diego. He saw me in the big mirror against the wall and waved me away.

I went downstairs. Everything I thought I knew was turned on its head. Doing nothing, saying nothing, meant I'd let some door slam. What Devon was doing upstairs meant that Karen's world was forever off-limits to me. There was a price to be paid for being Devon's friend. Somehow I had failed.

I was determined to do the right thing by Karen. I pushed the two couches together to make a sort of bed. I lifted her out of the chair and laid her delicately along the length of couch. She was as pliant as a rag doll. Her hair had tumbled from its sculpted elegance into pools of blonde silk around her shoulders. The distant beckoning oasis of sex was now an airy mirage. Any touching, any advantage taken, would be a violation.

I lay next to her, soaking up the quiet, watching the rise and fall of her chest. It was strangely soothing just to be there beside her: no talk, no effort, just closeness. For all her childishness, her gullibility, her selfishness, there was a core of beauty that made everything OK.

An innocence that put her above those faults. She slept soundly now beside me, a slight snuffle from her open mouth, her breath brushed across my face, warm and sweet. Somewhere upstairs there was this sound. A dull, banging noise. It went on and on, following me into a deep sleep.

# CHAPTER
# TWENTY-TWO

THIS NOISE. SWELLING. Getting closer. The sound of voices. Angry voices. I opened my eyes to the dazzling brightness of mid-morning. It took a moment or two to work out where I was, and who it was lying beside me. The voice was a man's but I didn't recognise it. It was answered by Angela's in a similar, outraged tone. I sat up just as Devon came running into the room. He was naked and carrying all his clothes in his arms.

'Trace! Trace! Get up man. Alien attack! Alien attack!'

I clambered out of the double couch set-up, immediately aware of the stupid penguin suit I was wearing. Then it all flooded back into my weary brain. Everything that had happened last night, Devon's part in the disaster, and even, at a guess, who was doing the yelling upstairs.

I looked back at Karen. She still slept on soundly, the sleep of a child, careless and deep. Even with smudged mascara, collapsed hair and a dribble-stained pillow, her face was angelic. I had this intense feeling of loss – almost grief. It was all over.

Everything seemed to be tumbling around me. I scooped up my casual clothes from the corner where I'd left them before the ball.

Oddly though, Devon had calmed down, and was dressing at an almost leisurely pace. He even stopped with his trousers at half mast to light a smoke. It was me who felt panic. The last thing I felt like was a fight with some outraged rich dude-claiming all sorts of crimes against his daughter and property.

A door upstairs slammed and a red-faced man in a pilot's uniform stormed into the room. Devon, unperturbed, put his foot up onto the piano stool to do up his shoelaces while I scrambled around gathering the rest of my things. The captain stood in the doorway, hands on his hips, struggling to contain his anger.

'You two aren't going anywhere,' he said. 'You've a lot of questions to answer!'

I was thinking hard, trying to work out some feasible escape route. He couldn't hold both of us here. We could rush him. Devon sat casually at the piano like he was about to play a request. He seemed amused by the captain, almost pitying.

'Whoa! Ground control to Captain Haddock, chill captain, chill. This is not your crew you're talking to. You should be thanking us. We're knights in shining armour. We rescued your lovely daughter and her sleeping friend here from the creatures of the night.' He slowed down now, sounding calm and cold. 'Now you're back you want to play Big Daddy. Fine, your call, but don't play it with me or Trace.'

'Load of codswallop.'

'Do you know what I reckon, Haddock?' Devon continued. 'I reckon you should fix that bed up there. Jesus, do those brass knobs bang when you're really going to it. I guess you'd know.' He winked at him, as if they were mates.

The captain looked as though a jumbo jet had just landed on his back lawn. He opened his mouth but no noise came out.

Devon shot me the 'we're out of here' head movement and tossed his smoke onto the Persian carpet. 'And furthermore, no ash trays.

Man, call yourself a host? What kind of hotel are you running here?'

While Angela's father was retrieving the smouldering butt, we walked to the front door. Panic overtook me then. 'Run Devon!' I said, darting down the front steps. He refused. My desperate need to put distance between us and the captain took 50 metres to work itself out. I waited, chest heaving, for Devon to amble on over. 'Is he coming?' I gasped.

'Course not. He's not going to do anything, couldn't you tell?'

No, I couldn't tell. In fact I felt like a runaway kid. We strolled on down the hill.

'Jesus, what a night, what a fuck-up!' I said more to myself than anything.

'I dunno, I quite enjoyed it.'

'Oh yeah, what about this morning?'

'Especially this morning.'

I looked at him. He meant it too.

As we reached the main road the traffic became busier and the day began to take hold. I was thinking how things between Karen and me had gone down the toilet again. We were doomed. Devon must have noticed me brooding.

'Cheer up old sport!' he said. 'It's a big day for us and it's started well. A good shot of adrenaline to clear the head. Those richies, they got thick skins. I don't know why you worry so much. All they care about is stuff. Did you see his moral high ground vanish when I threw the ciggie on the carpet? That says it all.'

I guess I didn't look convinced.

'Good sex?'

I didn't answer.

'Oh oh. Brewer's droop?'

'No. I'm not into screwing someone who's unconscious.'

He grinned at my huffy voice and shook his head. 'Trace, Trace,

Trace. What are we going to do with you?'

He dug into his pocket and said, 'Catch!'

I fumbled to grasp the heavy, cube-shaped object. It was a wad of 20 dollar notes, as thick as a phone book, all folded in half.

'This is your legendary block,' he said. 'Euphoric Enterprises attracted corporate investment last night.'

'What corporation?' I said, trying to guess how much was there.

'It's a gang … thug money. Drugs for thugs, Trace. That's about ten G you're trying to count … but it won't get split up, just passed on when the time comes. Intact. Part of another deal. It's an old block, lots of the notes are pre-plastic. I doubt whether you could even spend them now. Anyway, it's a working day for you and me. We've lots to do. That's why I decided to tag along when I bumped into you last night. It was an accidental meeting, Trace. You were fucked by the fickle finger of fate! Lucky eh?'

I just stared at him.

'Well, you may not think it was so lucky this morning, but you will, I guarantee it.'

He kept tossing me this block of money as we were walking along through the midday crowds of Broadway. Making light of it. Ten grand in gang money. It had probably paid for people to be 'disappeared'. Been used to keep the feds away from plantations. Bought truckloads of pain.

I was out of my depth. I knew it but I couldn't do anything about it. Stealing the dak was kind of fun – in a scary sort of way – but this stuff, it was just sweat and ulcers.

I was in with Devon now. He called the shots. I didn't like it but what could I do? You can't just pick out the parts of a friend you like and ignore all the rest.

AFTER I HAD returned the clothes to the hire shop we went to a big department store and bought a food processor, several rolls of resealable plastic bags, and some really expensive kitchen scales. It came to over 300 dollars. The shop assistant, a motherly type, was interested in the sort of cooking we were planning to do.

'Herbal recipes,' said Devon proudly.

Eventually, at home, we commenced the slow process of slicing, dividing and separating out the various elements of dak. Devon maintained it was not going to be a wholesale operation. There was a new boutique approach to dope that we were going to usher in.

'Remember. Gone are the days ...' he said, sounding like an infomercial '... when the euphoria market was covered by just one product: Mary Jane, the Coca Cola of dope. No sir. The marketplace has been invaded from many quarters. The boy scientist approach. So easy to set up your own little meth-lab. Speed. Then there's smack and coke. All the hard lines. You don't want to go there, Trace. It's really ugly.'

He opened a new bag and poured it out onto the carpet. The stink was so strong it made me feel like chucking. He looked up at me with a grin.

'But wait ... there's more. The humble cannabis plant can offer a complete range of experiences, provided it is divided up and blended judiciously. It alleviates pain, promotes sleep, eases tension, cuts off the damaging peaks and troughs of the bi-polar depressive. Non-addictive, non-polluting, home-grown. In short, it is the drug for all seasons.'

I knew Devon had worked as a journo, but now he was sounding like a fucking medical textbook. Like he'd written one. The guy was a mystery to me. Always would be.

Johnno's ten black garbage bags jammed the kitchen. As we began to weigh it and bag it I suppose for the first time I had a clear view of how much hooch we had in our possession: right in the epicentre of the biggest market in New Zealand and less than two kilometres from the city's police nerve centre.

'We have to start thinking beyond all this, Trace. We don't want to stay in this high risk/high return theatre of capitalism. We need to go somewhere where the risks are more moderate, the returns slimmer. We need to use this to creep somewhere respectable.'

'Yeah, it might lengthen our life spans.'

'Don't be dramatic. The only assassins we'll have to worry about are Mr Cholesterol or his mate Dr Cancer.'

'How about Wes, Devon? When are you going to see him? Tonight?'

'No. He was too tetchy. I never picked him for a bossy old prick – just a nosy one. I know what he was doing. He was trying to clear up something he had heard. He was digging. When I didn't come through, tell him everything, I was threatening his authority. He doesn't like that. He's a pompous old git really, behind that cool front. He likes young guys, standing around, listening to him … telling him he's the man!'

'I guess. I thought he sounded a bit ominous.'

'I reckon he was pissed because Joey let us in when he wasn't home. He wouldn't have dared do that a year ago.'

'A servant who knew his place!'

'Exactly.'

Devon was shaking all the buds we had picked off into the food processor.

I stopped what I was doing for a bit. 'I thought your connoisseur liked his buds intact. So he could hold them up and drool over them.'

'Your connoisseur might, but we are selling to the fast food generation. By rights we should be rolling it all into joints for them so they won't make dorks of themselves in front of their mates.'

'McDevon's Takeaways. We should design packaging and maybe

toys for the kids.' I could see it now.

'Yeah, little bongs shaped like Disney characters.' 'Suck on Donald Duck.'

We both laughed. It seemed ages since we had laughed. It was nice.

'So, tell me about the gang guy.'

'OK. It's like this. I guess the first thing is, news travels fast. I was expecting to see Travis with some proceeds. And as I'm waiting, right … this is before you lot turn up … I see this Māori guy all in black leathers, pacing up and down in front of the pub like a hungry dog. He was edgy, man.'

'He was wearing gang patches?'

'No, he was wearing really styley leathers, like stuff that had been made for him by a tailor or someone. I'm thinking, *What's up with him?* 'cause he was obviously waiting for someone, and he was dripping with nervous energy like he hated being out in the open.'

Devon paused to light up.

'Then I see Travis arriving and I head over to him. This guy heads for him too. It seems that someone Travis sold to has told a party who told this guy. And this guy is dead keen to score….'

'When did you find all this stuff out?'

'Over a few beers. He calmed down but he was still in a real hurry. That's why,' he said, pointing to the ten k block on the mantle. 'I guess he felt a little vulnerable wandering around with this.'

'What's the story with him?'

'He was from down the line originally, a crowd from Gisborne I think, maybe Wairoa. And anyway his dealer had stood him up, claimed a rip-off, blah blah. Too bad, how sad. So Travis had to drive me home and I was able to dash in and rark up enough quality crop.'

'What did Travis do? Wait in the car?'

'I got him to drop me outside the yuppie pub up on the main road. I ran in the front, out the back and then snuck down here.'

I didn't like it. 'I have the feeling this hideout's our only protection now. If any of these guys track us, we're dead meat.'

Devon looked up from the ounce bag he was sealing. 'Don't be para' man. I'm in control.'

'How much did you give him? Did you work out a per ounce deal or what?'

'About a kilo. This guy, calls himself Wiremu, looked a bit pissed when I showed him how much he was getting. I thought he was going to break into the block … a bit of a no-no that one … but after he had sampled, he knew he had struck real pay dirt.'

'It seems real pricey.'

'Yeah, well, you've read the papers. The feds have had a real bumper year with both indoor and outdoor busts. Nothing is better for prices than that. First law of economics: supply and demand.'

We worked late into the night. By the time we had finished we had a mountain of ounce bags. Devon made a fire of all the scraps in the sitting room fireplace so we didn't end up with a big residue of traceable material. I still felt funny about sleeping with the stuff or leaving it around the house. Too dangerous.

In the short term we put everything into a couple of rubbish bags and hauled them up into the big puriri tree at the bottom of the garden. It was a windy night. The bags made a dark shape, slowly turning. I dreamt about hangings and lynchings all night. The same thing again and again: being strung up, and then waking up feeling breathless and panicky, heart like it was being wrung in someone's fist.

# CHAPTER
# TWENTY-THREE

THE FOLLOWING MORNING I noticed that Devon was looking as ragged as I was. He had slept with the farmer's shotgun, loaded, next to his bed.

We agreed it was time we developed a self-defence plan to protect us and give us a chance to escape if we were attacked by anyone in numbers. There were two main prongs to this. The first was the strengthening of all the little house's doors, windows and locks. This was reasonably straightforward. I nailed trellis onto all the low window frames and screwed a metal strip down the door frame and over the catch. It was a relief to spend the day doing something constructive.

The second prong to our defence was finding somewhere else to park our vehicles, as being followed home was the greatest risk we'd face. There was a big block of council flats down the road: the last link with the rich suburb's working class roots. I reckoned there was bound to be someone there who didn't need their car park. We could probably squeeze the car and bike into one space. Devon volunteered to track down a garage.

FOR THE NEXT few days I tried to lose myself in the boring normality of work. The people I found really depressing when I first started now seemed reassuringly ordinary. Straight. I craved it.

Devon was different. His dealing with the gangs had left him totally pumped. He worked alone mostly, launching into a frenzy of selling. There was no stopping him; he was coming and going all hours of the day and night. He was hooked.

In a few days all the bags we had made up with Johnno were gone. Devon still as high as a kite, flying on pure adrenaline, me getting more and more nervous. My thoughts were doom-laden. Something had to give. We couldn't carry on like this without some sort of backlash from someone.

WHEN I CAME home the following Friday the house was full of the smells of food cooking: Devon had felt like preparing a roast. It was the first time since moving in that we had put the oven to its proper use.

Devon had a trip to make before we ate, though, and he wanted me to go with him. We were heading out to Glen Eden. It wasn't going to be a social call. Rebel had left three messages on the cellphone and the last one sounded like a summons. Something was up between them but Dev wouldn't tell me what. We arrived at the yard just on dusk. It sounded like a party was on. We could hear heavy metal belting out as we opened the gates. Rebel's big rotty, Boris, made a jump at us but was choked by his chain. I felt the sweat burst out of me a moment later in response, but it didn't even ruffle Devon's feathers. The door to the house was wide open and I could see the Taylors sprawled out on the couch, Lion Reds a fixture in their hands. There were others in the front room I'd never seen before: this guy in a suit and two skinheads. It was an odd gathering. On the table there was a slab of cold beers – busted open and half gone. The one thing that really stood out for me, even though it was parked in the corner of the room, was a shotgun.

I tried not to let on that I'd seen it but in a way it participated in our conversation.

I could sense the hostility. Something was known. Things had been said before we arrived, maybe some kind of agreement reached. I knew it was about us. We were given beers, but that was it. No fake hospitality tonight.

I looked at Devon to indicate that I wanted out, but he seemed unworried.

Rebel walked over to us and stood near the table. His voice was cold and sarcastic. 'What does it take to get you out here, Devon? There was a time when I couldn't keep you away. A bit different when you want something eh? one-way traffic.'

'Hear you've scored in a big way,' said the Taylor with the chipped tooth.

All eyes were on Devon, who was drinking, taking his time. 'That's what they're saying?'

'There's a lot of talk about you,' the other Taylor hunched forward. 'That it's all done by the block lot.'

'Sounds like hype to me. Remember the old saying, "Believe half of what you see, and none of what you hear." ' Devon's voice had an edge of sarcasm.

'Is it coming from the gangs?' the bad-teeth Taylor asked. 'Doesn't your info go that far?'

Rebel was sitting in the corner listening, as were the other two skinheads. The Taylor looked around the room and spoke again. Every word he uttered seemed loaded, almost pre-arranged.

'It might. So what've you got?'

'I have access to product now.'

'Wholesale or retail?' This was the guy in the suit. It was the first time he had spoken.

Devon turned to Rebel. 'Who's this? I'm not used to seeing people around here dressed like feds.'

'Oh Jig excuse me,' Rebel upped Devon on sarcasm. 'This is ... *Walter*, he's from the motor trade. How rude of me.' This said in a poofy voice. They all laughed. Everyone loosened up for a moment. Then Rebel turned to the two skins.

'And these two are ... *Tom and Jerry*. They're part of the motor trade too. A different part.' The bigger one sat forward and grinned. You could see his muscles flex beneath his black T-shirt. He looked like a boxer. The other one was leaner and his wrists were entirely covered with a mesh of tattoos. It was pretty obvious that they were enforcers for the suit.

Rebel continued, beginning to enjoy his new role. 'Colleagues, I'd like to introduce you to Jig and his friend Trace. Two cowboys fresh in Dodge trying to make their way in the big city.' He paused, waiting for some reaction from Devon. It didn't come. 'They used to be active members of the street racing brotherhood but we haven't seen them for a while.' Another pause. 'And they used to live in a boarding house in Sandringham but they haven't been seen there for a while either.' He turned directly to Devon. 'I guess you've moved up in the world, and taken your good fortune with you.'

There was a stained old dining table in the middle of the room which looked as if it had been used for everything except eating off. Devon sat down at it, trying to establish a more casual manner. I was planning escape routes.

'Have you been talking to Mark, Rebel?'

A direct hit registered on Rebel's face. It was like getting a glimpse of the other guy's hand during a poker game.

'He might've said something.'

'Let me tell you my side and you can make up your own mind.' Devon explained the kiss-off we had been given: *he does his dealing somewhere else.* I could practically feel Mark's breath and see those face tatts as Devon went through it all again, explaining where Mark's ultimatum left us.

Rebel crossed his arms, looking sceptical. 'I reckon it's time you reconsidered, Jig. We've missed you at Thunder Road. I hear some of the conditions have changed.'

'Who from?'

'Ahh, you want to know who from?' Rebel sensed he'd regained control.

'OK. Forget it then. What conditions?'

'You can deal on the strip but it's all done through Mark and Mr Sloane.'

'*Mr Sloane*,' Devon mimicked.

The guy in the suit betrayed some annoyance at this gibe, enough for me to see where he was connected.

'Yeah, *Mr Sloane*' (this time with emphasis) 'pushes a lot of business my way. It works out well. I'd recommend it.'

'It's the only way to go,' the suit chipped in. His accent was different from ours, a bit strange.

'The only way, huh?' Devon was gaining confidence. 'There's our way and the wrong way.' The suit put his hands

behind his head, and leaned back in the chair, as if that settled the matter.

'That's what Trace's dad used to say to him. You want to be our big daddy, huh?'

'Jig. Not the time to crack wise. I'm part of that deal. You come in with us or it won't be only Mark you are watching out for.' Rebel's voice was cold, the threat plain.

One of the Taylors sniggered. That made Devon twig. 'You've already been on surveillance, haven't you, Gaz?'

The other, quieter Taylor answered for him. 'It's a small world, Devon. Wherever we go, we seem to keep bumping into you.' The suit,

'Walter', spoke again. 'There are rules. Everyone buys into their spot. You keep on dealing without us and you're ripping us off. Simple as that.'

'Deal us in, Jig and it's cool. We'll all be one big happy family again. A brotherhood.'

'We get to come over for Sunday dinner?' Devon always went too far. Rebel looked pissed off.

'He's a funny man. Time to go.'

'Come back tomorrow and we'll work out a way of operating,' said the suit.

'And if you don't come back, we'll come to you.' The bigger of the two skins grinned, like a skull.

'Come out, come out, wherever you are,' whispered the other, his eyes wide.

As we stood on the steps Rebel added as an afterthought, 'oh yeah, Jig. One last thing. I don't want to hear that you've been dealing with the nigger gangs. We don't deal with those apes. That would be sorta like a betrayal.'

He and Devon stared at each other for a moment without speaking, then we left.

# CHAPTER
# TWENTY-FOUR

B Y THE TIME we got back home, the roast had shrunk to about half its original size but the smell was a relief: sort of welcoming. We were both a bit stunned but we divided up the meat as best we could with our blunt knives then sat in the sitting room eating off our laps: neither felt like saying much. After we had eaten, Devon produced a bottle of Jack Daniels, so we repaired to the back deck where we could stare out towards the Domain. Our green screen of contemplation.

Eventually Devon said, 'So the honeymoon's over. I've been thinking it through from every angle.' He tilted the bottle to and fro. 'We have to line up with someone. It has to be either Rebel or the gangs, and I don't trust my luck with the gangs. They're tight.'

'The devil you know.'

'True. Still it sticks in my throat, that's for real. Dealing with Rebel has been like, equal up to now. Everything done on contra. Stuff balanced out.'

'I've got a feeling that it isn't Rebel you're dealing with now,' I said, taking the bottle off him.

'So you think it's Sloane? or do you reckon there's someone pulling his strings?'

I tried to think who else could be involved. 'Could be. Could be the cops. I don't trust those bastards, that's for real. I picked that suit guy for a D. when I saw him. A wild arm of the drug squad. Those guys are so loose ... no rules ... just do what they want.'

'So what do you reckon?'

'I reckon we've still got to go in with this bunch. They know you, Devon.'

'And they're organised. I reckon the skins were trackers too, just like the Taylors, only from different scenes.'

'True, they were scary bastards.'

'I better go back tomorrow, see what sort of deal I can cut.'

He looked sombre. We knew that we had been forced into a corner and part of our dream had been ripped away.


DEVON WENT TO bed but I felt restless. I grabbed my helmet and headed out on the bike. A soothing ride through the quiet streets in the evening. Before long I found myself circling the area where Karen lived. I knew I had to see her again. My body ached for her – now more than ever. I ran over various options as I cruised along. Chance it at the front door? Ring up and see if I could lure her outside? I wasn't smooth enough to pull that off. That was Devon's territory.

I rode up to the house on spec, just to check out the lie of the land. As I neared the end of the street, her parents' car passed me, heading off towards town. I could see Raymond crouching over the wheel and peering short-sightedly through the windscreen. For the first time in days luck had dealt me a decent hand.

I parked the bike a few houses past theirs: always a good safety precaution.

I gave a nervous knock at the door. You can never be sure what's on the other side. I could hear talking. My heart sank a bit, but then I heard Karen call out, 'Who is it?' She was by herself.

'It's me, Trace.'

What had I been expecting? She wrenched the door open and threw her arms around my neck. Even in my wildest fantasies I hadn't been given this sort of a welcome. It washed away the events of the afternoon. We stood on the doorstep, kissing. Me in jeans, leather jacket, helmet dangling from my hand. She in a nightie and slippers. She felt light and frail. Birdlike. I could feel the warmth of her skin through the thin cloth. No talking. She pulled me inside. Nothing existed beyond her.

We found ourselves in her bedroom. On her bed. Everything else stayed pushed to some distant part of the universe and the only reality was our lovemaking. We may have talked. We may have paused and taken stock. I have no memory of it. All I can remember was a passion that was stronger than anything I have ever felt. A shared passion. Dimension had no meaning. We'd found a private refuge. When we finally emerged we were changed people. We knew each other in a way I had never known anyone.

Nothing could ever be the same.

The first thing I can remember saying was, 'How long have we got?'

She looked at her watch. 'Twenty minutes, half an hour at most.' The news was devastating.

Everything about her had a warm radiance. Her face glowed. No one could fail to notice. This was pure, stronger than any drug. It reached the dark, closed off places I never went to, I was blissed out and complete. My other life seemed, for a moment, years away.

Gradually something seeped in. The sad, leaden tick of the clock. Dragging us back from a warm, delicious dream.

'How did you know? How did you know to come to me?' she asked.

I shook my head. 'I just came. I didn't know anything. One moment I was riding. The next moment I was on your doorstep. When I heard your voice from outside, I thought, "She's home with someone else".'

'It was Angela on the phone. I'd just rung her up. It's been nightmarish here today. First my parents, then Angela's father... people yelling ... threats ... lectures ... more yelling. But Mum and Dad had to go to this conference. So I rang Angela. I mentioned your name, then knock knock. You're there. Magic!'

'Third time lucky.'

'It wasn't magic when I woke the other morning. You gone, Angela crying, her father threatening God knows what, my head full of hot rocks wanting to erupt. I just thought, blown it again. Nothing ever works out for me.'

'Me too. First time making a complete arse of myself. The second time being strapped to that whole ball scene. And then Devon showing up.'

'Who?'

'Devon, the guy I live with.'

'Diego?'

'Same. He has a Spanish ancestor he's pretty proud of ... so he plays it up.'

'Why didn't you tell me? Angela is in love.'

'You were a bit far gone, and anyway, I know better than to mess in other people's stuff.'

She thought about it and seemed to agree. 'Do you think I should tell her?'

I shook my head. 'She won't thank you for it.'

'Do you think Diego ... Devon will see her again?'

'Maybe. I don't know. That's his business ... he's got quite a bit on his plate at the moment.'

'But you're here.' Then she said as if only just remembering, 'We haven't got long. Let's organise something.' She thought hard, screwing up her hands with the effort. 'Are you on the net? E-mail?'

I laughed and she blushed. 'Silly question, I guess.'

'Are you working?'

She nodded. 'I am. At Dad's work, after school. I'm a filer … sort of a clerk person. You can't really ring me there.'

We both sat, aware of the time vanishing before us.

'Got some paper?'

We heard the sound of the car in the drive.

She ripped a page from the back of a novel she had next to her bed. I wrote our address and Devon's cellphone number on it and then we rushed to the front of the house. I could hear the back door opening as we kissed. I jumped off the portico that jutted from the flat front of the house and scrambled down the drive. I could see the lit windows from where my bike waited. Perhaps Karen might need me. I walked halfway up the drive and waited in the dark. But there was nothing. Whatever was happening now didn't include me so I wandered back to my bike. As I mounted I realised my helmet was still in her bedroom. Nothing was ever straightforward.

# CHAPTER
# TWENTY-FIVE

THE FOLLOWING DAY I slept in. I had been dozing off and on since about six o'clock, kept replaying a dream of this scene from when I was a kid. I had been locked in a shed by my father for stealing. It was the supreme punishment: the one he used when beating wasn't enough. The shed was full of garden stuff, stacks of newspapers, and junk that had nowhere else to go. The only soft things were a bunch of old coats which had hung on the back of the door since forever. I tried to make a bed out of these spidery clothes but there weren't enough to be comfortable. For hours I lay there, cold and miserable in the darkness, hoping to go to sleep. Somewhere under the floor boards was a rats' nest; they wouldn't stop squeaking and gnawing. I've never minded rats but these were close to my face. Just when I realised I'd have to spend the night there, this new noise came, faint but repeated. It worked itself into the scene but it didn't fit. I woke.

Someone was at our front door. Someone who wouldn't stop knocking. I dragged myself out of the bed, and bleary-eyed, went to the kitchen door. We had installed a peep hole. Devon's idea. There was this guy all in tight black leathers with a little rat's tail plait hanging down his back. He kept peering anxiously up the driveway. When I opened the front door he turned, surprised to see me. He must have been four or five years older than me. He was Māori, had a goatee beard, impressively groomed. What stood out though, was the gold. He wore a heavy gold chain, thick rings on his fingers, and his two front teeth had been capped with it. He smelled of those expensive aftershaves that people in offices wear.

'Yeah?' I stood there in shorts and T-shirt. 'Devon home?'

His voice was so soft it took a moment to work out what he had said.

Then I realised I wasn't sure. 'Wait here. I'll check.'

I went to his room and sure enough, Devon's bed was empty. Whether he had slept in it was anyone's guess, because he hadn't made it or changed the sheets since we had moved in. The dude had gone when I got back. I found him around the side of the house.

'What's up?' I was a bit pissed. I don't like snoopers.

'Is he in?'

'No.'

'I got this feeling someone was watching me when I arrived,' he said by way of explanation.

'Who wants him?' I asked coldly.

'Wiremu. I'll be back later.' He was already walking away.

It was an odd way to start the day but I hardly gave it another thought. My head was filled with Karen. Last night seemed like a dream and the only thing I wanted to do was to get back into that dream and stay there forever. I felt like one of those people who approach you in the street because they've found Jesus: those people who are dying to tell you how suddenly, their whole shitty world makes sense. Stoned on God.

I was hungry but there was, as usual, virtually nothing edible in the cupboards. There was butter but the bread was mouldy; there was milk but no cereals, and eggs that looked like they had been there when we bought the fridge. It didn't matter. Nothing could dent my mood. I went to take a shower but as I was taking off my T-shirt I could smell Karen on my clothing or maybe my skin. There was no way I'd wash that off. It was part of my happy bubble.

The need for food was urgent though, so I put my boots back on and found my wallet. The faint ringing of Devon's cellphone sounded as I was going out the front door. It came from somewhere in the sitting room. I'd just narrowed it down to a crack in the couch when it stopped.

I pushed the last call button and redialed, thinking it would be Devon with some new instruction. It wasn't. It was Karen. She was at Angela's and she wanted to be with me. Right then. I got onto the Norton without my helmet, not caring about the risks; I thought I was leading a charmed life at that moment. I didn't even care if Angela's father was home. As it happened he was in Singapore or L.A. Somewhere far away, anyway, so Karen and I were safe.

We hardly spoke for the first hour, driven by our desperate need to climb into each other's souls. Minutes or hours later, we surfaced, breathless, satisfied for a while that our core loneliness had been driven back a safe distance and we could relax in the afterglow. We went beyond the narcotic frenzy of lovemaking into a quiet, warm space like those pictures of tropical islands you see on travel shop walls. We lay there, nothing to say, touching and laughing, wanting to hold onto that moment forever.

Angela's room too, seemed enchanted. Part of the wall was covered in photos, ribbons, certificates, another with the posters of rock groups and actors who've since turned out to be one-hit, one-film wonders. The dressing table had a few little girl ribbons, hair ties and tiny toys, but was being overrun with the heavy artillery of make-up, perfume and creams. I tried to memorise every object, every colour, every smell. I wanted to lock it away in me forever. I knew I'd need it.

'I have to go.'

It came out of nowhere. It burst out as though Karen had been holding it back as long as she had the strength. Now the spell was broken and like cold sea water through the cracked hull of a submarine, the real world came flooding in. She had to go to work. She had escaped her parents with a thin little lie: she felt sick and would be late in. They hadn't said a word; her father left for his practice; her mother for the art school where she was learning to paint. Karen said that providing we were careful we could keep this going and that someday her parents would come around, would see things differently. That we had to be patient, and we had to be sensible, and we would have to be cunning.

I nodded dumbly but in my heart I knew that something was over. I didn't say anything; it would only have made it worse.

We made the bed and straightened everything up. The house had a sad, abandoned quality, as though the inhabitants had died and it had become a shrine to their past lives. Nothing was disturbed. Everything positioned with a military precision.

'How can she live here?' I asked.

'She wants to go. Her father drives her mad. He's a control freak. Drove her mother mad and now she says he's doing the same to her. I feel sorry for Angela.'

'Where is she?'

'She's working in Newmarket. We'll go and see her on the way to work.'

I STARTED UP the Norton, and Karen produced the helmet she'd somehow successfully hidden from her interrogating parents. We wound slowly through leafy streets that were lined with big old wooden houses partially hidden from the road. Low profile money.

Angela worked in a travel agency. Something the captain had jacked up, I guessed. Before we went in Karen pulled me to one side and said, 'Remember. She's desperate to see Diego. That's why we can use her place.'

'Devon,' I said, automatically. 'Can you do it?'

I nodded, not wanting to lie out loud. The idea that Devon would want any sort of commitment, let alone one with Angela, was beyond me.

Angela sat at a long desk answering the phone and directing calls. There were three other girls who looked just like her. We walked past these blonde watchdogs, who were all trying to make eye contact, wanting to find out where they could send us and what exclusions were in operation. Angela had a beaten, sad look behind her smile. Something that said she had grown used to disappointment, almost expected it.

Between incoming phone calls I assured her that 'Diego' was out of town at the moment but that we would all make a point of going out for burgers when he came back. She seemed satisfied. It wasn't the place for social calls. I could sense the hostility radiating out from the three toxic babes upstream from her.

When we emerged Karen said I had done well. I felt lousy: an unconvincing liar, promising something I couldn't deliver. We walked back to the bike and I dropped her near her father's surgery; she didn't want me to stray too close.

I HAD THIS feeling that said 'Why should we sneak about? What are we doing that's so bad?' I knew I wouldn't be able to keep up a back door-type relationship for long. There was something in me that would want to clear the air, to bring things out into the open.

# CHAPTER
# TWENTY-SIX

**B**ACK AT THE house things seemed much the same: no sign of Devon, and nothing had been disturbed. I made a coffee and sat down on the rear verandah wondering what to do.

Where could things go from here? All my ideas seemed to be built around running away and starting up fresh somewhere else. It felt like me and Devon had already stuffed things up so badly there was no future for us in this city.

And Devon expected something from me that I had never given anyone. A loyalty that cut deep into my independence. That bound us together like chained prisoners.

I wandered through the house looking at our rough old battered furniture. Some of it had obviously been left in the house through successive generations of tenants, outlasting them all. I supposed that we too would leave it behind when we were finally pushed out by Wes and when the wrecker's ball came crashing through the rusty old tin roof. It gave me that hollow feeling you get when you catch yourself thinking about how small you are in the big picture. About how brief your life is. How sometimes it seems nothing truly lasts past the blink of an eye.

There was a rattle at the front door and I jumped. It was Devon. He was glowing with excitement. I knew what he had been up to before he even opened his mouth.

'Come with me, Trace.' He led me outside to the big puriri tree in the back garden where we had hidden the remainder of the dope. It was gone.

'The guy I told you about came back. I met him in town. They're mad for it. He took the lot. I've got all this money in the boot of the car. Blocks and wads and cashiers' bags. I can't even count it. They took the lot man, everything I've got ... and for top money.'

'I thought you were out dealing with Rebel, making some sort of arrangement. I thought it was sort of decided.'

He had this wild look in his eye. I liked and feared its recklessness.

'Billy Revell and his crew will be dealt with. It's me and you Trace. We're the ones who have something everybody wants. We have the power. They can ask and they can wait.'

I thought about it for a moment. Like a lot of what Devon said, his enthusiasm made it sound OK, but it didn't add up. 'He was round here, you know.'

'Who?'

'Your gang mate. Wiremu.' 'When?'

'When I first woke up. There he was, pounding the door, and sniffing around the back.'

'How did he find out where we stay?'

'It's a worry. I thought you must have told him.'

Devon looked agitated. Then he dug out the old optimism from somewhere and said, 'It was going to happen sooner or later. I guess at least we're ready now. We know.'

'Ready for what? A siege?'

'Just ready. Anyway, what have you been up to? You disappeared.'

I told him about last night and this morning. There was no point in trying to hide it from him any longer. I was beyond his disapproval. Strangely enough, he seemed to accept it this time.

'Well at least you're screwing. I thought you were going to be one of those professional virgin types. "I'm saving it till I'm married." I was sure *she* was. Her old man, what's he called? Bernard? He can't lord it over you now. That's something. I hated to think that you were bowing and scraping to that type.'

'If Raymond finds out, we are going to have one angry doctor banging at our door.'

'It doesn't work like that, Trace. You're a jump or two beyond that. Or short of it,' he added.

I thought it might be time to follow up with the idea I'd had. 'Devon, I want you to do me a huge favour.'

'Oh yes. What is it? Let me guess.' He fixed me with his beady eye. 'I wonder if it's anything to do with Karen's little friend?'

I was amazed. 'How did you know?'

'Just call it masculine intuition.' He refused to give me any other hint.

'You made a conquest there, Devon. Now you're all she thinks about. In fact that's the only reason Karen and I are allowed to use Angela's place as a hideaway.'

Devon went into philosophical mode. He sat back and lit a smoke.

'You see Trace, everything's a commodity. Everything has a price. The dope. This house. Your *assignations* with Karen. You're paying a number of prices there, to Karen, Angela and now to me. Our youth and good looks have a value too. That's why the old bastards, who run things, make everything so hard for us. Because of this thing we hold over them.'

'A lot more years left on our clocks.'

'That's nothing. Just an illusion. Anyone can die tomorrow. No. It's our fresh faces and our hard, young bodies.' He grinned and pulled up his T-shirt exposing his brown stomach and chest.

'We trade with these.'

I looked at Devon. He seemed almost sinister for a moment. As if he knew so much more than me. More than I would ever know. He was older than his years. I didn't want to ask him about that. There are some things about people that are best left unknown. But it linked in with a murky feeling I had when we were on that first visit to Wes' house. And to the same feeling I'd had when the farmer held Devon at gunpoint on the dusty road next to the plantation. I tried to shake it off by getting back to my point about Angela and Karen.

'I just wanted the four of us to go out somewhere, do something fun. We should get out of town. I'm sick of this city.'

'Like where, Trace?'

'Up North. I mean the Far North. Stay in a motel by the beach.'

'Sex and sunbathing?' 'Sounds good to me.'

He thought for a moment. 'Like when?'

'I reckon the sooner the better. I guess as soon as I can organise something. What shall we do with the money? We can't leave it in the car and I don't think this place is as safe as it once was.'

That reminded him. 'Come and look. Let's play with it. I haven't even had a chance to feel it.' We wandered up the front path. Out on the street I surveyed the parked cars, looking for any that I recognised, but noticed Devon just wandered on, oblivious of everything. No wonder we'd been traced. The council flats where the car was kept were quiet too: just a few Island kids playing by the gate. When Devon opened the boot the shotgun was there in full view, lying on a bed of money bags.

'Jesus, Devon. What if you get stopped?'

'I drive carefully, man. Haven't you noticed? The only people stopping me are going to be bad guys.'

Bad guys, I thought. It's still a game. Who are the bad guys? He picked up a roll of rubbish bags and tore one off. I held it open while he rapidly tossed in all his takings. I kept thinking, 'What if someone walks down here now – what do we do?' He slammed down the car-boot lid and we headed back to the flat.

The bag was surprisingly weighty. I guess I expected the notes to flutter around like feathers in a pillow case.

Once inside, we tipped the cash out onto the dining room table. An impressive little heap. I remembered how only a few days earlier the table and half the room had been filled with bags of dak. And it had all come down to this. There were more than 20 blocks. Tight wads of money, each one soaked in pain and corruption. They weren't like money at all. They were like some radioactive substance that would rot us away on the inside. Devon picked up one of the discoloured wedges.

'I bet each one could tell a story,' he said, as if he could read my mind. 'Do you think this is real evil money, or just money that wears its true colours?'

'What do you mean?'

He looked thoughtful. 'Money is sort of like the source. The hard external form of what makes us do stuff. There's no such thing as good money or bad money. It just whizzes around the country from hand to hand: sometimes earned, other times stolen in one way or another. Is this stolen money? Did we steal it?' 'I dunno. It's just, you know, money from gangs: it's not quite like the pay packet from the hardware shop.'

'You used to tell me that you had to do all the shit jobs while everyone else just slacked around or stole stuff. Even the other labourers. Money doesn't flow into your hands the way it does for other people. Do you think Wes has to raise a sweat to get a heap of money like this? Money's like a river and he's dug a big channel, so it flows his way. Fills his pond. Like all the other fat cats. People like you and me are allowed a little drink there every now and then. The system's screwed. Once you realise that, Trace, everything makes more sense. You don't sit in front of a pile of dough like this feeling guilty.'

'I'm not exactly… .'

'You are. You don't think that a person like you should ever have this sort of money. It's just for the likes of Wes or your girlfriend's dad. You're being held back by a slave mentality.'

Devon always had a king-hit like that: personal, and right on the button. 'Yeah, but we ripped off someone's patch to get this. That was just straightforward stealing.'

'Stealing a few plants from the bush. The plants are only valuable because breweries pay the politicians to keep dak illegal, to make sure booze is still most people's drug of choice. It's a mainstay of what keeps the economy ticking over.'

'OK, so why doesn't the government just pay the growers then, and get their money that way? The money's out there. People are going to spend it getting off their faces on something.' 'Governments don't like dak. It doesn't go with the idea of everyone working hard and then rewarding themselves by imbibing an easily controlled beverage. Dak is more like a trip to where you can see the whole game sucks. Top to bottom. They don't like that. You aren't allowed to drop out of the game. I mean, we would all be living back in the caves before you knew it.'

'Well, not quite.'

'Yeah, but that's how they see it. That's why it will never be legalised.'

'It is in Holland.'

'Yeah but only in some places, even there. And anyway, they're like the exception which proves the rule.' Devon was sorting the loose stuff into piles. He tossed me a block.

'Hide this, Trace. Put it in a supermarket bag and go outside and stow it somewhere in the jungle.'

'What's the point of that?'

'I'm going to hide the rest at Gail and Martin's.'

'A bit risky.'

'A bit, but shit, it's better than driving around with it in the boot or leaving it here. Our little fort's not so secure now. Wiremu's been here. He'll be back. Then there'll be others. People have a good reason to break in now.'

I found a bread bag in the kitchen and wrapped it as tightly as I could around the wad of money. There was this dense patch of ginger plant which grew hard up against the fence next door. I squeezed the tight little parcel into its root system. When I returned Devon had put the bulk of the money back into the sack but he had stacked four or five blocks on the mantlepiece.

'Don't tell me where you put it. I did the same with my block earlier. They'll be our emergency escape parachutes. To be retrieved when all else fails.'

He saw me look at the blocks on the mantle. 'That's Johnno's cut. If we're going up North we can drop that off.'

'So what shall we do now?'

'I thought it was up North. For the four of us.'

'What? Right now?'

'Of course now. What did you think? In a few days when the weather cleared up?' he said sarcastically.

'No. It's just that this is only an idea. I haven't asked Karen or anything yet.'

'Don't worry. If she can't come we'll get some other girls. It's not hard Trace, you'll see.'

He was only half joking.

'It's a bit more than that with Karen and me.' I felt a bit weird saying so to him.

'You mean it's … *love*?' he said, mocking me.

'Yeah, I think it is.'

He sighed and shook his head. I was a bit pissed off. 'Christ Devon.

**187**

You'd think I'd caught some horrible disease.'

He smiled and nodded, as if that was exactly what it was. 'Come on, Trace. Let's go out and see the hippies.'

WE STASHED JOHNNO'S cut in a bag up the chimney and lugged the other one back to the car. I couldn't leave this place now without the feeling that a thousand eyes were watching me. It was like a mental illness. Paranoia. I hated it.

# CHAPTER
# TWENTY-SEVEN

W E LOADED UP the car and began the drive out to the Waitakere hills. On the way Devon stopped at one of those repossession shops in Avondale where poor people can pawn stuff when their dole won't stretch to the next Thursday. I waited in the car while Dev bought this clunky old stereo for three hundred dollars. He hadn't mentioned that he wanted one.

'What's that? A present for Martin?' I asked. We loaded it into the back. It was one of those old black stereos with big wooden speakers. It looked like crap to me. He pulled an ounce bag out of his pocket and held it up. 'No. This is a present for Martin.' He scrabbled about in the glove box and pulled out one of those screwdrivers with exchangeable tips and gave it to me.

'Here. Be useful. Take the back cover off those speakers.'

So I unscrewed as he wound his way out to Titirangi. When I had both covers off we stopped and he grabbed the bag of notes out of the boot. We were next to a primary school and a couple of kids ran over to the fence to watch us.

He gave me the bag and said, 'Stick the notes in the speakers Trace,

I'll talk to these kids.'

I filled both speaker cabinets with about an equal amount of money so they would weigh roughly the same. I was careful not to disturb the wires so the speakers would still work if Martin tried them out. When I had screwed the covers back onto the cabinets I saw that a woman teacher had joined Devon's little entourage. I gave a little blip on the horn and he came back and climbed in. The teacher was only young, not much older than us, and stood watching as we drove off.

'Did you get it all in OK?'

'Yeah, I divided it between the two speakers. What was all that about?'

'I forgot. You can't talk to kids any more. If you do you must be a molester.' He was angry. 'I mean, Trace, how fucked is that? You can't possibly talk to kids because you just like kids. It must be that you are dying to touch their willies.'

'Is that what the teacher thought?'

'To start with, but she was cool. I had to invent a past at the school to be on the safe side. "Does Mrs Moss still teach here? I had her in Standard Four" sort of thing.' Trace, remember stuff like that when you're feeling a bit off about breaking a stupid little rule. The whole game is stuffed. It's made all of us into sick bastards too.'

IT WAS LATE afternoon by the time we found the long driveway that led to Martin and Gail's house. It was one of those areas you get around the fringe of Auckland where there are no lawns or fences – just houses plonked in thick native bush. Their house was high up off the ground on poles. Four cars blocked the driveway.

'Looks like they might have visitors.'

'No, Martin is still in the auto repair business. The cars follow him wherever he goes. He's good but he's slow. Grab the speakers!'

We carried the stereo up the drive, squeezing past two identical Legacy wagons.

Devon, with his arms full of amp and CD player, nodded at the two cars.

'Looks sus.'

'Why?'

'You get an instinct for these things.'

We knocked and waited but there was no reply. After a while Devon stepped back and called out in a silly feminine voice, 'Yoo hoo! Anybody home?' upstairs there was a loud stereo banging out 'Stairway to Heaven'.

Soon we heard footsteps. I caught a glimpse of Gail through the side window. She was wearing nothing but a long T-shirt. Then she turned and yelled back into the house, 'It's Devon and his mate. They're bearing stereos.'

Martin came around the corner buttoning up a pair of black Levis. Barefooted, bare chested. We walked back to the sitting room.

'Jesus, man,' he muttered to Devon. 'Your timing's not very good. "Stairway to Heaven" is our sex mantra.'

'Sorry, man. You should put a sign on the door like they do in hotels. "Do not disturb. Fucking." '

We put the stereo down in the corner of the room and wandered out onto the deck which hung out over the driveway.

'Awesome views from here,' I said to Gail, who sprawled on a deck chair, her T-shirt not quite doing the job.

'You should see it at night. Auckland in lights, but you're at a safe distance from the contamination. It's been cosmic moving out here. A spiritual revelation. Sometimes we drag out our mattress. Sleep under the stars.'

'After sampling product I bet,' Devon chipped in.

I realised from the vacant way Martin was still staring at the city that he and Gail were well stoned.

'Where's little Martin?' I asked.

'He's taking a well-earned vacation,' said Gail. 'It's given Martin and me time to catch up on each other. It's cool.'

'So where is he?' asked Devon, 'Hawaii, the Gold Coast…?' 'Huntly,' said Martin, rejoining reality for a while. 'With Gail's mum. What's the story with the stereo? You can buy portable

ones now, Devon, they're much easier to handle.'

'Nice one, Martin,' said Devon, pretending to enjoy his wit. 'Actually, it's a hostage I've taken, against an outstanding debt. More of a reminder than anything. When he goes to play some sounds he'll think, "Must pay Devon for the ounce bag." That's the theory anyway. I may end up just flicking it. Thing is I don't want it at our place at the moment because burglars and tea leaves have been calling and walking off with anything not screwed down.'

'You get that in the poorer areas, actually,' said Martin with a fake ponce accent.

'Can you look after it for a while?'

'Sure, it'll be OK here.'

'Where are you guys heading?'

'Up North pretty soon, I reckon. We're due for a *vacation* ourselves,' said Devon. Then he added with ironic formality, 'Thank you Gail, thank you Martin. Here is a little something for your troubles.' He tossed Gail a little bag of buds. When we walked to the front door he added to Martin, 'And for intruding on your Stairway. Devonus interruptus.'

Once we were back in the car, I asked, 'What's on the agenda now?'

'Well, there are a number of things. Things business and things pleasure. We have to go to Warkworth, to restock and slip Johnno his cut. I still owe Wiremu a few ks. He'll be after that. Better restock the cupboards. umm … give something to Rebel and Co., to get them off our backs, and then,' he paused for effect, 'and only then, we can bury ourselves in the pleasures of female flesh.'

I felt a bit flustered. 'I don't know if it's even on … it's not like I've organised anything.'

Devon turned to me. 'Do you want this Trace, this mystery weekend?' A sudden seriousness had come into his voice.

I faltered. 'Yeah, of course I want it.'

'Then we'll do it. I'll organise it.' He reached over and pinched my cheek the way you'd do to a little kid.

'How are you going to do it?'

'Don't you trouble your tiny head about that. Just help me out with this other stuff first and everything shall come to you.'

And I believed him. There was something so persuasive about him.

# CHAPTER
# TWENTY-EIGHT

I GUESS IT must have been a week or so later that Devon announced that we were 'headed up North'. I was relieved. I thought he'd conveniently forgotten what he'd promised. So much had happened during the last few weeks in Auckland, it would be a blast just to be on the road again. Everything had been closing in on us. Getting faster and faster. I didn't feel safe anymore: not even at the cottage. I hardly slept, trusted no one. up at Johnno's it would be different. It was a place where time seemed to stand still.

WE WERE GREETED by the usual posse of dogs at the front of Johnno's property. His craggy figure moved among them so I felt able to get out and open the gate without them ripping my arms off. The whole place was bathed in the dense yellow light of sunset. We all took on a dusky brown hue, like those sepia photos you see of pioneers against fake backgrounds. The moment was about as real, too.

We made to go inside but Johnno was really excited about

something he wanted to show us. We wandered around the back of the house to where the big chunky form of a car was draped in a cover. Devon flashed me a certain look: the last thing he wanted to see was yet another Studebaker. Johnno flicked the cover off with a magician's flourish, to reveal a gleaming Shelby Mustang. It was a deep metallic red, with broad white racing stripes rising up over the bonnet and roof, and disappearing down its sharply raked fastback. It had massive chromed wheels and all those air scoops and badges that were big back in the seventies. A bit of a dinosaur really: huge and powerful maybe, but clumsy and primitive compared with the cars we raced out on Thunder Road. To say it was mint was an understatement. It was as though it had never been driven on the road. It was too clean. Johnno stood there, grinning like an idiot. Me and Devon made all the right noises.

'Isn't this just the duck's nuts?' Johnno chuckled.

'Where'd it come from?' asked Devon.

'I thought after all my hard work in our *joint venture* I'd reward myself with a seventies sex machine.'

'Oh yes?' Devon sounded pissed off. He knew bullshit when he heard it.

We piled in. The interior was a glittering mass of chrome instruments, logos, and flashy panel-work.

'Where's the key?'

Johnno had it on a clip on his belt, along with a dozen others. The Mustang's key had a silver running horse on a leather fob. Even the key ring was original.

Devon smiled. 'It really is your baby, huh. I guess you had to get rid of some of the others?'

He shook his head. 'This has got nothing to do with my collection. I just had to have it, because of the rarity. Only four in the country and this is the best one.'

'How'd you pay for it then?'

He looked rueful.

'Don't tell me you stole it?'

That wasn't it. He looked embarrassed. Then he came through like a little boy, 'fessing up.

'There was an ad in the *Trade and Exchange* Collectible Cars section. For a Studebaker Avanti. It's the car I've always wanted.

The last model they ever made before they went bust. Super charged V8 donk. Could do a hundred and eighty if it's geared right. It'd sort of complete my collection. So I drove down to Aucks to check it out. This was a few days ago. When I get there I find the owner's already sold it. Or it was gone … or something. Anyway, he had this Shelby.'

'I don't like the sound of this,' said Devon.

'No man, he was cool. He offered me a toke and we got talking and I gathered that he was after weed. I thought I would sweeten the deal by slipping him an ounce, and when he saw it he suggested we do the deal with dak, not money. It made sense.'

'How much did you give him?'

'A few kilos, but I laced it with cabbage to bring the weight up.'

'Shit!' Devon was furious.

'It wasn't much. There's plenty more.'

Devon wouldn't answer. He stood with his back to us, staring straight into the setting sun.

'Hey, whoa there Devon, it's my dope too, you know. You didn't do all this alone.'

Devon was beyond pissed. 'What was this guy called?'

'He called himself Spider. He was a tough little bastard, you know they never use their real names. What's the big deal? It's probably hot anyway. I'm never going to drive it anywhere. I just sort of wanted it, you know. A sort of rebound thing.'

'This guy was a sort of skinhead dude and he had a yard in Glen

Eden?'

'Yeah. You know him?'

'Sure do. Sure do,' said Devon softly to himself. So angry now, he could barely speak. I felt sorry for Johnno. All the pleasure had melted from his face, like some spell had broken. We stood around, both sort of embarrassed, waiting to hear what Devon was going to say next.

When he did speak again, he seemed to have lightened up. 'Could I borrow this tank for a little drive Johnno? Back in ten.' Johnno nodded and Devon fired it up. The deep burble that rolled out from under the bonnet is the sort of heartsong that any speed fiend instantly loves. But not today.

'Get in, Trace!' An order, not a request. His face was tense and stiff again.

We nosed slowly down the long drive and waited a moment at the gate.

'What's up?' I asked.

'I half expected to find Rebel and his goons waiting here.'

'Don't be para, man, it was probably just one of those coincidences. They happen. You're adding two and two and getting three hundred and sixty nine.'

He smiled and shook his head. 'Not quite, Trace.'

We trundled slowly down the road away from the state highway. The country round here was scrubbed and raw; the clearing of forests had left the land poor for farming. After a while we found ourselves passing through small pine plantations. They immediately brought to mind our night in the forest.

'Man, these things are springing up like weeds.' I was hoping to break the silence. 'They cleared the native bush only to replace it with this crap.'

Devon nodded disinterestedly and then said, 'Trace I've got a gut feeling, and my intuition is pretty reliable.' He stared solemnly into the thickening dark. 'Rebel must have known I had this mate up North somewhere. I could have told him about Johnno ages ago and forgotten it.' I could see him wracking his brains. 'The cunning prick worked out that Johnno's was likely where we were stashing the dak, set a trap, and our Johnno jumped straight in. I bet he lured him down with the promise of a rare Studebaker, one that doesn't exist, and then subbed in this tank.' His voice softened, almost to a sob. 'Johnno's pretty innocent you know, for all his roughness. He still basically trusts everybody.'

The light had drained from the evening sky so Devon turned the big car into a farmer's yard and we headed slowly back the way we came.

'They've been playing me, Trace. They knew it all. All the stuff I thought I had up my sleeve is gone.'

'Look at the bright side. If they had known where the dope was stashed they would have taken it by now. They can't have managed to track him back here.'

'True. Johnno wouldn't have told a guy like Rebel where he lives. He values his cars too much. Still, they've probably worked it all out by now.'

He paused.

'Fuck it, Trace. When we thought we held all the cards, they knew. They all knew.'

Devon had been worrying away about the big picture – but I was just concerned about the part with Karen in it. Concerned our trip up North was being washed away. 'We've still got the money and we've still got the dope. All we've lost is our secret hideaway.'

'Do you remember those two Subarus in Martin's driveway?' I nodded.

'You know I said it looked a bit sus?'

'Mmm.'

'They were a calling card, Trace. They said, "Rebel's been here".

Martin never works on new cars like that. Specially not pairs. I should have thought it through. And we've left all the money there.'

'Then we'd better go back and get it.'

'What's the point? They're Rebel employees now.'

He sounded very low. I wrenched my focus back to the task at hand. 'I don't think so. They're free spirits. It's about getting stoned and having sex. Grabbing all the chances they can get while little Martin is in Huntly "on vacation". They've probably forgotten the stereo's there. They had other business, remember. We should drive back now and grab it.'

WE DROVE QUIETLY back to the farm while Devon mulled everything over. The gate was closed again. 'Go on, Trace. Be a big boy, you open it this time. Fight your demons.'

I climbed out reluctantly and walked to the gate. No dog barks, so I guessed they were inside with Johnno. I flicked open the gate and sat on the bonnet as we rolled quietly down the hill. To the left of the house there was this low shape in the grass. It was a dog lying down. Me and Devon both reached the same conclusion simultaneously. It was dead.

'Let's get out of here, Trace, this is not fucking good!' Devon screamed, shoving the Mustang into reverse.

As I clambered in I saw two figures burst out of the front door. They were carrying guns. The wheels spun on the gravel drive and for a moment we were frozen, watching these guys closing on us, the taller one raising his shotgun. At that moment the wide wheels finally bit the road and we shot up the drive backwards.

There was a terrific boom and a yellow flash. The front of the car was hit by a blast of shot and the windscreen disappeared, along with one of the headlights. Bits of shot and glass poured into the front seat.

Devon didn't turn but raced the big car backwards along the curving drive. By the time we reached the road we must have been doing about 60 ks in reverse. He hit the brakes, but there was no stopping this battleship. We skidded straight across the road and hit the opposite bank with a thump. 'There go the tail lights,' said Devon. He yanked the T-bar back into drive and planted. The engine roared but nothing happened. I opened the door and looked back. The back wheels were slightly off the ground, raised by the impact with the bank.

'Quick Trace, they'll be coming. Weigh down the back.'

I jumped up and down on the fastback lid while Devon made the rear wheels spin. It did nothing. I could see the gleam of headlights going on at Johnno's. They would be on us in a moment. On an impulse I ran over and yanked the letter box out of the ground. I was able to squeeze the post under the wheels on one side and that, plus my weight on the back, made the rear wheels bite. Devon almost lost it again as he overshot. I was back in.

'Jesus, this bitch is hard to control. Like driving the Titanic.'

We were off just as the other car emerged from the gate. It was the grey WRX rally car: Devon's old car, right behind us.

'It's Rebel!' I yelled.

'This old clunker will never outrun that car. It's a race horse against a cart horse.'

The car was so close to us now that I could clearly see two faces in the dull glow of the instrument lights. It was the two skinheads that had been at Rebel's that last time.

We drove slowly along the middle of the country road that led to the main highway. The skins were waiting their chance on the wider road, content just to follow us. up ahead I could see the triangular reflection of the Give Way sign. We were running out of time and space.

Bits of windscreen glass were everywhere: in our clothes, our hair, and flying past our faces as the wind dislodged more pieces. I looked at Devon sparkling with the refracted light, his face covered with little dribbling cuts. He looked back.

'Sorry, Trace. This fuck-up's down to me.'

We stopped at the T-junction where the road was clear but Devon didn't move. I looked at him and then the skins. They didn't know what to do for a moment, then one jumped out of the car and walked towards us, shotgun at the ready, not sure of what we intended. At that moment, Devon planted his foot and we were a hundred metres ahead by the time they were mobile again.

There was a series of big straights on the road back to Auckland: favourite speed sites. Devon took the Mustang up to a hundred and fifty ks. I knew it was nowhere near fast enough.

'Is that all it will do?'

'Nah, it's got a bit more, but I'm saving it.'

I looked back. The other car was gaining on us so fast it was like we were parked. They would have us before we reached the end of the straight. The passenger's window was open and the gun barrel protruded at the ready.

'Hold on, Trace!' Devon roared.

A moment later they drew level. I could see the grinning face of the smaller skinhead, like this was what he was dying to do. I braced myself for the explosion that would end it all. Without warning, Devon wrenched the wheel down and the big car hit the little WRX with an impact that fired it straight off the road. There was a shower of sparks and then all I saw was the glow of their tail lights disappear as they went end over end down the steep bank. Devon locked up and lost the Mustang completely in a crazy spin. When the scream of tyres died and the smoke cleared, we were parked in the middle of the highway facing the wrong way.

'Yes!' I heard him yell. 'We did it!'

As THE CAR limped back to Johnno's the elation was short lived. There was a terrific rubbing noise coming from the front of the car and Devon said the steering was really funny and loose. We stopped at the turn-off to check out the damage. The stoved-in front guard had carved a big groove out of our front tyre and the wheels were wildly pigeon-toed.

Approaching Johnno's we drove at a mere crawl, not wanting to arrive. Devon flicked off the headlights as we moved down the drive and said, 'I want you in our car, ready to really boot it. Rebel may be in there, waiting. I'm getting the shottie out of the Holden.'

I thought this arrangement was stupid but there wasn't time to say so.

The night was so black and moonless you could hardly see a thing. I stumbled over a dead bull terrier as we reached the car. I crouched down and touched it. Still warm and wet. I didn't like dogs much, but still I felt sick. We picked our way over to the other car. The keys were in the ignition. I popped the boot and Devon pulled out the shotgun. He broke it in half to make sure it was loaded and then disappeared into the gloom. I knew he wanted some sort of showdown.

From behind the wheel I tried to visualise a path out of here. Something that avoided dead dogs and dead cars and cut through to the gate in a hurry. I kept waiting for the bang that never came. It felt wrong to be sitting there, waiting … I was too vulnerable, too exposed to anyone coming from the back. I wanted to be on my feet, so I eased out of the car carefully and stood by the open door. Still no sign of Devon. How long had it been? Five minutes? What could he be doing? I'd give him five more minutes and then go in.

Time stood still. I had never felt so lonely as I did as I waited by that car. When five minutes had almost passed I slipped slowly around to the front door. Even with my silent footfalls I could still hear no sound in the house. What had happened? I reached the verandah. There was this smell. Meths. Through the red patterned glass of the front door I could see a flicker of light. Then it disappeared as Devon burst out and slammed the door behind him. He was carrying a big polythene bag.

'In the car, Trace. Quick, move it.' We ran around the back of the house.

I started up the Holden and then threaded the car around the front and out onto the drive. I paused at the gateway to look back at the house. I could see the hot, red glow in the hall. There was no mistaking it now. I turned to Devon. He was looking too, his face glazed with tears. I gave his arm a nudge but he said nothing. We drove in silence for a full half hour. Just past orewa he said, 'Head for Martin and Gail's.'

A little voice groaned inside me. I thought we were headed home. It was about midnight now and I was hanging out for sleep. As we made the city, Devon pointed to a burger bar so I pulled over, suddenly aware of hunger. It seemed days since we had eaten.

We sat opposite each other, bathed in the sick, flickering light. Devon looked awful. Drained and sad. I waited for him to talk, had waited ever since we left the farm. After his second coffee he lit up a smoke and looked as if he was about to speak. A cleaner, who was probably about 13 years old, asked us to smoke outside. To Devon he didn't even exist.

When Devon spoke he did so softly, as if he was a long way away. 'I kind of hope those guys are still alive in the car, you know, stuck in it all night like in the TV ads, dying slowly and alone. That would give me …' he stopped, searching for a word. '… solace.'

He stopped again.

'Yes, I would like that.'

'What was in that house?'

'I had to torch it, you know. It was the only thing to do.'

'What had they done?'

He looked up and stared at me, pointing to his forehead. 'It's up there, Trace. It will be there till the day I die. Caught somewhere between my eyes and my brain. The image of his face… .' He trailed off and I asked no more.

I pushed my food tray away. 'I never picked Rebel as being that smart. Just because he read *Mein Kampf* doesn't make him Einstein. He's only a car thief. Little fascist prick,' I offered.

'It's not Rebel. It's that guy in the suit. Whoever he was. A real ominous bastard. The way they trapped Johnno, no way Rebel could've thought of that, let alone the Taylors. Out of their league. The way they lured him like a mouse. It was so clever … it was sick.' He stood up. 'Come on, Trace. Let's go. All we've got on our side now is surprise. They won't know what's gone down up North yet.'

I drove and Devon rolled a joint. He lit it and passed it to me. 'Just a little puff to settle your nerves.' I toked and passed it back: the last thing I wanted was to be stoned at this moment. He took one more draw, put the roach out in the ashtray then slipped it back into his pouch.

'The demon weed. What has it done to us, eh Trace? You could still be a shop boy mixing paint, and me a cub reporter making the coffee.' He looked at me. 'I bet you wish you still were.'

I shook my head. I tried to think of something stoical to say. 'Life's too short for regrets. It's like driving. What's around the next corner … that's all that matters. What was back around the last corner, that's history.' It wasn't entirely true, but I liked it and I hoped it might cheer Devon up.

'I guess that's my line too. In the end, you only regret the stuff you don't do.' I could tell he was trying to sound brave.

We were on the beginning of the big slope leading up to Titirangi. There were hardly any cars on the road. All honest people were in bed.

'What's the game plan?'

Devon thought for a while. It was obvious there wasn't one. 'I'm determined to recover our money. Now, more than ever. There's a good chance that Rebel and the suit already have it.'

'Do you think Martin's a back-stabber?'

'I don't blame Martin, but did things seem a bit weird to you the other day? Little Martin is *on vacation*. What five or six-year-old is on vacation?'

'Do you think he might have been snatched?'

Devon shook his head. 'No. He's probably with the olds in Huntly, but he's there to be out of the way. Something heavy's about to go down.'

'And those cars.'

'Yeah, that should have clicked right away. A better class of vehicle than the stuff Martin deals with. Imports eh? He has gone up in the world. He's been bought off, that's why he was looking sheepish. Nothing to do with being caught in the sack.'

'So it all comes down to Mr Suit?'

'Appears so.'

We reached the road Gail and Martin lived on so I pulled over and parked well short, bearing in mind the good view from the deck.

'Well, Trace. This *is* the next corner. Any ideas?'

'The way I see it there are three ways we can do this. Knock on the door. Bust in the door. Or lure them outside.'

'Who do you reckon the *them* might be?' 'I guess that's a key question.'

Devon pulled the shotgun from the boot of the car and we walked up the street to where the driveway began. I kept thinking that this wouldn't look good to any of the people in the other houses we passed … all it needed was for one person to spot us while they were going for a midnight pee.

The drive was long, about 50 metres, and threaded up a steep slope through overhanging bush. Its heavy foliage would shield us from view. There were no lights on in the house, but that meant nothing. Devon pointed mutely at where the two new Subarus had been earlier that day. Someone had been to collect them since the morning.

When we reached the end of the drive we had to cross open ground to get to the house. There was no way round it. Devon crouched in the shadows and signalled me on with the shotgun. I darted into the mouth of the carport, its gloom swallowing me instantly. As I stood there, my eyes adjusting to the deeper dark, I knew that if anyone was waiting for us, this is where they would be and that I would be completely vulnerable, outlined against the starry sky. I wondered whether Devon knew he was putting me into a situation where I had no defences. Suddenly it seemed as if he had been using me to test the water, while he lurked safely outside. For a moment I was swamped by panic. Did I really know him? As it happened, the garage was empty but for the red pick-up Devon had given Martin and Gail. I steadied myself against its steel tray, sweating with fear and with my heart pounding. I listened to the floorboards above. No sound. No movement.

There was a scrambling behind me. It was Devon making his dash across the gravel drive. I stepped out into the open so that he wouldn't pile into me. He was coming in blind too.

'What's the story?' he asked.

'I reckon we're clear. This is the place they'd have waited.

We would have run straight into them.' 'Dumb huh?' Devon brushed it off.

'A bit. Let's go in through the ranchslider on the deck.' 'How do we get up there?' It was three metres or so from the ground.

'I'll give you a boost.' It was putting him in the same situation I'd been in when I ran into the carport. He knew it too.

He dropped the shotgun and I crouched, holding onto one of the posts. Devon climbed on my shoulders. Skinny though he was, I found it difficult standing from a crouch. We both had to pull on the post in front of us.

'Come on Trace, mush!'

When I straightened my legs he was able to haul himself onto the outside of the railing.

'Do you want the gun?' I asked in a shrill whisper. 'Cover me!'

I had no idea how I was meant to do that from the ground. He was on his own, once again an exposed outline against the sky. As he disappeared from view I heard a murmur. It was soft and sleepy. I raised the shotgun at the edge of the deck, waiting to blast the first head that appeared over the side. There was no one. What was going on? I waited, frozen like a toy soldier, aiming at the top edge of the railing. Somewhere there was this ticking sound. I tried to locate its origin. Then I realised. It was coming from my mouth. My teeth were chattering uncontrollably. My fear was making itself known.

A head appeared over the edge. Involuntarily, I almost shot it. It was Devon, holding a speaker. He leaned over and I dropped the gun and moved closer. Slowly he lowered the speakers by their cables into my arms. Then he was over the balustrade, waiting for shoulders to ride down on. As I began to crouch, my legs folded and we both fell backwards onto the driveway.

'Good one, Trace!' he hissed loudly, rubbing his elbow. 'Sorry man. Weak legs.'

We gathered the speakers and the gun and headed down the driveway. I kept waiting for Rebel and the Taylors to step out of the bushes. For it to be all over.

We made the street. It was empty, the Holden gleaming white about a hundred metres away. I was dying to ask Devon what had happened, but we walked on silently.

He held his hand out for the keys and then he put everything in the boot. It wasn't until we were some way down the road that he spoke.

'They were asleep on the deck.' 'Shit. Rebel and Co.?'

'No. Martin and Gail. They had dragged their bed out to sleep under the stars. I had to step right over Gail's semi-naked body while I was holding the speaker cabinets. It was freaky. What happened to you?'

'I had an attack of nerves. It came out of nowhere. Teeth chattering, legs like jelly. It's a wonder I didn't piss myself.'

'How come?'

'Running into the carport. It was fucking stupid, like jumping into a black hole. Trusting your luck.'

'Sometimes you have to do that. There's no way round it.

Are you a bit pissed off with me?' 'A bit.'

'I would have done it, Trace.'

'Why didn't you then? Why did you send me in?' My voice sounded shrill and tense.

He went quiet for a while. 'If I had gone in there and got caught up with Rebel, what would you have done?'

'I dunno. Something I guess.'

'I know what I would have done. I knew it before you went in. I was ready.'

HE DIDN'T SAY what 'ready' meant, but I assumed he meant he would have used the gun. I suddenly recalled him standing over that farmer on the side of the road, with the barrel of the gun halfway down his throat. I knew he was right. I wasn't as reckless or as desperate as that yet. He was.

# CHAPTER
## TWENTY-NINE

**W**HEN WE WERE well clear of the Titirangi hills, I looked across at Devon.

'What's the plan?'

'It's home, James, and don't spare the horses. I reckon we've earned a sleep.'

'You'd be mad wouldn't you?' I flashed a look at him. He looked done in.

'What else can we do, Trace? Where else can we go? We aren't loaded with options. Anyway, the house is fortified. That's something.'

I thought about it. How much protection did a couple of cheap locks and a bit of trellis on the windows give? The stakes had risen from the days when we were worried about simple break-ins. Now it was us they would be after.

IT MUST HAVE been near daybreak when we finally reached the council flats where we stored the vehicles. The Norton was there, untouched. That was reassuring.

Devon said to leave all the stuff in the car, as it would be safer there. That was true but it didn't say much for our 'fortifications' as he called them. I noted he took the shotgun.

We approached the little house cautiously. Would we ever be able to go anywhere again without being on guard?

We were right to be jittery. The front door was wide open. Kicked in. We crept inside. I don't know what I expected but it wasn't this. Someone had really been busy. Everything had been smashed or ripped open: cupboard doors pulled off their hinges, cups and plates shattered. The TV had gone through the sitting room window. The couch had not only been slashed open like a gutted animal, but someone had shat on it as well. Devon pointed out the swastikas on the wall of his room and the word 'nigga' written there in tomato sauce squeezes.

He said with a cold laugh, 'I guess you could say that Rebel and I are no longer friends.'

I was too tired to feel anything. Shock? Sadness? Nothing. The place was still shelter. We heaved the dining room table up against the front door frame and wedged chairs in behind it. It seemed more secure than the lock had ever been. My bed was wet with piss, so we flipped Devon's mattress over and slept on the unslashed side.

It was odd sleeping together in the same bed. It was crossing a line that had been placed in my mind at puberty. He leaned the gun up against the wall by his head and promptly slipped off to sleep. I tried not to. Someone had to keep watch, so I lay there listening to his easy breathing as I ran escape fantasies through my overcooked brain.

I don't know how long I kept that resolution alive. I was awakened by the fierce yellow sun shining directly onto me and a fly practising take-offs and landings on my lips. Devon was nowhere to be seen. I lay there, slowly replaying the events of the past 24 hours. It seemed like years of life had happened in just one day. I wasn't old enough to have done everything that I had done. I knew what I wanted. It wasn't

money, it was Karen. I longed to be lying in her arms again, buried in that state of innocence, that blissful cocoon. But a screen had been torn away since I had last seen her, and now, this ugly world stood revealed.

Where was Devon?

I got up and walked through the house. Some order had been restored: furniture righted, broken crockery kicked into the corners, but the stink from the shit-laden couch still dominated the sitting room. Devon was on the back verandah with the speaker cabinets. He had emptied out one and was in the process of unscrewing the other.

'Sleep well?' he said with a smile. 'Man, were you out of it.' 'I tried to stay awake, I guess I never made it.'

'Some sentry!'

'You can talk. Money all there?'

'So far. I've no idea how much there should be anyway. I hadn't even counted it in block form.'

'Got any ideas, Devon? I sure haven't.'

'Yeah, it came to me last night. Cards on the table time. We know Rebel hates us and wants to kill us. Stumpy little prick. We've two choices. We can kill him, or buy him off.'

'So you're going to give him the money?'

'Not exactly. I am going to give him the rest of the dope. I'm sick of dealing, that's for sure. Don't think I'm cut out for it.'

'Johnno?'

'Don't….' He held his hands out as though to ward off a blow. 'Sorry.'

'I can't go there, Trace,' his voice was suddenly weak. 'Look, we'll sort this. Make the most of it. Try to put things right. Can't turn back the clock, though. We'll do that trip up North. I reckon then I'll have a clearer view.'

'Do you reckon? I'd sort of given the whole idea away. Seemed to me like a yesterday idea. The world's a bit different this morning. Like you said, "can't turn back the clock".'

'We won't be. I'll organise it with, what's her name?' 'Angela.'

'Right! Angie baby. You can count on me, Trace. If we can sort out the other shit today, then that'll be a breeze. You still got my phone?'

I tried to think. 'I think Karen might have it. I put it in her bag.'

'No worries. I guess I can afford a new one,' he said, holding up a wad.

'What are we going to do about this house?' 'Nothing.'

'Just walk away?'

'Sure. What do you suggest? Settle down? Raise kids? It's stuffed. Even without Rebel and his mates treating it as a shit house … it's lost it. It's fucked, man. We're out of here.'

'To where?' 'Questions, questions.'

He went inside and returned with a pillowcase. 'I reckon we have to think strategically now, or else we're finished in this town.'

'What do you mean, strategically?'

He threw the blocks of money into the bag. 'We have to align ourselves with one of the big guys. The real players. Someone who Rebel is scared of. Because he sure as hell ain't scared of us.'

'Who then?'

'I reckon it's got to be Sloane. I mean, who else is there? There's the suit we met at Rebel's: the guy who sent those skins to Johnno's. There's Wiremu, my man in the gang. Or Sloane through his mate Mark. Now that's someone Rebel wouldn't fuck with.'

'Who's left? Wes. Yeah, but you've pissed him off. Pity. He may be able to pull strings.'

'Though Wes is a cut above these boys. He's gone respectable now, did twenty years ago. Yeah, it would've been Wes not so long ago. Now, it's got to be Sloane.'

'Yeah, but we had this deal to supply him and we didn't come through. Don't forget that.'

'We will now though, and it will be a sweet one.'

Devon had reconnected with his old confidence. It seemed to be decided. I thought it sounded as risky as hell, thought we should run. But that wasn't Devon's style. He still believed he could deal his way out.

WE PACKED ALL the gear we could into the back of the car. There was no coming back. Before we left I walked through the rooms we had painted when we had first moved in. Such a buzz. No place would ever have the same magic.

'Come on man!' Devon said, giving my jacket a yank. 'Don't get sentimental. It's the past now and it's got Rebel's shit all over it.'

As if I needed reminding. What I needed was something to look forward to. Something that made me believe in the possibility of tomorrow. I'd never felt so down. Try though I might, I couldn't believe that Devon could pull this truce off. He knew it too. He knew I had lost faith in him.

'Where does Angela work?'

'In a travel agent's, on Broadway.'

'Well let's go there and set things up. Hey, we've earned this holiday, right?' Devon said, trying to buoy me up. His words seemed to have a hollow ring to them.

ANGELA WAS HANDLING a phone call when we arrived so Devon walked over and sat in front of the prettiest agent's desk. Seeing all these people at work made me realise it must be a week day. I couldn't remember the last time I'd checked in at the paint shop. That job seemed eons ago. The agent quickly cleared away the stuff she had been working on and broke into one of those automatic smiles. Her name tag said Roanne.

'How can I help?'

'Roanne, Roanne, I hope you can … but this won't be easy.'

'Try me, I like a challenge.'

'My colleague and I are planning a business trip to the Gold Coast and we don't have passports, tickets, anything. Can you do all that?'

'No problem. That's what I do every day.'

'How long will it take?'

'How good are you at filling out forms?'

'Not good.'

She smiled and stood up. I looked at Angela. She was watching us. Devon gave her a facetious little wave. Our lady returned with an intimidating sheaf of forms. 'You'll need to fill these out and we can courier them off. Providing you can get a birth certificate, everything else is just a formality.'

'We don't have current Auckland addresses. Can we do everything from here?'

'No problem. And what date did you think you would like to fly out on?'

'We would like open tickets. Business class.'

This created a new level of interest and helpfulness: more so when Devon paid the full amount in cash. Angela watched, intrigued, from the back of the shop, tied as she was to the phone headset.

'One more big favour.' Devon had this way of lowering his tone.

'Of course.'

'Would it be possible to have Angela help with these?' He held up the passport application guff. 'I'm useless with forms … she's a bright girl.'

'You know Angela?'

'Yes, biblically.'

Her jaw dropped, as though she had just lost a filling. 'Excuse me?'

'We used to go to Bible class together.'

'Oh. Well sure. Why don't you fill them in at her desk?'

'That's wonderful!' he said, almost purring.

'What are you guys doing here?' Angela asked in hushed tones. 'That's my boss. Is this some sort of con? Where are you going?'

'To the sunny beaches of Queensland. But that's not the reason we came here. I had other motives. I wanted to see you, Angela.' He spoke more and more softly until his tone was just a breathy whisper. 'After our night ... I've hardly slept ... I couldn't get you out of my head ... '

I watched him close in on her as he crouched down, his face near hers. Angela stared back, mesmerised, a possum in the headlights.

'Angela, look ... I've been spinning you a line. That whole Diego thing....' He glanced around the room. 'Shit, this is hard. It's like this. There's Spanish blood in my family, right? But I played the whole thing up to impress you. I know what you're going to say ... it was a crap stunt to pull, but Angela, the moment I saw you in that bar, I was history. You just blew me away. I would have done anything to be with you.'

I couldn't bear it. 'I'll just pop out for smokes.'

They didn't even appear to hear me. I walked down Broadway looking for a dairy but it was wall-to-wall fashion shops and coffee bars. The last time I had been here was the night before the ball. It seemed years ago. I was a different person then. Naive and excited.

Everything in front of me. Now I felt like an old man.

When I returned, Devon was leaning back in his chair sounding off to Angela and Roanne. He had that self-satisfied 'mission accomplished' look on his face.

'Ah, Trace. I was beginning to think you'd been gunned down by gangsters. Hahahaha. Look!' he said, holding up some forms. 'All done. Just a few things for you to complete.'

I sat down and filled in the bits that Angela pointed to. When we had finished she said, 'Six o'clock then?'

'And Karen?' Devon asked.

She smiled. 'I can talk Karen around. It's just daddy-phobia, and I know how to deal with that.'

'Cool!'

We left.

'See, Trace,' he said, giving me a big shove. 'You thought I couldn't do it. You thought I was all washed up.'

'No I didn't.'

'Oh ye of little faith!'

'So what did you tell her?'

'Mystery weekend. Starting tomorrow night. She handles the girls' end, I handle the boys' end. Sweet as.'

He had pulled it off. The difficult always seemed easy to Devon.

'So what about the tickets and the passports?'

'They'll be there. Waiting. Like our little stashes. All ready for a fast exit.'

'So where up North?'

'A mystery, Trace, is something you don't know the answer to. Just wait and see. Anyway, more importantly, let's get a new base. I reckon I'll sleep more easily if we can find a motel to hang at.'

# CHAPTER
# THIRTY

IT WAS AN uneasy afternoon. We both tried to sleep, to watch TV, and to think of something else to do, but it was no use. The wait couldn't be masked with any other activity. This was the last act. We both knew it. Make or break.

AT ABOUT SEVEN we went out for pizza. At least it was going somewhere. While we were eating, a bunch of young guys came in: a touring touch rugby team. There was a skull and crossbones and the words *Putaruru Pirates* embroidered on matching tracksuits. Me and Devon both stared at them from our booth. They were our age but seemed years younger, laughing and pushing each other, doing stuff that I guess we might have been doing under different circumstances. While the coach was paying at the cash register, a young Maori guy who looked a bit like Devon, sneaked up behind him and yanked his track pants down. All the others laughed as the coach fumbled with his wallet and tried to cover his bum at the same time. Me and Devon exchanged looks but didn't say anything. The same thoughts were in our heads.

As we were leaving, one of the team backed into me, pizza tray in hand. He said, 'Sorry man,' as he turned. When he saw us there was this alarmed look on his face, like we were threatening him. I caught a glimpse of Devon's and my own face in the mirror by the door. There was something hard about them. Something a bit ugly. The footballer had seen it. We had become something else.

BACK AT THE motel I showered while Devon organised the stuff for the trip up North. When I came out I was confronted by what was now a familiar scene. On the couch was the money, the floor was covered with ounce bags of dak and the shotgun lay across a chair. There was no glamour in it. The blocks of notes had a grimy malevolent look. Blocks of poison and pain. Nothing like the little wads of notes I used to get in my pay packet at the hardware shop. I was surprised it still worked as money. As for the dak and the shottie, well that just meant jail. No way around it. The scene looked like a police warning poster.

I dried off, watching Devon putting everything away.

'How much is it, anyway?

'A lot. More than I thought. Let's split it now, Trace. In case something happens.'

'Something like what?'

'Something unexpected.'

'Suit yourself.' I went into the bedroom to put on some clothes and when I returned Devon was just coming in from outside. He pointed to a supermarket bag on the table.

'There's your share.'

I looked at it without interest.

'I have to go out. I've got a few arrangements to make before we head to Thunder Road. I'll be back about eleven. You want to stay here or is there somewhere you want me to drop you?' Any warmth had gone. There was a distance between us. 'Arrangements?' Planning that didn't involve me. But I was

pleased it didn't.

'Yeah. Drop me at the flats. I need to get my bike.'

I put on my leather jacket and grabbed the bag off the table. It was weighty, as heavy as a bag of frozen food. We drove off in silence, Devon biting his lip: miles away. When we were about a hundred metres from our road, he stopped.

'I'll let you out here. There could be someone waiting in our street. The last thing we want to get is a tail. See you back at the motel at eleven?'

I nodded coldly. He was about to speak and then didn't. We parted without saying goodbye.

I APPROACHED OUR old street like it was a war zone. Each parked car contained danger, and who knew what lay behind the blank windows of the old villas that stood shoulder to shoulder from the corner. As I passed the driveway to our little house I had a quick glance down. It was impossible not to. Everything seemed the same but it was poisoned with sadness. With lost innocence. Down below the flats my old bike stood, awaiting my return.

My faithful steed. After all the stuff we had done during the past months, the Atlas was the only thing that was unsullied, even though, to be honest, it was probably stolen. I rammed the bag of money into a gap in the rafters at the back of the carport. You could still see a bit of plastic but what did it matter?

There was still time to get to Karen's work before she knocked off. I fired up the bike and powered out onto the street. For the first time in days I felt good again. Free from all of it. Able to disconnect. Minutes later I reached Raymond's surgery. It was located in an old house and the reception was where the front bedroom used to be. I stood outside watching the receptionist endlessly typing into a computer. Karen walked past the window. I waved wildly on her way back and caught her attention. Her face broke out into a dopey grin and then she looked behind her. She showed five fingers to me and I dropped back onto the footpath.

Minutes later she was out, and in my arms. Everything else faded into insignificance: the money and its other self, the dak, my anxiety and guilt, even Devon. It was just Karen and me locked together on the footpath. We parted and sat on a low wall holding hands. For a moment there was nothing to say and then words came bursting out. It was mostly questions. Questions I couldn't answer.

*Where have you been? Why didn't you call? What have you been doing?*

'Has Angela rung you?'

'No. At least not today. You've been in touch with Angela?'

'Yeah. Well, Devon has… .'

'She told you my news?'

'No.'

There was a pause, some reluctance maybe, then she blurted out, 'I'm off to the States.'

'What?'

'Dad has managed to get me a place at this big med school in Boston. It's like the best there is for medical science.'

I could see that this was her father's ultimate trump card. That Raymond had outplayed me. My last little avenue of hope had been closed down with one move. I had that sick feeling in my gut – the sort you get after a good kick in the balls.

'What about … you know … us?'

'I'll take you with me. You can live in my room. I'll hide you in my cupboard.' Her eyes were sparkling.

'Cool.'

She ruffled my hair. 'Stop looking all miserable. I won't have it. We'll work something out. You should be happy for me. The States! It's unbelievable.'

Despite everything else I enjoyed seeing her smile and laugh.

I GOT A remote buzz from her joy, even though it had nothing to do with me and a little doubting part of me had always known that something like this was going to happen – that there'd be no fairy-tale endings – only tears. I thought back to the last time I had seen her: how it had felt then that something was already over.

'When was this all arranged?' My voice was weak.

She was so excited. 'Well, Dad claims to have been thinking about it for some time, but I think he went through with the organising after that ball fiasco. I was waiting for the big telling off. The big grounding. But it didn't come. Instead – this.'

I had underestimated him. The picture of rich doctors that Devon had painted hadn't included their self-protection, their determination to defend their own.

'Wow.' It was all I could manage.

'I have to respect him for it, I used to think he was you know, sort of, you know, emotionally repressed, disapproved of everything … the ambitious father who had my future mapped out for me, but I was wrong.'

I almost squawked, 'You were? How?'

'Of course I was. He's like freeing me, so I can make the most of my potential. He's trusting me. He's given me wings.'

I have never felt such savage reversal. I thought of practical jokes. The exploding cigar. The rug pulled out from under the feet. The bucket of water balanced over the door. I went into a kind of daze, then began to notice cars going past on the street. The passage of time. I watched Karen talk without listening to her.

'So what was it that Angela was going to tell me? Come on. Tell me your news. Don't be such a clam.' Her voice finally cut through my mess of self-pity, self absorption.

I had lost my taste for the whole thing. It was all pointless. 'I'll let her tell you, Karen, it's her news. No big deal.'

'OK. You ring me tonight. On the cellphone. It's more private. I better fly. They'll miss me in a minute.' She noticed the look on my face, the sadness I was trying to cover up. 'Come here. Stop being sulky. Everything changes, we've got to change with it.' I knew she wanted me to play along with her. To pretend that we would somehow get together in the States. To pretend that this wasn't the end. She pulled me forward and planted a hard kiss on my mouth. More a gesture than a kiss. The slight click of banging teeth. I kept thinking the world had changed so much nothing could get to me. But then she was off ... walking away from me with a spring in her step. I was left on the pavement.


THERE WAS NOTHING else to do but ride back to the motel and hang around for Devon. It was going to be a long wait but I couldn't bear to ring Karen. She had too much power over me and she wielded it like a child. She had the power to injure me with the tiniest gesture. The careless word. The raised eyebrow. The TV seemed to be wall-to-wall car chases. I had lost my taste for them too. The real thing was so much less spectacular. And the real thing was deadly. There was a newspaper on the table. 'Complimentary,' the owner had said. It sat there, unopened, unread. I longed to know if there was any mention of Johnno or the guys we shunted off the road but I couldn't open it. I folded it once and threw it in the bin outside. One backward glance would finish me. The only way was forward.

A car pulled up outside the unit at ten-thirty. The engine noise told me it wasn't a Holden. I stood by the back door of the unit, wondering when to time my dash. The door unlocked and Devon strode in, grinning, expansive as ever.

'Settle man, it's me.' He turned back and Angela followed him in through the door.

'What's going on?'

'Look outside.' He had the smug look of the guy who has just scored. Outside, next to the Norton, was a big BMW. Seven series.

'Have you bought that?'

He laughed. 'As if. Never liked them that much. Old people's cars. It's Angela's dad's. The Captainmobile.'

She laughed. 'Hi Trace. We borrowed it. Dad hardly uses it anyway.'

'It's only got six thousand ks on the clock and it's nearly two years old.'

'Where's the Holden?'

'At Angela's. It as a good chance to split the cargo.' Devon had half a bottle of Jim Beam, so we chilled for a while.

I was dying to ask Devon what the hell he was playing at: why the car? Why Angela? He carried on like what he was doing was the most normal thing in the world. At last Angela checked out the toilet, so I put it to him.

It was important, Devon claimed, that we seemed connected, not just two tear away idiots with a huge stash of ripped-off dope. Like poker, it was all bluff and guesswork: we had to appear to be more than we were.

'A blonde chick and a BMW does that?'

'Hope so, Trace,' he said softly.

'How'd you persuade her to boost her dad's car?'

He smiled. 'I just asked. Hey man, don't go on the bike, come with us. We'll test it out on the strip if you like, for old time's sake. Remember when that stuff used to matter?'

It seemed like years ago.

I shook my head. 'I'll go on the bike.'

I didn't want to travel with them. It was all wrong.

THERE WAS SOMETHING reassuring about the strip, maybe because we had spent time there before all the shit happened. Maybe because the guys who raced had a sort of purity about them, a higher purpose. They were there to drag, to race, to lay rubber. No advertising. No controls. Your car. Your risk. Your life.

Dealing seemed scummy by comparison.

The lines were still forming. It was a bit early for racing but very busy. A few familiar faces seemed puzzled by Devon sitting on the bonnet of a big slab of German metal. He lapped it up. I guess this was the impact he was after. Some time later Sloane's kraut tank cruised by. Its blacked-out windows could have concealed a dozen guys. From the front, Mark's tattooed face clocked us.

Then I realised Devon's thinking behind bringing the BMW. He wanted to match cars with Sloane. To say, I'm as big as you are, as tooled up. It was all on.

The racing had started at this point but by now I was so nervous I hardly noticed. I wanted our own showdown to get underway. It wasn't so much the right thing to do but maybe the only thing. Devon had run out of options. We had to settle things so we could get on with new lives.

I looked down to where Sloane's car was holding court. I kept wondering what this Sloane guy was like. What it took to control a scene as loose and wild as this one. There was a massive cloud of smoke settling over the whole strip. It came from the woman burn-out champ showing her paces. How could anyone keep the wheels spinning for such a long time? A tyre blew with a loud pop and that ended it. Everyone cheered. They knew it took skill to do that.

The white smoke turned the night into a red fog of tail lights. I spotted the huge shadowy silhouette a long way off. It was Mark, and he was headed our way. I nudged Devon who was busy laying a bite on Angela's neck. Her round eyes rendered vacant by skunk, she was in happy land.

Mark offered me the bro' handshake without saying a word and then turned to Devon.

'It's been a while, man, the boss is pissed. Better come with me now.'

We followed behind him like naughty boys being led to the principal's office. As we approached the big blue car I saw the Taylor Twins. The one with the chipped tooth grinned but neither said a word. It was like we were the condemned. There was no escaping now, we were in all the way, face to face with the guy we'd been toying with for so long.

Mark knocked twice on the window. The back door opened and he signalled us in. Angela went first, followed by Devon then me. The interior smelled of leather and aftershave. In the front seat was Rebel and next to him was the guy in the suit we'd already met at his place. For some reason it had never occurred to Devon or me that Sloane was a suit. Where were the tattoos? The shaven head? This guy with his suit and tie, his shiny shoes and glass of whisky seemed so out of place.

Rebel glared but said nothing: waiting for the big man to control the negotiations I guessed. The door closed and for a while no one said anything. Then Sloane spoke. His voice was slow, deliberate, lacked any emotion.

'If I had known how difficult you were going to be to keep tabs on, Devon, you would never have left Rebel's.'

He stared hard at Devon, looking for some sign of response.

Then he went on.

'A friend of mine has a pet food factory. It has a machine that can turn a large animal into fish food in minutes. A bit like a mincer. It doesn't matter what you put in one end, it always looks the same when it comes out the other. It's not far from here.'

He stopped, letting the words sink in. Angela slumped in the seat, closing her eyes tightly but Devon lit up. I admired his bravado: no sign of fear, no attempt to make himself liked. If Sloane was thinking he would fall to his feet begging forgiveness, he was wrong. The silence lengthened before Sloane cleared his throat.

'What do you have to offer me?'

It was the wrong move. I could see it in a tiny alteration of Devon's body language. Now he held some small advantage.

'I've been thinking long and hard. The situation has changed since we spoke at Rebel's. A lot's gone down. Some really bad shit. There was stuff I was prepared to do then … but it's no longer on offer.'

Sloane held up his hand. 'Save it. I don't know what you've been practising in front of the mirror but this isn't a social call. All I want to know is whether you have enough of what I want, to buy me off. If you don't then you and your mate … and blondie here … will take a little trip to my friend's factory. And after that, how about a midnight cruise on the Manukau Harbour? Trouble is, you won't see much, because you'll be in forty litre buckets.'

I sat rigid, struggling to keep my face still, to keep the lid on every outward sign. My mouth was dry, and my whole body prickled with sweat.

Sloane's voice became louder and sharper.

'So don't fuck with me, Devon. I want the weed, the money and anything you might have bought with it. Then maybe … and that's just maybe … I'll let you walk away.'

It was the accent that I picked up on. Beneath the tough talk there was this accent I'd heard before. It wasn't like ours. Then it clicked. He was a private school boy. His accent was the same as Richard and Jason's. What were the odds that he had been to the same school? Behind all the wannabe gangster talk was a private school upbringing he couldn't hide.

I looked at Devon. His mouth was open but no words came out. Angela was pale, and had this sad blank look on her face, like she was trying to make herself invisible. I could tell that Devon had been outplayed: that he had nothing to bargain with. Show and bluff were not going to work this time.

Sloane's face broke into the smile of a reasonable man. The whole process had been easier and faster than he'd expected. I guessed he was relieved. I had to do something. My heart was beating like an over-revving engine.

'I've had a gutsful of this shit. I'm the one to fix it.' My voice sounded strange, like it wasn't really mine.

They all looked at me. This wasn't part of anyone's plans.

My own included.

'Yeah, this whole thing has got out of hand. I'm going to fix it now. No one's going to get hurt.' Then I added, 'There's been enough hurting.'

'Ah! Sense at last … from the silent partner. Maybe we should have dealt with you from the word go.'

'He's a bullshitter too.' Rebel spoke for the first time but Sloane ignored him. He seemed to have no status here.

'It's Trace isn't it?' Sloane's voice warmed. I nodded.

'What can you do, Trace? There's a lack of trust here. We've been ripped off by this guy too many times. He'd piss on your back and tell you it's raining.' Sloane relaxed a little. 'You guys have had your fun. It's cost me plenty. We were two years in setting up that crop. I had a guy living in the bush for four months. Pest patrol. Local farmers. The cops. All working together… .'

'A community project,' Devon couldn't resist. 'You fuck up!' shouted Rebel.

'…and you two walk in and rip off the lot,' Sloane continued, 'right in the middle of harvest. I was sure it was one of my guys, someone got greedy. There was some bloodletting in my team, but it all led nowhere. Then we figured it was our old rivals, the black gangs. They like to think they've got the whole scene sewn up. Like it's part of the Treaty of Waitangi!' He laughed and Rebel gave an involuntary snort. 'But my tame farmer kept maintaining it was a couple of white boys.'

'He was half right….' Rebel chipped in.

'I thought maybe he was involved, but the broken leg … it didn't add up. Then finally the dak began to make its appearance, it's got this trademark hallucinogenic stone. First it was here on the strip right under our noses, and then all over Auckland. Now the gangs are selling it by the shit-load.'

I'd heard enough. 'We've got money and we've got dope.

We've had a few expenses but most of it still adds up.' 'That BMW one of your expenses?'

'No. It's her dad's.'

The attention all rested on Angela who had buried her face in the back of Devon's neck.

'He's some big cheese in the cops.' It came to me on the spur of the moment.

'My arse!' Rebel, unable to contain himself.

'Get rid of him,' I said pointing at Rebel. 'I'll make a deal but I can't do it with him mouthing off every two seconds.'

Sloane was hooked. He turned to Rebel. 'I can take it from here. You wait with Mark.'

Rebel was a puffed up ball of fury. I heard him mutter, 'Fucken nigger,' as he climbed out. I guessed it wasn't aimed at Mark.

'You were at Collegiate?' I asked.

Sloane's jaw dropped. 'How did you know that? You know something about me?'

'A bit. Bartram there when you were there?' It was worth a try. 'Yeah, I took his history classes. Hated the place. I was a boarder.' He eyed me hard. 'The old story, my father thought it would straighten me out.' He laughed bitterly. Even the laugh had the familiar ring to it. The frat house laugh. A bonding

laugh that had little to do with humour.

'Well, let's sort this,' I said, wanting to keep the momentum. 'We've fucked up, and I want to put things right and move on.' 'A bit of sanity at last.' He flicked a look at Devon that was

pure contempt.

I shifted in my seat. 'We've brought the last of the dope. I'll have to pick up the dough on my Norton. We came in good faith. There's not much left thanks to your two skins torching Johnno's place but I reckon that's down to you, not us.'

He considered it.

'Yeah, well they certainly paid the price for that.' Sloane sounded almost sad. 'Go on then. The girl can stay here with me. We can get to know each other while you're off on your errand.' He reached over and gave Angela's bare knee a squeeze. 'I don't want him around though,' he said, indicating Devon, as though he was less than human. 'Rebel can mind him until you get back,' then he added, 'they deserve each other. Be straight with me, Trace. It's your one chance. You've got an hour, then I take these two fishing.'

Devon was so angry he wouldn't look at me.

Sloane dropped the window of the car. 'Rebel,' he said quietly to Mark, who went off to get him. There was a tense silence until Rebel appeared at the window.

Sloane turned to Devon. 'Keys!' He handed them over to Sloane who passed them out to Rebel. 'You wait with him in his car. I'm sure you two have lots to talk about.'

Me and Devon climbed out. I stared at Sloane and pointed at Angela.

'Police Commissioner's daughter. The car's a cop car too.' I don't know whether he believed me. I hoped so for Angela's sake.

As we walked back to where we were parked, the Taylors tagging along with Rebel behind us, Devon muttered to me, 'What the fuck are you doing Trace?'

'Trust me, Devon. Hang in there, we're going to make it.'

I knew I would have to be quick. He couldn't last much longer.

I fired up the Norton and rode carefully back along the rows of parked cars. It was as busy as ever: the wild street cars doing their thing and force-fed fours laying down nine second runs. We had been oblivious to everything in the back of the Merc. At the end of Whaitiri Street there was a car parked in the shadows. It was Carmody, the street racing cop. I wondered if there was any way I could involve him. It was all too difficult. We had been totally out manoeuvred. We should have lain low or left town. The thought of us all dealing together was an idea straight from Noddy-land. It was never going to happen.

# CHAPTER
# THIRTY-ONE

**B**ACK AT THE motel I scooped the Holden key off the kitchen bench. Something on the couch caught my eye. Devon's Yin and Yang necklace. I pocketed it and headed off for Angela's house. The streets were deserted and my mind throbbed with crazy ideas.

There was nothing about Sloane I trusted, least of all his word, but the idea of the machine that ground up bodies had a deadly credibility. Everything was coming down to the next half hour or so.

I WAS PLEASED that Devon hadn't parked right up Angela's driveway. The possibility of her father returning was too much to think about. I left the bike in the street and drove the Holden back to the cottage in Parnell. I planned to pull the block I had hidden in the back garden as well as the bag in the garage. At least then I knew that I had done everything I could to clear the situation. No amount of money was worth the risk with the hole we'd dug ourselves into. If Devon still pulled some crazy stunt, it would be on his head, not mine.

I parked in the garage of the flats and grabbed my cut from the rafters. Then I ran out onto the road, cramming it inside my jacket as I went. The only light on our old house was the glow of the town houses next door. It was going to be difficult to find the money. I went to the front door. It was wide open. Well worked over, I supposed.

The dank smell of the empty house covered another one – the faint smell of aftershave – that I only recognised after I'd stumbled in and turned on the dining room light. There in front of me was Wiremu. He was impeccable in his black leathers, sitting on the last remaining dining room chair, sawn-off shotgun lying across his lap. He looked the business. For a moment or two I just stood there. I had forgotten all about him since our meeting.

'Hi,' I said, feeling flustered and forgetting everything I was here for. 'Are you waiting for Devon?'

He sat there for a moment or two saying nothing, and then he spoke in his soft voice.

'Devon owes me. I'm here for the rest.'

He could see my eyes glued on the gun, and he smiled.

'It's not for you. Last time I came there were these guys doing the place over. This time, well, I'm ready.'

'Do you operate … alone?'

'Shit no. I've got my people. We're whanau, me and my boys. You never heard of the Scorpions?'

I had. They were one of those gangs that people talked about but that never made the papers. Didn't wear patches.

'Yeah,' I said, 'but I never met one.'

'What's your name, bro'?'

'Trace.'

'OK, Trace. Tell me what's happening.'

Where to start? There was no time to work out an 'edited' version so I told him the lot. From the beginning. He enjoyed the story, grinning and nodding his head from time to time. When I'd finished he laughed.

'You guys. You're babies, man. You thought you could unload all that weed and no one would know. Jeez. I done some dumb things in my time but you guys … you guys could teach me a thing or two. So what now?'

'I was about to hand over all we had to get Devon and Angela out of there.'

'And you thought they'd leave you alone?' He started laughing again.

I nodded.

'Uh uh. Don't believe it. I reckon as soon as you hand over all your stuff, you're fish food all right. Devon agreed to this?'

'He didn't. This was my idea.'

'Your idea.' He shook his head. 'Man, I bet he's pissed with you.'

'You might say that.' There was a pause. I couldn't think of what to say.

'Well, what can I do? They're waiting for me.'

'You can do what Devon should have done in the first place. Come to me and I'll put out the word. Where did you say these petrol heads hang out? Whaitiri Street? Thunder Road.'

He pulled out a cellphone and wandered outside onto the back deck. I could hear him talking but it was low and soft and much of it in Māori. He must have made three or four calls in rapid succession and then he came back in. He folded the phone and put it in his pocket. The shotgun was placed inside a tennis racquet cover that he pulled out from under the chair.

He was aware of my silent gawping and held up the cover.

'Anyone for tennis? Old sport.'

I made a funny noise. It might have been a laugh.

'It's all on. Let's move it. It's all going down in twenty minutes.'

There was a black Ford Fairlane parked at the end of the street, a real gangster wagon: lowered, blacked-out windows.

Once we climbed in, Wiremu's unhurried coolness all changed. We u-turned with a big screech of rubber and shot through the red lights at the end of the street. Wiremu was smiling. For the first time in weeks I thought that maybe I had grabbed back a bit of control. Maybe I'd lucked out.

Nothing had changed at Whaitiri Street. The drags were still going off every minute or so. Carmody's car had gone and we pulled in at the bottom end of the strip.

'What happens now?'

'We wait. The brothers are coming. Then we'll close the street down from both ends at once. We need to box our *Mr Sloane* in so we can have a little talk. We've got history, him and me.'

'You know him?'

'Oh yeah. I know Steven Sloane from way back. If he wasn't *useful* he would have gone into the Manukau himself. Long time ago.' He turned to me. 'It's all about being *useful*, Trace. That's where your plan fell down. You wouldn't have been *useful*.'

'So how's he useful?'

'Car imports. He and his old man. We've piggy-backed cakes of speed in with some of them. Dak seeds. All sorts of shit. It was a good arrangement before he began to see himself as "the man". Won't deal with us any more. I heard he gathered a little band of skins. It's got racial.'

He glanced in the rear view mirror. 'Here they come.'

I saw two big cars, and then a third pull in behind us. Wiremu finally hauled himself out and wandered over to the driver of the second car. Other guys all milled around in a state of excitement. I could see they were used to this sort of thing. Finally a fourth car arrived. It was a big old Chevvy that someone had chopped the roof off. Full of guys.

Everyone got out of their cars and gathered around Wiremu. They bowed their heads. It looked like a prayer or a chant was being said. This was followed by a cheer and the slapping of palms as they all ran back to their cars.

WE WOUND INTO the bottom of Thunder Road, the end that the races finished at. There were a few spent cars with bonnets up, the owners watching our sombre procession. up ahead two cars were rocketing towards us. I could see the rise and fall of the headlights as the cars were chopped through the gears. I remember thinking, 'He's not going to play chicken.' And then a moment later, 'He is'.

About 50 metres away the drivers separated and shot past on both sides of us. They must have guessed this convoy wasn't moving for anyone.

We were down among the cars at the bottom of the parked line now and I could see teenagers running for their wheels. They were out of here. It was like the cops had raided: the news passed up the line as if by telepathy. Stampeding sprint cars shot out in front of us and headed off into the night. It was a drill everyone knew.

Up ahead there was the flash of an explosion and a hard sharp blast. In the chaos it was hard to tell what was going on. A moment later the big BMW shot past us. No windscreen, passenger door hanging open. Even in the gloom and smoke I could make out Devon at the wheel.

'It's Devon,' I said to Wiremu, 'He's got away.' 'He'll keep. It's Steven Sloane I'm after.'

We reached Sloane's Merc just as it was pulling out. Wiremu squeezed past and stopped inches in front. The other cars spurted in behind. It was a slick manoeuvre.

The driver's door opened and Mark climbed stiffly out of the stalled car. Wiremu sauntered over to him in that unhurried way that big men have. I thought, 'Now it's happening.'

I was wrong. They said nothing but locked fists close to their chests and hongi-ed. There was some sort of tie in. I couldn't believe it. Sloane had gone from gangster to rich white man in a big car. His whole aura had been nothing. None of his friends had stood by him. He didn't have a gang, it was just image: something I'd grown in my head.

I tried to see what was happening up the road. The cars had mostly gone now; there were just a few stragglers who couldn't get their engines started. Somewhere there was the thin, distant noise of a siren coming, above the roar of engines. The Scorpions were all lounging about, joking and laughing. It had been a bit of an anticlimax. No battles tonight. Some lounged against the front of the big car talking to Mark. Whatever was happening didn't seem to involve me. The door of the big car opened and Angela emerged, looking shaken and drained, her clothes all askew. When she saw me she burst into tears and lunged into my arms. I stood there holding her, feeling her body heave with sobs.

After a while she spoke. 'Where were you? Where did you go? Where's Devon?'

It was too difficult. I didn't know where Devon had gone either, but I knew he was in trouble. The sobs weakened and died with the questions. We stood there, locked together.

Wiremu emerged from the big car, 'It's done, let's go.'

Our convoy pulled out. Wiremu flicked a 'Ka kite' at Mark who was in the process of getting his huge body back into the driver's seat of the Mercedes.

'Thanks,' I said.

'What?'

'Thanks for that. I thought we were all goners.'

'It was sweatless. Didn't get what we came for, though.' He sounded a bit sharp.

'I'll get it. It's in the back of the Beamer.'

'Yeah, but where? Did you see that ute take off after it?'

It didn't take much imagination to work out who that would have been.


WHEN WE MADE it back to the old Parnell cottage Wiremu gave me his number. I said I would call him when I tracked down Devon. Angela and I stood on the footpath, watching his Fairlane saunter off into night. Angela was in a bad way. She seemed to have had some sort of breakdown: was shivering and crying, unable to speak. There was no knowing what might have happened to her in the back of Sloane's car. One thing was for sure, though; she couldn't stay the night in her big empty house alone. I bundled her into the Holden and drove to Karen's. We staggered up the drive. The house was dark and silent. I hoped Karen's folks weren't home. I stood, indecisive, in the front entranceway, then rang the bell, long and hard. A light came on somewhere in the depths of the house. I had to leave Angela, crouched and snivelling on the doorstep. No more dinner invites for me.


BACK AT ANGELA's house it was a relief to be reunited with the Norton. It didn't take long before I started to feel more like my old self again. I put all my focus into riding, tuning into the gutsy chuckle of the exhaust, finding just the right lines for the corners. Its soothing familiarity allowed me to review my options. What could be done? Where should I go? It had to be the motel. Our last refuge. If Devon managed to shake the Taylors loose, he would head there.

Turning into the double lane bypass road at Greenlane, I rode straight into a blockade of police cars re-routing traffic. Cops everywhere. Reflective raincoats, flashing lights carving the darkness, and hordes of hot cars: the remnants of the drags. There had been a big accident.

I was signalled over while a fire engine squeezed past. Two others were already at the scene. There was this ominous, grinding feeling in my gut but I didn't let my mind visualise the unbearable. No. Not yet. I wanted to live extra minutes, extra seconds believing he was OK. Believing he had got away. I rode up onto the footpath and parked my bike.

Torn between having to know and the fear of finding out, I stood with the hungry crowd locked into the impromptu drama. I was once more on the outside, a spectator. Somewhere a voice untangled itself from all the other voices. It was familiar, close. unignorable. Even with his back to me I knew it was Rebel. He was excited, recounting a story to the Taylor Twins. His muscular back mimicked the angry gestures of his fists. Carefully, I backed away, all the fight gone from me. The only thing I wanted was to find Devon and get back to the motel.

I turned and made for the bike. My legs, weak with exhaustion, fought to gain speed. Something about my movements caught the attention of one of the Taylors. I pushed the Norton off its stand and off the footpath. There was no time to kick-start – they were too close – but the momentum was enough to bump-start in second gear. I felt someone grab the belt of my jacket for a moment before the bike's torque kicked in and jerked me clear.

Two hundred metres down the road I had to wait at the intersection for the police to wave me through. In the mess of lights I could see a ute pulling out of the line of parked cars. It slowed and the figure of Rebel darted across the road and jumped onto the back, a scary animal grace in his movements.

Up front the police seemed to have forgotten about me and the two cars waiting to make a left turn. I squeezed inside the cars and round the corner, narrowly missing the cop's outstretched arm as I thrashed back towards Newmarket. I rode straight through four sets of lights without even slowing down. Behind me I could see the ute doing the same thing.

Broadway was deserted. A canyon of shops all waiting for tomorrow. On an impulse I plunged into the exit of a big car-park building. The sleepy attendant's cries were drowned by the thunder of the engine in the echoing space. Two or three levels down I was able to duck out the entranceway into the street a block away. Clear at last. No way they could follow me now.

By the time I had reached the waterfront promenade I felt safe again. I rode slowly, breathing the salty air and reaching out to the splintered me hiding deep inside, as if my body was just a shell of who I was. It was all over at last. I could feel neck and back muscles relax and the tension gradually ease from my frozen face. I stopped for a while where the water was lapping against the sea wall somewhere below me. The dim forms of moored boats were bobbing about in the bay. It was time to head back to the motel.

The streets were virtually deserted now. I reached the top of the Parnell rise and waited at an intersection for the green. My head was fuzzy with fatigue, I knew I was near my limit. A ute passing in the opposite direction jolted me awake. I was no more than three metres away from it. I knew who it was without even turning my head. I hoped somehow my stillness would make me invisible. It didn't. The suck of the big car's throttle was followed by a screech of brakes as they made an abrupt u-turn. I knew then that I was really in trouble.

I clicked the Norton into first and screwed back on the throttle. The front of the bike reared high in the air so I backed off a little to bring it down. By the time I plunged down the steep slope of Ayr Street I was doing nearly 80 ks. Coming out of the gentle right hand bend, a big concrete roundabout loomed. How could I have forgotten that? The front wheel locked up as I desperately tried to damp down the speed. There was no chance, no hope of stopping. I powered on through, relying on luck. It held. No other cars. The muffler clipped the raised edge of the roundabout, leaving a shower of sparks as I pushed the bike over to the limit, but I was through.

In the long straight next to the mangroves the ute gained on me again. I was heading into unknown streets. Too much chance of stuffing up. I turned around and doubled back cautiously. The big Falcon passed me on the blind corner. It was something they weren't expecting, and I was close enough to see them gawping at me in anger and disgust: the Taylor Twins in the cab, one of them framed by a rifle barrel, Rebel on the tray. There was one last chance. I would try to lose them in the Domain. Its trees and huge lawns, the little service roads and multiple entrances all favoured a bike. This time I took it easier around the road island; I couldn't risk an error. up the hill, the bike was pitifully gutless as the ute closed the gap. Finally,

I played red light roulette before plunging into the dark green vastness of the Auckland Domain.

I could hear the ute behind me but I daren't look back. The sky was beginning to lighten. As we were winding down the twisting hill towards the Stanley Street Tennis Stadium I did something that surprised even me.

On one of the corners there was a little service road, chained off, where the park staff had their compost pits. Me and Devon had often walked past it. To the right of the post where the chain was attached there was a gap wide enough for a person to walk through. I aimed at it and then flicked off my lights and disappeared into the void. At once, I was lost in the blackness of the forest and the weightlessness of falling. Ecstatic deliverance. For just an instant my senses were stripped of meaning, my body unattached to the world. I was beyond safety or danger, in another realm.

Then I reconnected. Slammed by the branches of trees, the ground, and the bike all at the same moment. Three onto one. It was almost funny. The bike rode on by itself, carving a passage down the gully. I rebounded against the trunk of a small tree and dropped to the ground.

The relief of being clothed in the blackness of the forest sped through me though I was stunned and aching. I began drinking in the stillness and silence which lay just beyond my perimeter of pain. My helmet had gone and there was a stickiness in my hair. I was surprised to see blood on my fingers. I'd felt nothing much as the bike had crashed its way down into the ravine. The rich smelling leaf litter mingled with the darkness. Somewhere down the gully I could hear the clicking of the cooling engine. I lay back and looked up through a break in the tree cover.

The stars. How long since I had looked at the stars? Really looked. I saw this child hiding in an ancient wash-house. It was me, on my grandparents' farm. There were no windows and on a bright day I would run in, slam the door and see, in those first moments of darkness, my day time constellations. Spears of light pouring through the holes in the tin roof. Just as beautiful: a universe of my own making.

Inside my leather jacket I felt the plastic bag, stuffed with the hard mass of paper. unbelievable wads of bank notes. The smell, slightly disgusting but thrilling, wafted out through the opening and mixed with the scents of fresh sweat and old leather.

Into this poured a noise that set my teeth on edge: the distinctive burble of a V8 somewhere across the park. They were back. And looking for me. I tried to sit up, but couldn't. A moment of panic. What had happened to my legs?

I heard the scrunch of wheels as the V8 turned into the service track.

Suppressing all feelings of pain, panic and exhaustion I lay still. Above me I could hear the relentless thrum of the motor and then a beam of light lit up the trees like daylight. It was the ute's roof-mounted spotlight. I closed my eyes and imagined myself melting into the earth.

Hoping: my last line of defence. It was all I had.

I could hear the Taylors and Rebel talking, calm now, determined, and close. They were held back by the chained-off road so the light beam was locked inches above my face. Someone ran down the path. A moment later his triumphant voice came. 'It's here. I've got the bike!'

I knew it was only a matter of time now before they found me and it was all over.

The other two ran down the slope and there was excited speculation about where I might have gone. One person, Rebel I think, walked back up to the ute while the other two disappeared deeper into the woods, down one of the many jogging tracks that fed into the surrounding streets. After a few moments all was quiet again.

# CHAPTER
# THIRTY-TWO

I WAS WOKEN by voices and the chug of an engine. As the dazed randomness began to reorder itself in my mind I remembered Rebel and the Taylors, the night chase, the search. They were back again. Back for me. I tried to move, this time with more success. I found myself in a sitting position. My chest ached and I had to breathe shallowly. I wiggled my feet and, with an enormous sense of relief, I could see there was movement in my boots. Dizzy and stiff with pain, my hair prickly with dried blood, a thick crust around my left eye and ear, but I was upright. The ravine below me was still beyond my line of sight so I grabbed the thin trunk of a lancewood and pulled myself up. About 30 or 40 metres down the bank, a tractor was parked, and two guys around my age were examining my bike. I could see from where I stood that the forks were hopelessly bent. There was no prospect of me riding it out of the park. I called to the guys and their heads shot around guiltily, shock clearly visible on their faces.

'Give us a hand.'

They both bounded up the hill towards me.

'Shit man, look at you.'

'How long've you been there?'

'I'll get an ambulance.'

I raised my hand. I told them I was on my way to the hospital when I came off. Could they give me a ride over there?

It seemed that their supervisor was away for the morning and they could do whatever the hell they liked. Such a good attitude, I thought. They took an arm each and helped me pick my way down to where they were parked.

The Norton was fixable but the damage was major. I felt like I had killed off the last of an endangered species. One less Norton Atlas in the world.

The two guys made a sort of bed for me out of bags of leaves on the tractor's tray. We bumped our way up the hill, back to the main road through the park. Whatever I had done to my chest registered in every lurch. The blond one, Jeff, rode along with me, making sure I didn't fall off. He explained that they were both on P.D. and they couldn't stop long. If anyone found out about this it might be added to their stretch. I envied their mateship, making the most of what came along no matter what. It was like the way me and Devon had been.

The hospital was only a few hundred metres from the entrance to the park but it seemed longer. We attracted some amused attention as we stopped outside the main doors and they unloaded me. We stood for a moment at the revolving doors. On an impulse I said, 'The bike's yours if you want it. I'm finished with it.'

They looked at me doubtfully and then realised I wasn't joking. We tried to shake hands but the pain was very sharp. I watched them for a moment as they roared down the driveway, then I limped through to outpatients.

It was a quiet morning so I was put in a room more or less straight away. A nurse had me take off my clothes in the prep room, saying an intern would be along to check me out. I rolled up the bag of money inside my jacket and waited on the edge of the bed, just wearing socks and underpants. My chest was a mess of blue bruises and red scratches. After a while a doctor arrived. Someone familiar was by his side. It was Richard. We both did a double take at the sight of each other. I had forgotten that he was a med student.

'Hi, Richard!'

The supervising doctor was surprised too. 'You two know each other?'

Richard nodded and went bright red. He looked annoyed.

I had strayed into another area of his life.

IT TURNED OUT that along with bruising and lesions to the head, I had a couple of cracked ribs. In an hour I was washed, strapped, stitched, and bandaged. Next stop was x-rays but I was starting to feel better and had had enough. There was only one thing on my mind that moment and it wasn't cranial x-rays.

I headed to the front desk to see if Devon had been admitted. The receptionist, a stern-looking woman in her fifties, took one eyeful of me and decided she didn't like me.

She said no one of that name had been admitted but then reluctantly added that there was another Santos. His name was Te Arepa and he had been checked in with burns and head injuries last night.

Could I see him?

No. He was in critical care and only family had visiting rights.

I was whanau. I got the 'I don't believe you' stare. What relation?

Half brother. The others would be here later.

We stood there for a while, eyeballing each other and then she said that there was a little waiting room at the end of the critical care ward but I wasn't to go in until the next of kin arrived. Level five.

I almost ran to the lift but rapid movement was like someone jabbing my ribs with a screwdriver. There was a mirror in the lift and I could see why she was reluctant to let me go anywhere. My bandaged head and staring eyes … I looked like an escaped mental patient. On the fifth floor there was another nurse's station. An intern about my age was chatting to a nurse, who was a bit older.

'I've come to see … ahh …' (forgetting his name for a moment) '… Te Arepa Santos.'

I was obviously interrupting something. 'You are?' the nurse asked.

'Trace Santos, I'm his brother,' I said, getting used to the lie. She leaned towards me. 'He's through in room nine. His coma is induced until he's stabilised. He's on life support …still in a very critical state.'

I wasn't prepared for what I saw in room nine. I imagined he would look a bit like me, with bandages and bruises, but he didn't. He lay face forward on a little sort of hammock that supported his head. There was a tangle of wires and tubes and monitors around him that made getting close to him almost impossible. I had to sit on the floor next to the bed to see his face.

'I was coming for you, Devon. Why didn't you wait? Why didn't you trust me? It was my turn. I could've got you out….' The talk just poured out of me. I didn't know what was coming next … it was a dam-burst of questions, pain, disappointment.

How long I carried on like this I have no idea, but after a while a doctor's head peered around the corner of the bed to find me on the floor.

'Oh, excuse me. I didn't see you down there. I thought it was Te Arepa talking. You're the brother?'

I nodded and climbed stiffly to my feet. My injury was making itself known now that the codeine was wearing off.

The doctor glanced at a clipboard and then placed it back on a hook at the end of the bed. 'The prognosis isn't good. All we can do is wait at this stage ... wait for things to stabilise before we can even begin any remedial actions.' He watched me. 'You look as though you've been in the wars yourself. Were you in the same accident?'

'Sort of.' I didn't want to talk.

'The policeman in the other car died at the scene, so the police are following Te Arepa's progress closely too. I've told them that he's a long way from talking to anyone.'

It sort of hit me, that. The policeman died. Along our trail of casualties, Death was gaining on us.

Another doctor and nurse arrived and the first doctor turned to me and said, 'You wouldn't mind waiting in reception while we go through our tests? It's a little tight in here.'

I found the cafeteria and had some food with my codeine. I had lost track of the last time I had eaten anything and the first few bites of my pie made me feel like vomiting. I took my coffee out into a bleak little courtyard so I could smoke. High up in the monolithic building in front of me Devon's survival was being plotted. Nothing dramatic. Just tubes and fluids, cables sending impulses to bleeping monitors, his food now reduced to a clear liquid, and fed in through the arm. I bet he was dying for a smoke.

When I got back the nurse on level five said I couldn't go through yet. To wait with the others. Then she disappeared. Against the wall sat a Ma¯ori man in his sixties and a girl about nine. The guy was looking at me as if expecting something so I went over to introduce myself.

'I'm Trace Santos.' I reached my hand forward and he stood up and held it. He leaned towards me until forehead and nose gently touched mine. We paused for a moment, silent and still, as though he was reading the contents of my head. Then he straightened up.

'I'm Ra, Te Arepa's koro. This is his sister, Aroha.'

We sat and then he said with a smile, 'Now, what branch of the whanau do you come from?'

Feeling a fool I thought it best to 'fess up and clear the air. I explained how I had just used the name to get in. How it was next of kin only. I thought I must have violated any number of protocols in using their name.

'I'm … his friend.' The words shrank to a whisper.

'Then you *are* whanau,' he said definitively and that was an end to it.

'Me and Devon've been living together, here in Auckland. He never told me about his family, just about his Spanish ancestor, the pirate.' It sounded stupid now, somehow.

'We're from a little place on the Coast. Te Arepa hasn't been back for years. He left school … too early, and then struck out alone, I suppose trying to make a name for himself. And he certainly has.'

'I never knew he was called Te Arepa. He was always Devon to me.'

'That was his Pakeha name. He called himself that when he went off to the boarding school. He was teased there, eh, about being Māori.'

There was so much about Devon I wanted to know but this was no time to ask questions. Part of me knew that he would never be able to answer them himself.

We waited. Hour after hour. It became clear that nothing was going to happen today or perhaps even tomorrow. It would be a long vigil.

It was hot in the hospital but I couldn't take my jacket off because it concealed my bag of money. My loot. It was beginning to plague me. I was sick of it. It was a heavy uncomfortable lump on my body, like a growth; it was the ugly driving force behind everything that had happened here. I longed to be free of it but also couldn't part with it. That would make all the whole trail of pain and death we had travelled meaningless. All for nothing.

As EVENING FELL, I slipped out of the hospital into the trees of the

Domain. I found this ancient puriri tree by the pavilion next to the duck pond. It was so old it must have been part of the original bush which had somehow escaped destruction. About four metres up a branch had fallen and there was a shallow hole with some other little tree growing out of it. The area was fairly public, but no one was around right then so I made a tight bundle of the bag and threw it in, basketball style. A shot that would have done credit to a Michael Jordan. From ten metres back there was still a bit of the white plastic bag visible but I no longer cared. It was taken care of. I had shed an immense load and walked back to the hospital feeling like a free man. It was only back in the lift that the heavy coat of grief once more descended on me. This wasn't a healing place.

BACK IN DEVON's hospital room Ra and the little girl were playing euchre on the floor. Devon was strung above them so he could watch too, if his blank eyes could relay the information. I joined them. I hadn't played cards for years. These two were real sharps: flicking through the hands so quickly I could barely see what was happening before it was all over. As we played Ra talked of Devon.

'When he was about Aroha's age he wrote this poem. The headmaster at our little school couldn't believe he made it up ... even though he did it in front of him. He came to me and said, "Ra, this boy has a gift, a taonga. He would be wasted at the local high school. I want to apply for some scholarships for him." Well, I thought about it: his mother dead and his father in the jail, all the local kids ending up with joints in their hands before they hit high school ... and he had such promise. But then surely it was me who should be grooming him? I could see in his face, the tipuna staring out at me. First one, then another. They too were waiting for a decision ... but it was hard. Finally, though, I made the mistake of so many of my generation, thinking that the good Pakeha education would save him. Armed with that and coming from a strong whakapapa he would be able to make his way in the world. Not follow his father's path to the gangs first and then on to jail. The well-trodden path.'

He looked up at Devon. 'I was wrong.'

We played on for a while, not talking. Little Aroha was writing the bigger scores on a piece of paper. She had some serious competition going with her grandfather. I was out of the equation.

'He loved the stories about our Spanish tipuna. The so-called pirate. He pumped me for all I knew and when the facts ran out I would embellish the stories. The man grew into a legend and colonised Te Arepa's mind. Te Arepa became Spanish, not Māori any more and when he went off to school … he forgot about us, about where he came from … but chased this pirate. The dream of treasure. Like a conquistador in search of a new Eldorado. When he was fifteen he was determined to leave school. I wanted him to go on to the university but he wouldn't even consider the idea. I told him, your talent is language, we need a lawyer in the family, but by this stage everything took too long, and he was in a hurry. At fifteen you know everything.'

His hands made an expansive gesture and he smiled. 'At my age, after a lifetime of learning, you know nothing.'

We had to leave again while the doctors checked Devon out. In the waiting room the heat made me drowsier by the minute. They were a long time with him. Aroha put her head in her grandfather's lap and went off to sleep as quickly as a light being turned off. I looked at Ra's face in repose. It had the heavy-featured monumental quality that you see in meeting house carvings. There was a hugeness about the man that made you feel instantly safe. I had never come across this in a person before.

'What's your real name, Trace?'

His voice startled me. 'My birth certificate says Edward, but I've always been Trace.'

'King Edward,' he muttered. 'I'll call you Eruera.'

I was awakened by movement through the dimmed lights of the waiting room. I realised that Devon was being wheeled away to the operating theatre, but no one told us what was happening. Aroha was still asleep but Ra watched silently. His was a weary vigil.

The nurses' station was closed so there was nothing to do but wait. The clock said it was after three but time had long since ceased to mean anything. Hour followed hour. We sat in silence now. At five-thirty the eastern sky was beginning to brighten when the swish of the lift door made us both sit up together. It was the doctor. Without him saying a word we both knew Devon was dead. Ra placed Aroha's head gently on the couch, then rose slowly and stiffly to his feet.

'Mr Santos…' the doctor began '… I'm sorry. There was no time to come and get you. Te Arepa passed away twenty minutes ago. We have been trying to revive him but there has been a major shutdown … .'

Ra stood and proclaimed '*Ka ura he ra. Ka to he ra!*'[1] to the dawning world. Then he turned to me and said, 'Eruera, you stay with Aroha. I need to go to Te Arepa.'

He left me and walked off with the doctor. I looked at the little girl, at the deep untroubled sleep of childhood. She would awaken to an adult world. The still pond of innocence was waiting for this, the first stone, to break its reflective beauty: to know that we all must die.

---

1 *A sun rises. A sun sets.*

# CHAPTER
# THIRTY-THREE

A S I SAT in the quiet room the veil of grief descended on me like a frost. It ate itself deeper and deeper until it sat on my heart. All other emotion disappeared. No longer did I feel fear or anger. My limbs were heavy and any will to move had gone. It was as though I had been set in concrete.

Ra re-entered. He spoke to me but I heard nothing. He went. Hours passed. Daylight came. Aroha awoke. She looked around for her grandfather and then sat silently beside me. A nurse came and crouched in front of her. They went off together. When they returned Aroha was carrying a cup of tea and a roll. She offered it to me. I shook my head. We waited again. Ra returned with another man. The four of us wound our way downstairs to the front lobby. We waited while Ra spoke to the front desk and signed papers, and then two men appeared with Devon on a trolley. Out the front in the covered area was an old pick-up. They loaded Devon's body onto the back. I climbed on with him. They tried to get me into the cab with them but I stayed there with Devon. We drove to a house in the south of the city where a family waited for us on the verandah. There was wailing and crying. Devon was carried in and placed on a bed. I sat next to him on a chair. The family tried to persuade me to come and eat but I knew it was no good.

Later he was placed in a coffin and we headed for the Coast. I travelled in the back of a station wagon with my hand on the edge of the box. Other people had come and they travelled with us in procession. It was a long way. We arrived as the sun was setting and formed a group at the gateway to the marae. Speeches were made. Songs were sung. The wharenui was small and old, lined with framed photos. Mattresses were placed next to the casket and people came and sat with me all night; some for an hour, others slept there.

When I woke in the morning my hand was still on the side of the box, stiff and set. Ra came and eased it off. He led me to some showers and indicated he expected me to wash. I stood under the water for a time but it did no good. The water on my skin felt remote, as if it was not managing to wet me. When I emerged my clothes were gone and new ones were in their place. These looked as if they hadn't been worn for a while. The coat smelled of mothballs. Ra reappeared and took me to the kitchen. It was full of people preparing food. They all greeted me but all I could do was nod back. A chair was placed near the big wood-burning stove. I was given a mug of tea. It took a long time but eventually I was able to drink it and even eat some porridge. But that was all.

I went back to the meeting house. It had filled up since I had been away and it was difficult to get close to Devon. I sat a row back beside some weeping women. It was good to be next to this noisily grieving group. They made the noises I longed to make, but couldn't.

Later that day the ceremonies began. I held my place next to the coffin. I seemed to be regarded as a fixture. They moved Devon and me out onto the paepae so we could both hear the speeches. Although I couldn't understand much it was comforting to hear the layers of language descend upon us like layers of bedding.

I noticed among the seats of speakers was a man with a policeman on each side of him. It had to be Devon's father. Green eyes but his face more like Ra's. Monumental, carved, warrior profile. When the speeches finished he was a pallbearer and we faced each other across the closed coffin. In his face I saw pain and anger. He nodded at me. The urupāwas some distance from the marae but we walked it in procession. I stared at the backs of the men in front, not caring how long it took or where we were going. I was content to just walk and follow.

As we left the entranceway to the marae there were more people: some onlookers, local people who had just stopped because they were passing by, and others dressed up but who had arrived late and couldn't enter. I noticed, numbly, that Wiremu and a couple of Scorpions were with this group.

It was a slow walk and the load was surprisingly heavy. By the time we reached the gates I was beginning to struggle. The days and nights of grief had taken their toll. At last we lowered the coffin next to a freshly dug grave. I sat next to it, my hand firmly around the handle. Women came forward and kissed the coffin. After a while Ra came forward to free my hand so that the box could be lowered into the hole. He held my arm. All around us were wild cries and weeping. I was silent and my eyes were dry. I felt locked up, frozen, unable to perform any show of grief. Back at the marae I was able to eat at last and the bitter cold which permeated me began to thaw. People came up to me and tried to talk but I was unable to utter a word in response.

That evening Ra took me for a walk. We went up to the freshly turned earth that marked Devon's grave. Ra took a small stone adze from his pocket and handed it to me. It was made of a glossy, black stone, almost like glass. It was beautiful, heavy and cold. A groove had been carved into the thin end, and a string fastened to it so that it could be worn around the neck. It seemed impossibly old. I tried to hand it back but Ra turned and walked to the edge of the urupā. I stood there with the adze seeming to fizz in my hand. He returned with a small sprig of mānuka and placed it in the top pocket of my coat.

'Listen, Eruera. When the leaves fall from this twig of mānuka you will know it is time to put your grief behind you. Time to move on.'

He walked to the corner of the fenced-off area and washed his hands at a tap.

Then he left me. As soon as his outline faded away I looked at the adze lying there in my open hand. It demanded my grief. And then it came. First tears, silently running down my face; then huge, convulsive sobs erupted painfully to the surface from deep within my body. Like some monstrous presence was leaving me, battering its way out. The noises I made were not my noises. They were scarcely human. I fell onto the soft mound of heaped earth and flowers and let my body perform its long-suppressed ritual.

When I eventually stood my chest ached and my eyes were gritty and sore. But I felt light. My feet barely touched the ground as I walked down the hill from the urupā. There, in the gloom, Ra was waiting at the gate. Together we walked back and rejoined the hākari. Devon's dad had gone but I met his cousins and aunties … and other people, whose relationship was explained to me in great detail. After a while we all sang and for the first time I began to feel fully human again.

Wiremu was standing near the food slide in the whare kai. I went over and we shook hands and hongied. It was the natural thing to do now. He said to call him when I got back to Auckland. That he had something to tell me, but this wasn't the place or time.

The following day I joined Ra in farewelling people as they left to return to their homes. I felt the sadness one feels when old friends depart, and yet I had only just met these people. I stayed on for a few days after everyone had left, doing jobs in the garden and helping clear scrub. Aroha, who lived with an aunt, went back to school, while Ra and I stayed on in the wharenui. He was a rangatira and spent most of his time travelling between relatives and attending to affairs of the iwi.

The tough little leaves of the mānuka were beginning to curl and as he had predicted, it was time to move on. I was going to hitch back to Auckland so we walked together to the main road. The traffic was thin in this remote part of the Coast but he flagged down someone he knew who was going to Whakatane. It would be easy after that.

As I was about to get into the car he stopped me and said, 'Eruera. Before long, your heart will burn for utu. For revenge. It's the natural thing. You mustn't listen to it. No good will come from it.'

I told him that I had no taste for revenge, that there was no one I wanted revenge against. I had other plans.

We hongi-ed and parted.

# CHAPTER
# THIRTY-FOUR

A UCKLAND HAD A harsh impersonal air after the warmth of the Coast. Too many people, too much noise. I knew that I could no longer stay. Those tickets which Devon had booked would be my way out. Angela wasn't in the travel agency when I went in to pick them up. I needed to see Karen one last time. Not to explain, but just to say goodbye. To wish her well. I rang the cellphone I had given her but was greeted by the recorded voice saying, 'The number you have dialled is not currently switched on or within the receiving area'.

I walked to her father's surgery and sure enough I could see her in the front room, wandering backwards and forwards, doing those menial tasks that clerks do. I sat on the fence and waited for her to look out the window and see me. The last thing I wanted was a confrontation with her father. It took longer than I expected, so absorbed was she in her jobs. Her face didn't register pleasure, just anxiety. She signalled me away. Moments later she came out to where I was waiting a little distance down the road.

'I didn't think I would ever see you again.' There was no warmth in her voice.

'I've come to say goodbye.'

The words were brushed away and her face clouded with anger. She no longer looked like Karen but like someone else.

'Have you any idea of the shit you dropped on us? What you put Angela through?'

I tuned out, having no interest in responding to this. It was her father talking.

'We've had half the Auckland police force tramping through our house, Angela's father blaming me, my parents accusing me of doing all sorts of things behind their backs… .'

'Devon's dead,' I cut in.

She stopped for a moment, as if this was news. Then she started again.

'So's the policeman he hit.' The shutdown response. 'His wife's been on TV. There was an appeal from her to the boy racers to stop before more people die. The mayor has closed off Whaitiri Street ever since….'

'He's dead, Karen.' My voice flat and steady.

She stopped and let out a huge sigh. 'I'm sorry, Trace. I wish I could say that I feel sorry for him too, but I don't. The trouble he's caused….'

I walked off. This had been a mistake. I wished our last, blissful, time together could have stayed intact. The treasured, final memory. Now this one had eaten into it. Our lovemaking had eroded into mere sex.

BACK IN NEWMARKET I sat in a coffee bar smoking and taking stock. The first flight out was early the next day so I had a bit of time to kill and a couple of things to do. In a newspaper lying on the counter I found a statement about the accident on the opinions page. It was an article written by the mayor. He and the widow of the dead cop, Mrs

Carmody, were forming a task force to close down the street racers.

Mrs Carmody explained that she knew where the racers were coming from; her husband used to be one but he had 'dedicated his life to stopping this senseless and dangerous activity'. The mayor's comments were mostly things like 'dicing with death', 'an accident waiting to happen' and 'take it to the track'. I guess he wanted to appear hip. There was no mention of drugs or money or guns. I noted the date. The day before my birthday. Twenty tomorrow and no one to celebrate with.

Near Grafton Bridge there were a number of backpackers' hotels. I paid double rate to get a room to myself. I had no luggage: all my other stuff had been left behind in the motel in Mt Eden. The money was beginning to call me again now I was in its orbit. It couldn't be left. It had to be dealt with. There was simply too much of it to leave where it was, but I knew now that no matter what else happened, I didn't want it.

As it was a sunny day the Domain was full of tourists and office workers on their lunch break. The duck pond area was teeming with Koreans getting their photos taken. I had no time for stealth, so I must have made an interesting photo for some Asian family's album, hauling a café table up against a tree, and then with the aid of a chair, retrieving the bag of money. I strolled off through their midst with a jaunty stride, carrying over a hundred thousand dollars in a bag worth about five cents. In a nearby post office I crammed it into a post bag and sent it off with a note containing two words: 'Pirate treasure'.

I sent it to Ra, care of the marae we stayed at. I hoped he might use it for Aroha's education, but that was his call. He was just as likely to throw it into the river. Nothing could be better, though, than the feeling I had squeezing that package into the parcel slot.

THERE WAS ONE last thing which would wrap everything up: one last action I wanted to carry out, before I walked away from the places, the memories – the world I'd known with Devon. I had to go back to the little Parnell house and lift the money I had hidden that last afternoon I spent with him.

Before I did this I would ring Wiremu as I had promised. I knew, now that the bulk of the money had gone, that there was nothing for me to give, there were no items of trade. I wondered what it was he wanted to tell me.

As it happened Wiremu was after the remaining dope. I told him he would have to scrape it out of the burnt car.

And the money? That too.

'Yeah right,' he said.

'What was it you were going to tell me?' I asked. 'Where are you staying?' he asked.

I hung up. I was disappointed. I thought somehow he was better than that. Sort of noble.


IT MUST have been five o'clock by the time I arrived at the familiar street that was once our sanctuary. I guess I should have anticipated what I saw, but I didn't. Where the house once stood there was a gaping crater. The path and the outline of piles were all that remained of a house that had spent 90 years looking out on the overgrown gully. It was as though someone had done the job of erasing every trace of my summer with Devon. up against the footpath a large sign advertised a row of three-storey town houses to be built at the site, and the developer, Elysian Fields Corp. So that was the name Wes traded under. It sounded right. He had this thing about death.

Using the outline of the old house it wasn't hard to find where I had concealed the money. The ginger plant, whose roots I had used to hide the tight little wad, had been smashed by the wheels of a machine and the bag was partly visible. I guessed it was only days before some young builder's labourer like myself would have stumbled upon it. Winning Lotto without even buying a ticket. No, fate was not that friendly. There was a heavy price to be paid for this money and it had been well and truly paid. I stuffed it inside my shirt and was about to walk out onto the road when a white Bentley purred up in front of the gate. I immediately fell back behind the big tree that marked where the land fell away sharply to the railway line.

It would be interesting to see Wes in the daylight. Part of me thought that he had the vampire's aversion to full sun. But nothing happened. The car remained shut up so I imagined that inside Wes was jabbering away trying to impress some would-be investor. For rich people like Wes, every occurrence, no matter how disastrous to others, blew fortune his way. Devon had cleared a path. He had removed the tenants and now he too had gone. As with the little house itself, soon there would be nothing left to mark his passing except a small upward movement in Wes' fortune.

What happened next lit a fuse I could never put out. The door of the Bentley opened to reveal the suited figure of Steven Sloane. What was he doing in Wes' car? At first I thought he might be a customer and that any moment Wes would spring out, but it didn't happen. He was alone. He had to be some sort of partner. Then it all made sense. No matter how careful we were, we could never hide. We were followed so easily: when we thought we were ahead, we were in fact always one step behind. There was an enormous unfairness about it. As if we were playing cards against someone with a marked deck. We never had a chance of winning. He picked his way around the site, carefully avoiding anything that might soil his smart shoes. He stopped not three metres from me and spread out a plan on the fallen remains of our chimney. His hair, his face even his fingernails had a plastic perfection about them. He had the blemish-free good looks of an American soap opera star.

I longed to tear him to pieces. To feel his flesh rip between my fingers. He straightened up and took a number of slow steps backwards until he was almost close enough to touch. My body began to shake as the rage grew inside me. Here we were, one on one, no advantage of numbers or weapons. It would be clean and fair. Then, as if some inner alarm bell had rung, he strode briskly back to the car.

My moment had passed.

I HOPED THE walk to the backpackers' would calm me but it did nothing. I kept remembering Ra's caution, about utu, but it still burned within me. I lay for hours in my hard little bed, in the stark room, staring out at a street lamp. Waiting for the night to pass. Waiting to be on that plane and away from all this. But it was no good. My thoughts kept coming back to the unfairness of Wes pulling the strings at a safe distance. Ropes around our necks. Devon's mentor, his idol, was finally his killer. I had no idea how it all held together. But I knew that Rebel and his little Nazi cell out in Glen Eden were only pawns. So was Sloane, the private school boy. It all came back to the cold, hard eyes of Wes, sitting safely in his eagle's nest of a house looking down on everything. Laughing. Wherever I went I knew that this would follow me. I sat up in bed. It had to be resolved.

# CHAPTER
# THIRTY-FIVE

IT WAS A long walk. What took a few minutes on the bike took over an hour on foot. By time I reached Paritai Drive it was some time after eleven o'clock. The door was opened by a boy I had never seen before. Fresh from somewhere in Asia, he could not have been more than 14. Like his predecessor he was dressed in white cotton, but seemed to be wearing a lot of gold. Chains, ear studs, rings on his fingers and toes: early days in their relationship, I guessed. The present-buying stage.

'I've come to see Wes.' This was greeted by a blank smile of incomprehension, then he gestured me in. I had the feeling that this boy was only days out of some hell-hole in Manila. A FOB as we used to say: fresh off the boat.

In the lounge Wes lay back on some sort of antique recliner. Feet elevated, head almost horizontal. He was wearing his regulation white bathrobe and carpet slippers but he had his head back with a flannel draped over his face. He looked vulnerable.

'Who is it?'

I made a shoo, shoo gesture to the boy who seemed pleased to retire.

'It's me, Wes. Trace Dixon.'

There was a pause; you could almost hear the cogs of his mind grinding into action.

'To what do I owe the pleasure?'

'I feel we have unfinished business.'

'Oh yes?'

'Yes.'

'And what might be the nature of that business?'

He hadn't moved a muscle since I walked in, the flannel still covering his face. His calm was intimidating.

'You don't know?'

'Well Trace, I know what unfinished business I have with you, I just want to … reassure myself that we are talking about the same thing.'

'I'm here about Devon.'

There was an almost imperceptible sigh beneath the flannel and a minute shake of the head.

'Trace. Listen carefully. In the parlance of your generation, it's "game over" as far as Devon's concerned. I say it with some regret, as I liked the boy, and all I can say by way of commiseration is "it happens".'

'So that's the end of the matter?' 'Yes.'

I wasn't sure where to go from here or even what I wanted Wes to say, but I could tell this particular path was sealed off.

'Well what do *you* think is our unfinished business?'

Wes took the flannel off his face and sat up. He was smiling. He had won some sort of little opening gambit and was entering the game with enthusiasm.

'Like all things in this hungry little world, it comes down to money. You have some money, I believe, quite a hefty sum. I want it. It's mine.'

'How much do you think there is?' 'Possibly half a mill, I am informed.' 'Who informs you?'

He shook his head as if I had made a basic gaffe. 'We don't mention names in this business. They're irrelevant anyway, what it comes down to is information. The bearer of that information is only important from a sort of book-keeping perspective.'

He wandered across to the bar and poured himself a glass of wine from an opened bottle. There was no offer of a drink today. It pleased me.

'I have a wide array of associates. From judges right through to people whose only talent is for inflicting pain. The process of making money is what keeps us all in line. We are all loyal – if in no other sense – to that process. You know the expression "keeping it honest"? Well in my circle it's making money that keeps us honest, predictable. Not laws or moral codes. Those dictates have a different purpose, and I salute that purpose.'

He raised his glass as if making a toast.

I watched him, fascinated. The vulnerable old man I'd seen on a reclining chair when I first arrived was gone: changed to someone who was in charge. And he knew it.

'I'll only say this once. Listen carefully. It's like this. Devon blundered into our world and he dragged you in after him. You were like his Man Friday. He didn't know how things worked. He continually overestimated himself. He imagined that you could rip off a large amount of ...' he paused, searching for a word, 'product and sell it on without being detected. *I mean, they can't run to the police can they?*' He stopped for a while as if marvelling over the naivety of the logic.

'His assumptions, all of his assumptions, were wrong. The drug scene is very regulated at that level. How do you think they keep the prices up? Many livelihoods were damaged by what he did, what you both did, and these were people with a lot to lose. And yes, Trace, they can run to the cops because in some cases, they are the cops. To think otherwise is not naivety, it's stupidity.'

'So it's nothing to do with you, eh? You're above all that?'

'You sound petulant. I didn't invent the game. I didn't make the rules, but I accept them. They apply to me too. I know what the inside of a cell's like. I know what you have to do to survive there. Sit around and cry "not fair" and you really *are* history. But enough of this, let's get to the point. Thank you for coming in, Trace, it means I won't have to send for you. That can be very stressful. What I am charged with doing – on behalf of others – I get no direct material benefit from this, Trace – is recovering as much of the missing proceeds as possible. We call it *damage control.*'

'You think I have it?'

He looked immediately caught, as if he hadn't thought of something. He lost his slow dead-pan delivery.

'I hope you do. For your sake.'

'Were you the one who told them about Johnno? Who set those two goons onto us?'

'Trace, there is nothing to be gained from this. I have a deal which I have been wanting to present to you. Can we skip the rewinds?'

'It *was* you. Nobody else knew about him. So it was just a matter of setting your mate Sloane the task of retrieving the dak. You wouldn't even do that yourself.'

He raised his hand to shut me up. 'Not my *mate*, Trace. My son.'

I sat there, open mouthed.

'What did Pope say? "A little learning is a dangerous thing ... fools rush in ..." You're angry because you're stupid. I treated you two like equals, but that doesn't mean you *were* equals. In wealth or power or knowledge there was no comparison. It was only your youth I found attractive... .' He stopped for a moment and then added sharply, 'And that certainly isn't the case now.'

He put down his drink and sat on a bar stool with his hands resting on his knees. The sharp, white spotlights washing down on his bald head made him look every inch the evil genius from cartoons. I almost laughed at the thought: the unreal sight had helped something to turn for me.

'The deal is this, Trace. It's the best deal … the only deal in fact. Drop off what you have. Keep a block for yourself … call it educational expenses and then get the hell out of here. Don't let your face be seen on these streets again.'

'What was it like? Being able to sit in this chair and tell Sloane, tell your son… ?'

'Listen to what's on offer, Trace. Do it now. Time's running out for you.'

'I've got something for you, Wes, something Devon might have wanted returned.'

I pulled the Yin Yang necklace from my pocket. 'I don't want it.'

'Maybe you can give it to your new houseboy. He looks as if he likes presents.'

'Get out of here, Trace. This is over.'

'I'm going, Wes, don't worry, I don't like it here. But before I go, you're going to wear this medallion. I reckon it sort of stands for how things were. The black tadpole, the sign of evil, that's you. The white one is Devon … and the little spots, they're your common ground.'

I walked quickly across the room and put the necklace around his neck. In his watery blue eyes I saw something I hadn't seen before. Fear.

It released something inside me. Something terrible.

I threw my arms around him in a bear hug, imprisoning his arms at the same time. I wanted to squeeze hard – hard enough to crush the life out of him. But instead I slid my arms down and picked him up off the floor. He seemed so light he was almost weightless. His screams and kicking came from somewhere far away. I walked slowly out onto the deck.

In front of us were the matchless views of the harbour, the dark familiar form of Rangitoto in the distance. A view to die for. Carefully descending the three or four steps to the lawn, we progressed slowly to the edge of the cliff. The winding harbour front esplanade murmured 30 metres or so below us, the traffic still busy. I became aware of Wes' frantic kicking.

'Relax, Wes! Remember what you told me? The right to live here is what it's all for. All the deals, all the channels you've carved, that drag the money in. Enjoy!'

Standing sideways and pivoting with my hips I saw I could toss him a reasonable distance out, but he would still bounce several times before finally hitting the road below. I remember thinking how someone was going to have a good story to tell when they got home that night. 'We were just driving home, around the last corner before the bridge, when splat!'

As Wes had said, it was 'game over'.

I swung back to get some real momentum. At the same moment there was a stab of pain in my chest. I paused. It was the adze. Searing me like a hot rock pressed against bare skin. I thought of Ra. I thought of what he had suffered and then I recalled his final advice. 'Eruera. Before long your heart will burn for utu. For revenge. It's the natural thing. You mustn't listen to it. It's no good.'

The kicking had stopped. Wes had given up and lay limp, a dead weight in my arms. He was just so much tired, old flesh, and one day soon, without my help, he would die too. That would be an end to it. He represented nothing that I feared any more and his death would make no difference to me. I placed him almost gently on the grass and he groaned quietly and held his chest. As he lay there I looked out to sea. I felt the adze, strangely cool now. The million dollar view didn't seem so special now. I turned and walked back to the house.

# Ted Dawe

IN A ROOM off the lounge the Asian boy was playing a computer game in front of a giant TV. 'You may thank me for this, one day,' I thought as I slipped quietly out the front door.

# EPILOGUE

I T'S DIFFERENT over here, and I'm a different person. It's like a frontier, where anything's possible. On the Gold Coast it's one season, all year round. Summer. The days are all fine and warm and one runs into another. I can see why so many old Kiwis come here to retire. It has the boring predictability of heaven itself.

I like it here for other reasons. It's a place for the clean slate, to put all the fuck-ups, all the grief, behind you and aim at doing something fresh. I've got this little flat 50 metres from the beach. I live alone but I'm not lonely. Better to be alone than chasing some dream girl, dancing ahead of me into a fake future. I've got a job with a rental car outfit: it just hires convertibles and Harleys. People love it. Cruising along the esplanade, the hood down, seeing and being seen. Or maybe playing at being a hog-riding bad boy for the day. Fantasy stuff. They pay big though. It's given me this business idea which I've already started. I'll have a motor bike rental agency which specialises in big British bikes. Not for noters, but for people who know the real thing. People who like the rattle and roar of great bikes.

I used the last of the money to buy a Bonneville and a BSA

Goldstar. A few weeks ago I found a Trident; now it's just a matter of getting the owner to part with it. Of course what I'm really holding out for is another Norton Atlas but that's going to take a while. Five bikes should be enough to get started. I'll set up somewhere along the beach front. I've already thought of a name. You guessed it. Thunder Road.

It's been nearly a year since Devon died. I must think of some way of marking his anniversary. I guess what Wes didn't know, or had long forgotten, was that it isn't 'game over'. Devon got so much wrong but they were just details: behind the surfaces, the talk, the act, there was something glowing, something golden. He's a song that will hum in my heart forever. His cheeky, brazen grin. The arrogant confidence never fazed by what life threw at him. The vision to stick his head up and see a world beyond the glass dome. The courage to go out and live in that world, no matter what.

It was a long journey from the quiet, misty valleys of the East Coast to the midnight frenzy of Thunder Road. But it was in those frantic bursts of speed and screaming tyres that Devon found himself. In the blinding rush to oblivion, where, for a few seconds, we are released.

# Acknowledgements

To Jane McKay, whose belief and enthusiasm drove me on.

To Bernard McKissock-Davis, Ross Browne, Sion McKay and David Blaker who laboured through my earlier attempts.

To Neville Byrt and Julia Brown who helped polish my later ones.

To Tipene Pai who checked te reo. Kia ora e hoa.

To the boys at Dilworth School who road-tested this beast and gave it the thumbs up.

To Barbara Larson and all her staff at Longacre Press who embraced this project so enthusiastically.

To Emma Neale, whose sensitivity and erudition had so much to do with how this book reads today.

To Professor J M Coetzee for his time, grace and advice. To you all, my deeply felt thanks and appreciation.

# About the Author

As the child of schoolteachers, Ted Dawe moved around New Zealand a great deal – from Mangakino, Ruatoria, Tokoroa, otaki, Darfield, New Plymouth and finally Invercargill. He currently lives in Auckland with his family.

He's had numerous jobs: he's been a builder's labourer, university student, world traveller, high school teacher but his favourite job was floating above London's Hyde Park in a hot air balloon. These days he is the Director of Studies at a foundation college in Auckland; a job which he enjoys. Ted Dawe travels, surfs, plays tennis and loves cars and car people, but admits to driving a motor scooter to work.

*Thunder Road* was written over 40 days, one summer. Although it came to him in a rush, he had been mulling over the story for some time. The character Devon reminds Ted Dawe of his cousin, Jak, a dynamic, over-confident street racer who died in a car accident.